# Dew on the Thorn

## Jovita González

Edited and introduced by
José E. Limón

Recovering the U.S. Hispanic Literary Heritage Project Publication

Arte Público P
Houston, Te
1997

This volume is made possible through grants from the Rockefeller Foundation, the National Endowment for the Arts (a federal agency), the Andrew W. Mellon Foundation, and the Lila Wallace-Reader's Digest Fund.

*Recovering the past, creating the future*

Arte Público Press
University of Houston
Houston, Texas 77204-2090

Cover design by Mark Piñón

Mireles, Jovita González, 1904-1983.
    Dew on the thorn / Jovita González ; edited with an introduction by José E. Limón.
        p.    cm.
    Includes bibliographical references.
    ISBN 1-55885-175-5 (alk. paper)
        1. Mexican American families —Texas—History—19th century—Fiction. 2. Mexican Americans—Texas—History—19th century—Fiction. 3. Landowners—Texas—History—19th century—Fiction.
    I. Limón, José Eduardo. II. Title.
PS3563.I6947D48    1997
813'.54—dc20                                                    96-14240
                                                                          CIP

The paper used in this publication meets the requirements of the American National Standard for Permanence of Paper for Printed Library Materials Z39.48-1984. ∞

# CONTENTS

## Dew on the Thorn
Jovita González

# FOREWORD

The Special Collections & Archives Department of the Texas A&M University-Corpus Christi Bell Library is proud to be part of the recovery of *Dew on the Thorn* by Jovita González de Mireles (1904-1983), noted South Texas folklorist, educator, and long-time Corpus Christi resident. Its publication will contribute to the public's growing appreciation of her work. The original manuscript is part of her papers and those of her late husband, E. E. Mireles (likewise a distinguished Corpus Christi educator and author), which comprise one of the Department's more valuable research collections.

*Dew on the Thorn* has been recovered through the type of cooperative effort necessary to bring to the public the documents of the Mexican American past. The González de Mireles Papers were graciously donated to the TAMU-CC archives by Isabel Cruz, employee and friend of the Mireles couple who inherited the materials after Mr. Mireles' death in 1987. Ms. Cruz was ably guided in her choice of repositories by Ray J. García, Corpus Christi lay historian. The public spiritedness of Ms. Cruz and Mr. García, as well as their concern with memorializing the Mireles, saved the manuscript from destruction. Once the collection was made available for research, Dr. José E. Limón authenticated the manuscript's value and served diligently as its editor. Under the direction of Dr. Nicolás Kanellos, Arte Público Press and its Recovering the U.S. Hispanic Literary Heritage Project worked with both the editor and archival repository to bring the publication to fruition.

Texas historians Cynthia Orozco and Arnoldo de León must likewise be recognized for their role in this recovery effort, as they did much to foster TAMU-CC's interest in locating the González de Mireles Papers. The support which TAMU-CC Special Collections & Archives received from such local groups as the Spanish American Genealogical Association (SAGA) and the Nueces County Historical Society must be acknowledged, as well as the help of Dr. Clotilde P. García, Vicente Carranza, and Mel G. Lemos. Archives Assistants Alva Neer and Grace Charles are to be commended for their outstanding work in administering the collection. These individuals and organizations should find satisfaction not only in bringing deserved recognition to Jovita González de Mireles (and E. E. Mireles, who faithfully preserved the manuscript after she died), but also for advancing our understanding of the Hispanic literary tradition.

—Thomas H. Kreneck
Special Collections Librarian/Archivist
Texas A&M University-Corpus Christi

# PREFACE

Jovita González (1904-1983). Who was she and what about this book, her book —*Dew on the Thorn*— probably written at various intervals between 1926 and the late 1940s, recently recovered through the generous support of Recovering the U.S. Hispanic Literary Heritage Project, and now brought to publication by Arte Público Press and the U.S. Mexico Fund for Culture. In addition to this book and another called *Caballero*, she has also left us a brief unpublished autobiography, so with these autobiographical comments which follow, let us permit her to answer these questions, at least in part. I shall have more to add in my introduction, but suffice it to say, for this prefatory moment, that the publication of these two long-lost manuscripts and the biographical recovery of this life may now allow us to identify an important Mexican American literary intellectual—active between the two world wars; a precursor for more contemporary Mexican-American letters—who through circumstance passed into literary near-anonymity. She is anonymous no longer. Let us begin to listen to her, for she has much to tell us about who we were, who we are, and who we might imagine ourselves to be.

—José E. Limón
The University of Texas at Austin

*Jovita González*
*1904 – 1983*

# JOVITA GONZÁLEZ:
# EARLY LIFE AND EDUCATION[1]

## Early Life

I was born in Roma, Texas. My father, Jacobo González Rodríguez, a native of Cadereyta, Nuevo León, México, came from a family of educators and artisans. His father, Pablo González, taught poor boys the trade of hat making. When, as a young man, my father finished the equivalent of our high schools, he was awarded the General Bernardo Reyes scholarship to study in Belgium. However, his mother's illness prevented his going, and his cousin Emilio Rodríguez went in his place. I mention this because upon his return, Emilio established in Monterrey the first normal school in northern Mexico. I did not know my grandfather Pablo. He died before I was born. At a very young age, my father was sent by his superiors in Monterrey to become the director of the boy's school in Mier. There he met my mother, Severina Guerra Barrera, the daughter of Francisco Guerra Guerra and Josefa Barrera Barrera. Both my maternal grandparents came from a long line of colonizers who had come with Escandón to El Nuevo Santander. One of my ancestors, Don José Alejandro Guerra had been surveyor to the Crown.

And so it was that my father at twenty and my mother barely eighteen were married at Mier, Tamaulipas. Why was my mother, a descendant of a Texas landowner, born in Mexico? It is not hard to understand. After the Treaty of Guadalupe Hidalgo, fearing the reprisals of the new conquerors, most of the *colonizadores* on the Texas side crossed the Rio Grande to live among their kinsmen in Mexico. However, at the close of

[1]The hand-written manuscript of this autobiography is in the E. E. Mireles and Jovita González de Mireles Papers, Special Collections & Archives, Texas A&M University-Corpus Christi Bell Library.

the Civil War my grandfather, with financial aid from his mother, the widowed Ramona Guerra Hinojosa, returned to Texas to regain or buy some of what had been their land. At a place where the Indians had found a dead snake, he purchased land known as Las Víboras. That was the beginning of his ranch in Starr County. This period was an exodus of the old Texas ranchers back to their homeland.

Homes were built, families grew, and the ranchers wishing a Mexican education for their boys looked for a teacher. The man was my father, married to one of their own and with the culture and training of Mexico.

With Las Víboras as his headquarters my father made plans for the school that was to bring Mexican education to the border boys. Books were ordered from Mexico and the curriculum from that country was followed.

What about the girls? They were taught at home. We were fortunate to have with us, at intervals, Mamá Tulitas, our paternal grandmother. She brought to us fantastic tales from medieval Spain. Before our eyes passed Christian damsels wooed by Moorish Knights, Crusaders fighting for the Holy Sepulchre, the Cid receiving his spurs from *la infanta* doña Urraca, the unfortunate Delgadina* *"que paseaba de la sala a la cocina"*, as she was followed by her infamous suitor. Perhaps more important was the Mexican version of *Cinderella* which we loved.

My family had two sets of children. The three older children were much older than the last four, of which I was the oldest. My sister Tula and I did everything together. We went horseback riding to the pastures with my grandfather, took long walks with father, and visited the homes of the cowboys and the ranch hands. We enjoyed the last the most. There were Tío Patricio, the mystic; Chon, who was so ugly, poor fellow, he reminded us of a toad; Old Remigio who wielded the *metate* with the dexterity of peasant women and made wonderful *tortillas*. Tía Chita whose stories about ghosts and witches made our hair stand on end, Pedro, the hunter and traveler, who had been as far as Sugar Land and had seen black people with black wool for hair, one-eyed Manuelito, the ballad singer, Tío Camilo; all furnished ranch lore in our young lives.

I must add someone very special, mi Tía Lola, my mother's sister. As a young widow, she had come to live at Las Víboras Ranch. She was a handsome woman with a will of iron and a vast store of family history. It was from her that we learned many things that made us proud of our heritage. But all these things, as much as we loved them, did not

---

*Ballad from the Middle Ages. Delgadina was wooed by her father.

provide us with an education. As a poor man, my father felt that the only heritage he could leave his children was an education. The three older, now grown, had a fairly good education in Spanish. But my father and my mother realized that my sister Tula and I were not getting the proper training girls in our family should have. True we rattled off in Spanish *La Influencia de la Mujer*, a poem which began with Judith, the Old Testament heroine, and ended with Doña Josefa Ortiz de Domínguez, the mother of Mexico's independence. We knew about Sor Juana, the Mexican nun who in the seventeenth century addressed men as "foolish men who accuse women without a motive." But that was not enough.

We had learned to sew and crochet, and that was not enough either. So after talking it over with Mother and grandfather, he decided that the family should move to San Antonio where we could be educated in English.

However, before leaving, Tía Lola and grandfather suggested mother should take us to Mier to see Mamá Ramoncita, our great grandmother, perhaps for the last time.

I have a clear picture of her lying in a four-poster bed her clear-cut ivory features contrasting with her dark sharp eyes.

"Come, get closer to me, children, so I can see you better," she said. "Your mother tells me you are moving to live in San Antonio. Did you know that land at one time belonged to us? But now the people living there don't like us. They say we don't belong there and must move away. Perhaps they will tell you to go to Mexico where you belong. Don't listen to them.

Texas is ours. Texas is our home. Always remember these words: Texas is ours, Texas is our home."

I have always remembered the words and I have always felt at home in Texas.

## Education

Previous to our moving to San Antonio, I had attended, for one year, a one-teacher school in English, taught by Miss Elida García at the San Román Ranch. Even though the English I learned was elemental, it helped me a great deal. This, together with my knowledge of Spanish, enabled me to enter the fourth grade at the age of ten. With the aid of a dictionary and my father's constant help, I was able to be promoted at the end of the school year. Another thing that helped us was the fact that all our neighbors were English-speaking. By attending summer school I finished the equivalent of the high school course when I was eighteen.

The following summer I enrolled in what was called a Summer Normal School. As a result, I acquired a teacher's certificate two years.

I went to Rio Grande City and with the help of my grandfather and my uncle, Encarnación Sabinas, County and District Clerk, and Mr. Sam P. Vale, then County Superintendent of Schools, I was given a position at the city schools. Since I lived with my uncle and aunt, I saved all my money except $5.00 a month for incidentals that went to my college fund.

The following fall I enrolled at the University of Texas. After finishing my freshman year I returned home to San Antonio. Again I was out of money. The following two years I taught at Encinal, as Head Teacher of a two-teacher school. After this experience I decided to go back to college. So I entered the summer school at Our Lady of the Lake in San Antonio. The dean of the college, Mother Angelique, became interested in me, and needing a teacher of Spanish to teach in the high school department, offered me a scholarship for the following year. For teaching two hours a day and a class of teachers on Saturday, I would get a private room, board, and tuition. My worries were over. However I had to consider the courses in Spanish I had started at the University of Texas. While there I had studied a course in advanced Spanish under Miss Lila Casis, and once having her as a teacher I could not consider anyone else. To enable my studying at the university during the summer, I began to tutor at Our Lady of the Lake.

The summer of 1925 brought me a far reaching experience. I met J. Frank Dobie. Heretofore the legends and stories of the border were interesting, so I thought, just to me. However, he made me see their importance and encouraged me to write them, which I did, publishing some in the *Folk-Lore Publications* and *Southwest Review*.

At the end of my sophomore year I was offered a position teaching Spanish, half a day, at Saint Mary's Hall, an Episcopal school for girls. In this way I could help my family some, and study in the afternoon. I continued my summer studying at the university and enjoying my friendship with the Dobies, Miss Casis and Dr. & Mrs. Carlos E. Castañeda, the latter old family friends.

After getting a B.A. degree from Our Lady of the Lake in 1927, I became a full-time teacher at Saint Mary's Hall.

Two years later, through Miss Ruth Coit, Headmistress of that institution and Dobie, I was awarded the Lapham Scholarship to advance further research along the border and to study for my M.A. at the university. In this way, again I would be among friends, relatives, and my family in the valley.

The summer of 1929 was spent traveling in Webb, Zapata, and Starr Counties. To facilitate matters I had asked the Catholic Archbishop Droessarts and Bishop Capers, Episcopal bishop of the same city, for letters of introduction to the clergy of the border counties. Whenever anyone in Starr County asked who "the strange young lady with long hair and a book full of notes was," the answer would be, "She is *Maestro* Jacobo's daughter," or "She is don Francisco Guerra's granddaughter from Las Víboras Ranch." That was the open sesame. In the other counties, Archbishop Droesarts' letter was enough. My thesis, *Social Life in Cameron, Starr, and Zapata Counties* is the result of that year's study and a lifetime of love and understanding for my people, the border people. Dr. Eugene C. Barker, my thesis Master, was somewhat hesitant at first to approve the thesis. It did not have enough historical references. To this my friend, Carlos E. Castañeda commented—"This thesis will be used in years to come as source material." When Dr. Barker signed it, his comment to me was, "an interesting but somewhat odd piece of work."

As a result of the thesis, and again through the recommendation of J. Frank Dobie, I was awarded a Rockefeller grant in 1934.

In 1935, Edmundo E. Mireles, whom I had met as a student at the University of Texas, and I were married in San Antonio at the mission of La Purísima Concepción by Bishop Mariano Garriga.

For four years we lived in Del Rio where Edmundo was principal of the San Felipe High School and I taught English.

In 1939 we moved to Corpus Christi where Edmundo, a year later, organized the Spanish Program in the elementary grades, from the third to the sixth grades. It was slow going at first, for this was a period when the walls of racial prejudice still had to be torn down. However, the movement of Spanish in the elementary grades spread through Texas, the Spanish southwest, and other parts of the country.

My husband and I collaborated in writing two sets of books for the teaching of Spanish in the elementary grades. *Mi libro español,* a series of three books, was adopted by the State of Texas. The second series of six books, *El español elemental* was also used in Texas and other parts of the country.

Until my retirement I taught Spanish and Texas History at W.B. Ray High School in Corpus Christi. We have been happy.

# Jovita González's
# Texas and Northern Mexico

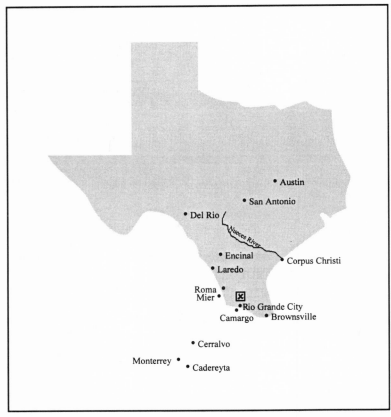

- Austin
- San Antonio
- Del Rio
Nueces River
- Encinal
- Corpus Christi
- Laredo
Roma
Mier
- Rio Grande City
Camargo - Brownsville
- Cerralvo
Monterrey
- Cadereyta

☒  Approximate location of the Olivares ranch

# INTRODUCTION

Along with the rest of her now published work, we may take Jovita González's autobiographical remarks as yet another example of her literary writing.[1] As autobiography it has its own inherent interest, even as it bears directly on the material that chiefly comprises this book, *Dew on the Thorn*. In these brief personal remarks she tells us much, though not as much as we might need to know, to establish a relationship between her rendered life and the work at hand. As Janet Varner Gunn has noted, "It is...the case that autobiography can never exhume all of that buried life making up the past. But just because all of the past cannot be presented does not mean that it is therefore absent from the autobiographical text."[2] My purpose in this introduction is to draw on and expand this already interesting autobiography, especially by making what is seemingly absent more present as a way of understanding the full significance of *Dew on the Thorn*. Thus understood, I want to use her autobiography as a reference point as I focus on three categories of thought and experience central to González's life and to *Dew on the Thorn*. These are history, folklore, and her South Texas "sense of place," to borrow a useful phrase from another South Texas writer, the distinguished Rolando Hinojosa, although in closing I also want to give some sense of González's relevance to certain contemporary issues.[3]

*Dew on the Thorn* may best be understood as a moderately unified set of literary, which is to say also fictionalized, sketches fashioned into a short novel and set in the Mexican-descent community along the United States-Mexico border in southern Texas, where the Rio Grande begins to make its way into the Gulf of Mexico (see map). Here, as she tells us, Jovita González was born and raised and spent most of her life, save for a few college years in Austin. Although then and now an agricultural and ranching area, she lived the greater portion of her life in three of the region's cities—San Antonio, Del Rio and Corpus Christi.

The highways that today link San Antonio to Del Rio and Corpus Christi, respectively, in effect form the boundaries of the South Texas area. But as she indicates in her remarks, her sense of place also involved her close-knit family, one bearing a resemblance to the Olivares, the fictional family that is at the heart of this novella.

The story opens in 1904, the year of González's own birth, and traces the lives of this ranching family, its patriarch, Don Francisco, and their close associates over the course of approximately two years. During this period, the principal concerns of this group are three-fold, general and particular, and these give *Dew on the Thorn* its plot development. Of particular concern is the potential disruption of the romance and betrothal of Don Francisco's daughter, Rosita, to young Carlos, son of Don Ramón Aguilar, a neighboring rancher and *compadre* to Don Francisco and his wife, Doña Margarita. In Chapter III, "Border Honor," we learn of cattle thieves plaguing these and other ranchers in the area, but to our shock and theirs, we discover that young Carlos may be one of these thieves, bringing instant dishonor and shame to these proud feudalistic families who trace their lineage in this area for some nearly two hundred years. The problem of Carlos, Rosita and this rupture recurs unevenly throughout the text, only to be resolved in the end where it is interwoven into yet another specific emplotment: a story of bewitchment involving a young boy named Cristóbal and a new character named Carmen.

These two specific emplotments are contextualized in a general framework of historical change. The first two chapters are substantially taken up with these people recalling in detail their Spanish-mestizo ancestors who settled this area in the 1740s as part of the last major Spanish exploration and expansion in the Americas. They speak of the relatively autonomous and tranquil existence of these isolated settlements—save for the Indians—even as the area became part of Mexico after the expulsion of the Spanish from the northern part of the Americas. As this community begins to enter modernity in the mid-nineteenth century, we are made to sense its first real crisis—the coming of the United States into their lives.

In a bargain with a Mexican government far removed from the interests of this community, Stephen F. Austin brought the first large numbers of Anglo-Americans into Texas, settling them north of the Nueces River but in close proximity to the South Texas area. By the mid-1830s, these new people were in open revolt against Mexican rule while, for the most part, the South Texas Mexicans remained aloof from this encounter. As noted in the narrative, General Santa Anna inflicted a major defeat on the Texas rebels at the Alamo, only to be himself defeated later at San Jacinto, effectively ending Mexican control of Texas, at least north of the Nueces River. But we also learn that the new Republic of Texas claimed the land south of the Nueces to the Rio Grande, a claim contested by Mexico but supported by the United States which was about to annex Texas. This dispute and the annexation process soon led to the U.S.-Mexican War and the incorporation not only of South Texas but also the lands that became the Southwest of the United States. Invading U.S. troops crossed South Texas and occupied it on their way to central Mexico, setting in motion conflicts and contradictions within the Mexican community that became the narrative stuff of *Caballero*, an historical romance novel that González co-authored with a woman named Eve Raleigh also during the 1930s and '40s.[4]

But although disruptive and at times deadly, this invasion and the years that immediately followed turned out to be not the greatest crisis for the Mexicans of South Texas. David Montejano, the leading historian of Texas, himself from Del Rio, San Antonio, and now Austin, tells us that "in the Nueces River region where considerable numbers of Mexicans and Anglos lived, the tragic aftermath one expects of war—recriminations, dispossession of land and belongings, violence and revenge—was much in evidence," one needing only to add violence and revenge especially as inflicted primarily on Mexicans.[5] We see an example of this kind of racial violence inflicted directly on the Olivares family in Chapter I as one of them is murdered on his way to San Antonio. However, a kind of relative peace prevailed right after the war among the Mexican settlements along the Rio Grande like the Olivares ranch. Indeed, as we see in *Caballero*, intermarriages between Mexican women and ex-soldiers from the American army were not that unusual, with the latter remaining in South Texas and becoming integrated into Mexican society. *Dew on the Thorn* itself gives us the fictive, narratively recurrent example of John Warren Preston, and Chapter XVI recalls the real historical case of Henry Clay Davis, who co-founded Rio Grande City after marrying a wealthy Mexican woman.

This period of relative tranquillity came to an end toward the end of the century as the second and much larger wave of Anglo-Americans, principally from the Mid-West, came to South Texas looking for cheap land and exploitable labor. They inundated the area, bringing with them their dominating political, educational and cultural institutions, as well as a greatly intensified racism. Again, Montejano:

... the agrarian development of this period can be seen as the last in a series of crises that eroded the centuries-old class structure of the Mexican ranch settlements. By 1920, the Texas Mexican people had generally been reduced, except in a few border counties, to the status of landless and dependent wage laborers.[6]

The Mexican narrative life of *Dew on the Thorn* is inserted precisely in this historical juncture and in the face of this new period of change as the narrative opens in 1904 and closes approximately three years later as the change is intensifying.

That *Dew on the Thorn* should have such an historically informed character should not be surprising for such an author. Relative to the standards of the time, at least for state universities, González was a trained historian of Texas, having taken, as she tells us, the M.A. in history at the University of Texas at Austin. Indeed, her M.A. thesis wholly informs *Dew on the Thorn*. At moments literal passages from the thesis are incorporated into the fictional narrative; at others, actual historical personages, such as Don Blas María de las Garza Falcón, appear among fictive ones. Eugene C. Barker, the eminent Texas historian, directed the thesis, although the record suggests that Carlos Castañeda may have been her true mentor for this project.[7] As González tells us in her autobiography, all did not go well with Barker; witness his dismissive comment on her thesis and Castañeda's defense of her. Although her autobiography does not elaborate, from another source we learn more about this encounter as we see González in an ethnic and gender struggle similar to that of her characters in this novella. According to an interview she gave in 1981, Barker "appreciated her discussion of Spanish land grants, but objected when she launched into the social history of the descendants of the grantees."[8] Beyond her discussion of land grants, the rest of her thesis is concerned predominantly with a careful delineation of the customs and traditions of her community and a narrative of racial and ethnic conflict, both of which make their way into *Dew on the Thorn*. We can imagine why Professor Barker, born and raised in Texas and committed to his sense of Texas history, objected. We can also now see the prescience of Castañeda's retort in González's influence on young historians today, such as David Montejano.

González tells us that it was J. Frank Dobie who recommended that she write her thesis under Barker, even as she also acknowledges her indebtedness to Dobie for his crucial assistance in developing another aspect of her career—the collection and inscription of the folklore of her native community—for which she gained her most significant public presence from 1927 to 1955. In the mid 1920s, when she and Dobie met on the Texas campus, he was a faculty member in the English Department and was launching his own formidable, if problematic and complicated, career in folklore. He focused initially on Mexican and Anglo cowboy lore, but increasingly concentrated on the latter. Indeed, it is as if he might have planned to turn over the former domain to his new Mexican-American protégée from his own native South Texas. Over the course of the next twenty years, he was a close mentor to her, soliciting and editing the papers that she read at the annual meetings of the Texas Folklore Society even as a graduate student. Several of these papers she later published in the series of the society which Dobie edited. He was also something of a personal friend, he and his wife hosting González for dinner on many occasions and supporting her by underwriting bank loans and providing letters of reference for scholarships. Dobie was also instrumental in promoting her candidacy for the presidency of the Texas Folklore Society, which she held from 1930 to 1932.[9]

As can happen with protégées and protégés, González adopted Dobie's approach and style in the collection and rendering of folklore which is evident in the work she published during these years. But it is an approach interestingly complicated in *Dew on the Thorn.* We can best appreciate Dobie's outlook and folklore practice if we contrast it to two other then competing perspectives with which he and most of the membership of the Texas Folklore Society quarreled. An anthropological approach espoused by Franz Boas, for example—and still important today—would see folklore, especially narratives, as imbedded in culture and as a kind of mirror of that culture that reflected society's fundamental values and beliefs. A competing perspective fostered by literary departments, and in the United States, articulated principally by Stith Thompson of Indiana University, saw folklore, again especially narratives, as literary artifacts, but concerned itself less with their cultural content and relevance and far more with comparatively analyzing their distribution over time and space; hence it was named the "historical-geographic" method. This distributional analysis would be carried out by keying on universal motifs and tale-types prominent in the narratives. Both perspectives stressed the rigorous collection of texts in the field, faithfully translated, when necessary, with minimal grammatical/syntactical alteration, and their close analysis, albeit for different purposes.

In contrast, Dobie's approach was also literary and cultural, but in a very different, much looser or flexible way, depending on your point of view. Here memory, conversation and presumed camaraderie prevailed in the collection of material. Here the tracing of motifs or the detection of "values" gave way to an aesthetic appreciation of what Dobie often called "flavor" in a text, and a culture was to be appreciated rather than analyzed for its ability to produce aesthetically and morally pleasing texts or, in the title words of one of the Texas Folklore Society publications, "a good tale and a bonnie tune." To give a non-folk audience a full appreciation of such folklore, texts were often re-written, somewhat at least, in a more literary English with minimal analytical or historical commentary. Indeed, Dobie and his followers were often well-pleased enough just to read such a text as a formal paper at their meetings, usually in an ideological aura of representing an aesthetically and morally interesting "folk." However, Dobie also believed that such folklore could also serve as the basis—the core—of more developed narratives, such as novels and short stories, written by an educated, English-literate author. Dobie openly placed his practice in that literary-folkloric tradition represented by Sir Walter Scott, Washington Irving, W.H. Hudson, and W.B. Yeats. This he himself attempted to do with Mexican folklore and, with mixed success, in a book called *Tongues of the Monte*, a folklorically laden, novelistic and romanticized account of a trip into Mexico which avoids any engagement with matters of social conflict and political economy.[10] Commenting directly on González's work, Dobie had this to say: "I look for two things in folklore. I look for flavor and I look for revelation of the folk who nourished the lore... If a thing is interesting, that is all the excuse it needs for being... Some day, it is quite likely Miss Jovita González will plunge in and trace her charming stories... back to the Middle Ages, but I hope she will not do this until she has extracted all the dewy freshness that the Mexican folk put into their tales."[11]

Dobie's influence on González's earlier published work and public presentations is clear. It is likely that his *Tongues of the Monte* played some role in her decision to write *Dew on the Thorn* as an extended narrative incorporating some of the folklore in her earlier work and some new material based on the field research she carried out in 1934-35 with a Rockefeller Foundation Fellowship. She had received the latter with Dobie's recommendation as well as that, interestingly enough, of economist Paul Taylor at Berkeley, whom she had met during his own field research in South Texas on Mexican labor issues.[12] But some of the material is also derived from her memory of her childhood, as the autobiography suggests.

It is this kind of folkloric writing tactic that gives *Dew on the Thorn* its special texture, as almost every chapter furnishes the occasion for rendering a folkloric event, even as the principal plots are developed. As such, and even in a literary English, the novella is still a rich literary ethnography of a wide repertoire of folkloric practices from Mexican South Texas, although it occasionally lapses into sentimentality and idealization. Wherever possible, I have tried to indicate the folkloric material that González published separately with references to her appended bibliography at the end of this book and have identified the folk narratives she uses employing the motif-index of folk literature developed by Stith Thompson, which is a compilation of major motifs appearing in folk narratives from around the world.

Dobie's influence, however, was by no means total, and we now know of her political divergence from him in their relations at the University of Texas-Austin, a divergence also manifested textually in *Dew on the Thorn*. As she reported to McNutt in the previously cited interview—a view omitted in her autobiography—she never attended any of Dobie's classes, by mutual agreement:

> You see, it was an agreement that we made, that I would not go into one of his classes because I would be mad at many things. He would take the Anglo-Saxon side, naturally. I would take the Spanish and the Mexican side.[13]

But a more significant, though correlated rupture, is to be found in the manner in which *Dew on the Thorn* contests the wandering romantic nostalgia of *Tongues of the Monte* even as it emulates its incorporation of folklore. In González's regionally focused treatment, folklore is not simply added as a quaint adornment to the narrative of a romanticized text. As I have argued in analytical detail elsewhere, almost every folkloric instance in *Dew on the Thorn* is pressed into service as an imbedded commentary and plot development of the principal conflictual themes of the book. The male tale-swapping session of Chapter V is closely related to the political crisis engendered by the coming of the Americans; Nana Chita's performances in Chapter VI serve as a commentary on the status of women; and, in later chapters, the folk story of the woman who lost her soul is intimately joined to the resolution of the crisis involving Carlos and Rosita. Taken by themselves as they were in some of her independent articles published under Dobie's eye, these folkloric instances are only inherently aesthetically/morally interesting; imbedded and textually managed in *Dew on the Thorn*, they are artistically implicated in a running political commentary on ethnic, gender, and class relations.[14]

In this sense we may now also read *Dew on the Thorn* as anticipating, in part, the use of memory, literature, and folkloric history in Chapter I of Américo Paredes' *With His Pistol in His Hand: A Border Ballad and its Hero* and in the fictive sketch of Gregorio Cortez based on folk legend in Chapter II of that classic book.[15] Yet, there is a definite sense in which she enlarges the range of Paredes' work even while writing earlier. Commenting on the latter, Renato Rosaldo says:

> If taken literally, Paredes' view of the frontier social order seems both pre-feminist and as implausible as a classic ethnography written and read in accord with classic norms. How could any human society... function without inconsistencies and contradiction? Did patriarchal authority engender neither resentment nor dissent? Read as poetic vision, however, the account of primordial south Texas-Mexican society establishes the terms of verbally constructing the warrior hero as a figure of resistance. It enables Paredes to develop a conception of manhood rhetorically endowed with the mythic capacity to combat Anglo-Texan anti-Mexican prejudice.[16]

With *Dew on the Thorn*, and notwithstanding its idealizations and occasional sentimentality, it is as if Jovita González is answering Rosaldo with an "It couldn't," and "Yes, it did," to his two respective questions, and in doing so, making herself far more a critic of our time. For in these folkloric sketches, we are also offered a different vision of an internal Texas-Mexican world, a conflicted Texas-Mexican world where the invading Anglo is not the only source of conflict. We discover, for example, a critique of an oppressive class hierarchy where peons and Indians are disparaged by their Mexican "betters," a disparagement also often couched in racial terms. (Yet, in chapter VI we also find a racist lapse in González's figuration of African-Americans.) And we find something else yet, a theme that surely was produced by González's tutelage under parents who taught her about Doña Josefa Ortiz de Domínguez and Sor Juana Inés de la Cruz, "the Mexican nun who, in the seventeenth century, addressed men as foolish men who accuse women without a motive." This story makes us witness to a critique of a patriarchal order that continually subordinates women even as we are given vivid portraits of strong and creative Mexican women. In her anticipatory enlargement of Paredes's work, we also note her partial anticipation of much of the current intellectual-political moment that goes by the rubric of "Cultural Studies." Her eschewal of a unified singular subject of history; the genre mix of literature, popular culture, history, and ethnography; her clear commitment to a complicated assessment of political and cultural contradiction; her critique of several orders of domination beyond but not excluding race, especially gender—all of these should make her a more familiar voice to us in the present moment.

But finally, there is yet more that she anticipates and that also makes her a familiar figure to many of us who are also Mexicans in the United States involved in intellectual labor and who, in some sense, have also lived out some version of her autobiography. Like her, many of us have made the passage from a rural to urban setting as our parents sought better opportunities in this country for us. For although, like the Olivares, her ancestral family possessed some wealth, principally in land, the record suggests that their later circumstances were far more modest and might be well described as "lower middle class," a descending condition that perhaps occasioned her recurrent textual sympathy for the peons in her books. Recall that she was forced to withdraw after her first year at the University of Texas at Austin for lack of money. She then attended Our Lady of the Lake College in San Antonio where she could live at home and support herself and her family by working as a teacher. In these years, again, like many of us, later as a student she was also active in community politics with the League of United Latin American Citizens (see González 1933). Eventually, with a scholarship, she once again left the relative security of home and the heavily Mexican city of San Antonio to cross a great cultural and racial divide when she resumed her studies in Austin, this time armed with a hard-won competitive scholarship to work on her M.A. How many of us have not known this passage in our own efforts for a higher education, whether from South Texas to Austin, from northern New Mexico to Albuquerque or East L.A. to U.C.L.A? And, this is so especially if one is a woman.

For there is in González's career a particular anticipatory experience pertinent only to Mexican women in the United States. As she notes early on, her parents made the far-sighted decision that their girls should also have a good education beyond the domestic arts and what they could teach them in rural South Texas, although as she and we have already noted, the latter included an exposure to the work of Sor Juana Inés de la Cruz, the great colonial feminist. Later, the record suggests that her gender played a role in her daily negotiations with Dobie about her published work, as Dobie worried about and therefore asserted his cowboy masculinity, lest he be thought effeminate for teaching in an English department.[17] Her published work from this period, all of which he reviewed, shows an almost exclusive concern with masculine experience, as Gloria Velásquez-Treviño has also affirmed.[18] But as I have already noted, in the present work, as in

*Caballero*, we see the return of a female repressed in a great range of women figures.

Her gender was to have an even more decisive role in the production of these two books. In the period 1935 to 1938, González made two critical decisions whose net effect was to shift her career away from her work in Cultural Studies to public school education. As she notes, in 1935 she decided to marry Edmundo E. Mireles, a fellow student at Austin. They first lived in San Antonio where they both taught, and then moved to Del Rio, Texas where he was offered a better-paying job as a principal. Four years later, he was on the move again to another and still better educational administrative position in Corpus Christi, as she also notes. What she does not tell us in her autobiography is that in 1938-39, while they were contemplating the move to Corpus Christi, she explored the possibilities of further graduate study toward a Ph.D. at Stanford, California-Berkeley or the University of New Mexico, but following what were likely complicated marital negotiations, she decided to go with him to Corpus Christi.[19] She would spend the remainder of her professional life until retirement as a teacher of Spanish and Texas history at W.B. Ray High School in that city. There she became known as a formidable teacher and a person active in social affairs centering on the Mexican community. As she says, she also helped her husband in the preparation of Spanish-language instructional texts.

We learn a great deal about González from her autobiography, but it is now time to take account of its most fundamental omission, for there is not a word in this autobiography of *Caballero* and *Dew on the Thorn*. Yet the record shows—and we have the present evidence—that in such time as she had away from her teaching duties with their nightly obligations of grading and class preparation—the Mireles' financial circumstances also required summer teaching—and her culturally required duties as a "housewife," she continued to work on her manuscripts whenever she could, agonizing over their state and her failure to find a publisher for them.[20]

She closes her autobiography by referring to the last years of her life with her husband. "We have been happy," she says. I have little grounds to doubt her word, nor should we in any sense diminish her contributions as an already published writer, a teacher, and community leader. Yet today, as a professor of Mexican-American cultural studies at the University of Texas at Austin, I cannot help but wonder about what possibly could have been, if the cultural imperative of marriage had been less imperative or more flexible for a woman of her time, and if she had then chosen the road less-traveled and pursued her Ph.D.

Everything about her academic record suggested nothing less than resounding success, especially had she selected either Stanford where she had identified Professor Aurelio M. Espinosa, or the University of New Mexico where Professor Arthur Campa awaited, both of course distinguished scholars of folklore and of U.S.-Spanish-Mexican descent.[21] But why did she not select Austin for the Ph.D. where she had wide-spread and influential campus support? I cannot prove it, but strongly suspect that she was aware of the academic "rule" that an institution does not normally hire its own Ph.D.s, and that she indeed fully intended to return to Austin, but now as a faculty member armed with a Ph.D. from another institution. "I have always felt at home in Texas," she says. Had she done so, to my knowledge, she would have been the first Mexican-American woman Ph.D. and among the first, male or female, joining that first generation that included Espinosa, Campa, Castañeda and George I. Sánchez.[22] With her clear interest in the fortunes of Mexicans and women manifested in her texts, she would have been in a unique position to generate a cadre of new Mexican-American academics, especially women. But she did not choose this road and now we can only speculate and wonder. What she did do, given her life, was to leave us a record of achievement to which we can now add her two book-length manuscripts, *Caballero* and *Dew on the Thorn*. It is far more than we could have reasonably expected from an individual living under her constraints in her time. We can only be grateful.

As academic authors still do, González sent proposals for her two books to various publishers and persons, hoping for critical commentary and, of course, eventual publication. In a letter to one Dr. John Joseph Gorrell in Pittsburgh, Pennsylvania (otherwise unidentified), Jovita González describes her two manuscripts, first *Caballero* and then the sketches she calls *Dew on the Thorn*. Of the latter, she says:

> Now as to the sketches. They deal with a border family of Mexican ranchmen, descendants of a family that held a grant from the viceroy. Date 1906. This was the time when the Americans from the middle west came in great numbers to develop what is now the Rio Grande Valley. They found these ranchmen, impregnable in their ranches, holding tenaciously to the traditions of their forbears. What I have tried to do is to show life as it existed then. There is much folklore, perhaps too much; as you know, writing folklore is about the only thing I can write. The characters in these sketches are the same. Each could be independent, yet there is enough sequence in each to make the reader want to know what is to happen next. The first chapter, which I have called *The Stronghold of the Olivares*, gives a little of the family background. Others are, *The Perennial Lover*, the story of

an old don who amused himself writing love letters until he was finally caught by a woman, rich in years and in flesh. *The Woman Who Lost Her Soul*, this deals with ageless superstition brought to Spain from the Moors, and still prevalent among our lowly Mexicans; *Saint John's Eve*, with all its beauty of tradition. This sketch, in my mind, is as fresh and as fragrant as a rose wet with dew. *The Good Eve*, Christmas Eve, that feast so precious and so holy to the Mexican Catholic. There are twenty-five in all. I have entitled this collected, *Dew on the Thorn*. The dew, the beauty of faith, of lore and of tradition, amidst the sufferings of life.[23]

As it turns out, González appears to have actually written only seventeen, most of which I found bound as one unit in relatively good order in a box with other materials not directly relevant to the manuscript in the E.E. Mireles and Jovita González de Mireles Papers. I believe that González finally decided to write seventeen chapters because Chapters 1 and 17 have the clear character of opening and concluding chapters. Chapters VI and XVI were not in the original set with the others, and I found them later in a separate part of the archival collection. Her letter to Gorrell identifies them as part of *Dew on the Thorn*, and they make narrative sense in the work as a whole. The manuscript as a whole has the character of a work still in progress, but very close to completion as her letter to Gorrell also suggests. As with any work in progress, this author was not always completely satisfied with her work, so that occasionally a few passages are either crossed out or marked "rewrite" in the margins. Chapters VII and VIII were in particularly poor condition, heavily edited although still legible. Further, some of the chapters were numbered and re-numbered or not numbered at all, as González possibly thought of more chapters to write. Finally, Chapter XI appears to be missing along with several pages in other chapters. I also found slightly different versions of some chapters. It is my judgment that deleting the marked passages would have the effect of destroying the narrative movement of the book, since González did not write any alternatives; their deletion, in a few cases, would also deprive us of important historical and cultural information. For these reasons, I have noted these passages with brackets and footnotes and have maintained them in the text. I have also offered other clarifying information in other numbered footnotes. All asterisk footnotes are González's. I have numbered the chapters in the order which I found them and inserted V and XVI in their narratively appropriate places, while noting the absence of XI in the table of contents. In these editorial decisions, I believe I have produced a coherent narrative whole—even with what appears to be the missing chapter—in the spirit of what

González said to Gorrell: "The characters in these sketches are the same. Each could be independent, yet there is enough sequence in them to make the reader want to know what is going to happen next."[24] Centrally motivating all of these decisions is my larger judgment that *Dew on the Thorn* is an important cultural document by a significant Mexican-American woman intellectual and artist, deserving of publication even in its present edited form. As Tey Diana Rebolledo has recently noted, the literary life of Jovita González has gone too long unrecorded, and it is my hope that this book will improve matters.[25] I only regret that Jovita González did not live to see its publication, which her life circumstances delayed and which she so ardently desired. I trust she would approve this publication of her engaging story set among her people.

# Notes

[1]See her appended bibliography. The original of this autobiography, found in the E.E. Mireles and Jovita González de Mireles Papers, Special Collections & Archives, Texas A&M University-Corpus Christi Bell Library, is not originally part of *Dew on the Thorn*. I recovered the manuscript for *Dew on the Thorn* after a long search that began in 1986, when I started doing research on González's folklore work. See footnote 9.

[2]Janet Varner Gunn, *Autobiography: Toward a Poetics of Experience* (Philadelphia: University of Pennsylvania Press, 1982):14.

[3]Rolando Hinojosa, "The Sense of Place," in *The Rolando Hinojosa Reader*, ed. José Saldivar (Houston: Arte Público Press, 1985):18-24.

[4]Jovita González and Eve Raleigh, *Caballero: An Historical Novel*, eds. José E. Limón and María Cotera (College Station: Texas A&M University Press, 1996).

[5]David Montejano, *Anglos and Mexicans in the Making of Texas, 1836-1986* (Austin: University of Texas Press, 1987):29-30.

[6]Montejano, p. 114.

[7]See Mario T. García's chapter on Texas-Mexican historian Carlos Castañeda in his *Mexican Americans: Leadership, Ideology and Identity, 1930-1960* (New Haven: Yale University Press, 1989):231-251.

[8]James Charles McNutt, "Beyond Regionalism: Texas Folklorists and the Emergence of a Post-Regional Consciousness," (Unpublished Ph.D. dissertation, University of Texas at Austin, 1982):252.

[9]José E. Limón, *Dancing with the Devil: Society and Cultural Poetics in Mexican-American South Texas* (Madison: University of Wisconsin Press, 1994). Chapter II, "J. Frank Dobie" and Chapter III "Jovita González." See also Francis Edward Abernathy, *The Texas Folklore Society, 1909-1943*, Vol I (Denton, TX: University of North Texas Press, 1992).

[10]McNutt, Chapter 7. "Eclectic Provincialism: J. Frank Dobie and the Texas Folklore Society," 215-267. See also Simon Bronner, *American Folklore Studies: An Intellectual History* (Lawrence: University Press of Kansas. 1986) :54-93.

[11]J. Frank Dobie, "Just a Word," *Introduction to Man, Bird and Beast*. ed. J Frank Dobie (Austin, Texas Folklore Society Publications, 1930):6.

[12]Correspondence in the E.E Mireles and Jovita González de Mireles Papers, Special Collections & Archives, Texas A&M University-Corpus Christi Bell Library.

[13]McNutt, p. 251.

[14]José E. Limón, "Folklore, Literature and Politics: Border Writing in Jovita González's *Dew on the Thorn*," *Recovering the U.S. Hispanic Literary Heritage*, Vol II (Houston: Arte Público Press, 1996).

[15]Américo Paredes, *"With His Pistol in His Hand": A Border Ballad and its Hero* (Austin: University of Texas Press, 1971 [1958]).

[16]Renato Rosaldo, *Culture and Truth: The Remaking of Social Analysis* (Boston: Beacon Press, 1989):151.

[17]McNutt, p. 180.

[18]Gloria Louise Velásquez, "Cultural Ambivalence in Early Chicana Prose Fiction," (Unpublished Ph.D. dissertation, Stanford University, 1985).

[19]Correspondence in the E.E. Mireles and Jovita González de Mireles Papers, Special Collections & Archives, Texas A&M University-Corpus Christi Bell Library. I am currently at work on an intellectual-political biography of González and her husband to be called *"Our Life's Work": Jovita González, E.E. Mireles and the Politics of Culture in Texas* (under contract to the University of Texas Press.)

[20]Ibid.

[21]Ibid.

[22]Again, see García for a larger assessment of this generation.

[23]Correspondence in the E.E. Mireles - Jovita González Papers, Texas A&M University-Corpus Christi Bell Library. Note that González changed her mind about the year 1906, changing it to 1904.

[24]Ibid.

[25]Tey Diana Rebolledo, *Women Singing in the Snow: A Critical Analysis of Chicana Literature* (Tucson: University of Arizona Press, 1995):26-27.

# Dew on the Thorn

---

Jovita González

---

# CHAPTER I

## The Family of the Olivares

> *"Soy como el roble, me doblo
> pero no me quiebro."*
>
> *"Like an oak I may be bent,
> but not broken."*

Rich in the traditions of a proud past, and still rich in worldly goods, the year of Our Lord 1904 found the Olivares on the land which His Excellency Revilla Gigedo, Viceroy of New Spain, had deeded to the head of the family in 1764. The grant which extended into territory destined later to become Texas, was located thirty miles east of the Río Grande, and ambled leisurely along through fertile plains and grass-covered prairies to within five miles of the Nueces River.

Yet in spite of their long permanency in the country, this family, as was also true of all the border families, remained more Spanish and more Mexican than if they had lived in Mexico. A series of unfortunate circumstances which had made the Olivares cling tenaciously to the traditions of their people, had also made them look upon all Americans with distrust and dislike.

The first of the Olivares, Don Juan José, had come in 1748 as Surveyor to the Spanish Crown. At that time the Indian infested region north of Nuevo León had been created into the new province of Nuevo Santander. Later, a military expedition led by Don José Escandón was sent by the Viceroy with a two-fold purpose, namely to subdue the warlike Indian tribes and to look for suitable locations for settlements in the region between the Río Grande and the Nueces River.

Efficient and thorough in the work assigned him, Don Juan José accompanied his friend and commander through the wilderness of the Indian country. Together they explored the region, together they braved the dangers of the frontier, and together they fought and subdued the Indian tribes.

"The country must be colonized by all means," Altamira, the Auditor of War had told them. "Use whatever means you find within your reach, but colonize." Following the orders of the Viceroy and Altamira, Don Juan José thought of a plan, "Why couldn't we," he told Escandón, "get these northern *rancheros* interested in the movement? Why not offer land to those who want to expand the frontier to the north?"

Escandón approved of the plan and together they interviewed the ranchmen. These frontiersmen, who like new Lots were ever on the lookout for the means of extending their grazing lands, became interested in the colonizing scheme. At their own expense and at no cost to the Crown, these daring ambitious men offered to colonize towns and ranches along the Río Grande in exchange for all the grazing land they desired.

Together again, the Surveyor and the commander founded several missions and towns along the coast and hills of what is now Tamaulipas, and together they saw the foundations of the towns along the Río Grande, Camargo in 1748, and Mier, Revilla and Dolores one year later. While exploring the country Don Juan José learned to like the flower-covered prairies along the Nueces and the brush-covered land of the Río Grande.

He saw many promises in this land that invited him to remain and he asked Escandón, not only for permission to stay, but for a grant of land. Escandón acceded to his wishes, but with regret, for he was greatly attached to the man who had shared with him the dangers of the new frontier.

The Commander returned to the capital of the province; the Surveyor remained. And with the title of *Capitán*, Don Juan José, accompanied by the other ranchmen, formed the vanguard of this last frontier of the tottering Spanish empire. The need of more land for his rapidly increasing herds of cattle and flocks of goats and sheep, induced him to lead a roaming existence; the outlet for his nomadic wanderings being the grass-covered plains which extended to the east, towards the Nueces River.

He and his friend, Don Blas María de la Garza Falcón, founder of Camargo, drove part of their cattle across the river and established themselves at the Carnestolendas ranch.

By 1761 they advanced to within five miles of the Nueces River where they founded another settlement, the Petronila. Imitating their example, other ranchmen followed them and they also founded ranches in the valley south of the Nueces. Confident that his friend Escandón would approve their actions, Don Juan José, as Captain, encouraged more of the ranchmen in their northward migrations. His confidence in Escandón was well founded, for when the Commander returned, not only did he approve their actions but asked him, Don Juan José, to survey the land that he might legalize their possessions. He fulfilled his promise when *La Visita Real* issued the Royal grants in 1764.

Like Captain Olivares, the founders of these border towns and ranches were in the majority *criollos* or Spaniards. They were *gente de razón\** and the settlements they founded were destined to prosper and succeed because of "the desirable character of its citizens, and because even though small in number they were of good family and well to do."[1]

Captain Olivares, as did most of the *rancheros*, made his headquarters at Mier; the family lived there, but whenever the Indians were at peace he took his family on occasional visits to the ranches across the Río Grande.

A man of great physical strength, he spent most of his time going through his possessions; he loved the sense of ownership. He liked to feel that he had brought to this out-of-the-way corner of the Spanish Empire, the culture and civilization of the Spanish race. Sometimes alone, sometimes accompanied by *peones* and *vaqueros,* he traversed the wild Indian country with the same facility as though he were traversing the plains drained by the Guadalquiver\*\* of his native Sevilla. The journeys on horseback, the wounds he had received in the Indian campaigns, the exposures and privations he had suffered in the early days rapidly sapped his strength. At fifty he was almost an old man. Realizing that his days were few, he asked to be taken to Cerralvo where he had first met his friend Escandón. He died there in the bosom of our Mother, the Holy Roman Catholic and Apostolic Church, in the year 1773.

His oldest son Don José Alejandro succeeded him. Carrying out the wishes of his father that he should strengthen his ranches, specially those in the fertile plains beyond the Río Grande, he moved his family there and established himself permanently at what he called *El Olivareño*, the stronghold of the Olivares. His life, long, and uneventful,

---

[1]Escandón to the Viceroy, April 17, 1749, Provincias Internas Archivo General de la Nación, México, Historia, Inspección de Nuevo Santander, 1757, pp. 55, 64.

\*Literally, people reason. The Spaniards and their descendants differentiated themselves from the native element by calling themselves *gente de razón.*

\*\*The Guadalquiver River drains the southern part of Spain.

was one of peace and contentment. Changes of government meant nothing to him. The Mexican War of Independence came on and passed
unnoticed by the *rancheros* who continued living with easy-going
placidity. Thus, Don José Alejandro could tell nothing about the War of
Independence, except that he had married during the first year of it
(1810) at the age of fifty-seven, and that his son Cesareo had been born
one year later. Whether as subject of his Catholic Majesty or citizen of
the newly created Mexican republic, his chief interest remained ever the
same, to protect his family from the Indian invasions and to increase his
holdings. Don José Alejandro died of old age and contentment, at peace
with the world and himself, at the age of ninety-three.

His son Cesareo, the child of his old age, now a man of thirty-five,
continued his father's work. As was expected of him, the new leader of
the family went to Mier to look for a wife and married Doña Ramona
Hinojosa, a girl noted as much for her beauty as for her wealth. As the
only heir of her uncle Don Marcelo, she was the richest landowner in
northern Mexico.

While at Mier, Cesareo heard the most astonishing news. The
country north of the Nueces was being colonized by men who were not
of the Mexican race. He was told these men were *Americanos*, men
from the north, who came seeking homes in a land that was not theirs.
What surprised him most was that the government in Mexico had given
them permission to come. There were rumors also that these blue-eyed
strangers wanted to keep the land for themselves and were preparing for
war against the country that had given them hospitality. How true, he
thought, his father's homely proverb had been, "Raise crows and they
will pluck your eyes out." He had also heard of a powerful man who
was ruling the country, Santa Anna, who, he was told, had as much
power as the King of Spain had ever had.

He brought his bride home and life went on as placidly as before.
But soon rumors of wars began to spread. The foreigners had openly
declared their wish to take the country for themselves and many battles
had been fought between them and the Mexicans. One day, a man from
San Antonio came. He told them what he himself had seen with his own
eyes. Santa Anna had destroyed all the Americans with his army and
there was nothing more to fear from them.

Don Cesareo was sorry they had all been killed. Like the good
Catholic that he was, he had even said a few prayers for the repose of
their souls.

But that was as it should be, he thought. Why should they have
come to a land that was not theirs? Did they not have a country of their
own? Poor foolish men, these foreigners be, he mused, to think they

could take anything away from Mexico. Mexicans were courageous and could fight! Hadn't they heard how the Mexicans had driven out the mighty armies of the king of Spain from their country? He shuddered at the mere thought of the approach of these Americans. These men who were heretics should not come to Christian territory. He had read in a history his father left him that the Americans were the same as English, and the English had always been the enemies of Spain. One of his ancestors, if he remembered right, a captain of a Spanish galleon, had been killed by the English pirate Drake. Not only were they enemies of Spain but at one time the English had even dared to oppose the Pope, and all because he would not allow their king to have more than one wife. And if history was true the king's lawful wife had been a Spanish princess. Ah! these *Americanos* had a deathly heritage. They were the born enemies of every thing Spanish, and consequently they were the enemies of the Mexicans. Certainly, thought Don Cesareo, God, who was a Catholic, could not allow these people who were His enemies to take the land away from them!

When news came that Santa Anna had been defeated and that his troops had been forced to leave the country he felt as though the world was going mad. He could not believe it. It was impossible! How could these interlopers, these vandals take what had been given his ancestors by the king of Spain?

For a while nothing more was heard. Perhaps the news was not true. And then one morning when he and his *caporal** were riding through the pastures they had been accosted by a stranger who told them he had come to take possession of their land. And when he had replied that the stranger must be mistaken because he, Don Cesareo, was the rightful owner, the foreigner had taken out his pistol and had killed the *caporal* without any warning.

"Let that be a lesson to you Mexicans," the man had said, "that's how we shall deal with any one who opposes us, and unless you leave the country you shall be treated the same."

That had been the beginning of the struggle for possession of the land the Mexicans owned and the Americans coveted. During the period of lawlessness that followed, when both Americans and Mexicans stole freely from each other, the latter as a conquered race paid the greater price. While the American ranchmen prospered and profited, the Texas-Mexican landowners were forced to abandon their land. Only a few remained and those that stayed were those too powerful to be disturbed or those whose land was considered worthless. As a natural

¹*Caporal* means Foreman.

result frictions were constant along the frontier and the favorite pastime of both Mexican and American ranchmen was to see how much damage they could do to each other. A Mexican found stealing cattle from an American was hung. An American doing the same from a Mexican merely added a few head to his herd.

[Then the Cortina incident occurred. The son of a wealthy Spanish-Mexican family, Juan Nepomuceno, like all the Texas-Mexicans of his time, resented the conquest of their territory. But in spite of his resentment he and the men of his family had become American citizens. One day as he was riding through the streets of Brownsville, he came upon a deputy sheriff dragging a Mexican who had been his, Cortina's servant. In no gentle terms he asked the deputy to let the man go, and in no gentle terms the officer replied, "I'll do the same to any 'greaser' that crosses my path. I'll even do it to you." Cortina's answer was a shot. He then rescued the prisoner and rode across the river where he was acclaimed as a great hero. He became the self-appointed champion of the Mexican ranchmen in Texas who saw in him the leader that would free them from American domination and rule. As might be expected, this Robin Hood of the border became the idol of a certain element in the Mexican frontier. Assuming the role of a liberator he issued a proclamation explaining the purpose of his enterprise. This was, he told them, to punish the infamous villainy of the Americans who had banded together to rob and persecute the Mexicans for no other reason than that they were Mexicans, and to organize a society in Texas whose chief effort would be the extermination of the tyrants. Overnight Cortina became a great man. Not only was his position considered impregnable but he had defeated the *gringos*. The Mexican flag was floating from the flagpole in Brownsville and numbers were rallying to his standards. He became the champion of the Mexican race—the man who would right the wrongs of the Mexicans and drive the hated Americans to the Nueces.[2]][3]

But the climax to the Olivares, misfortunes came when Don Juan, Don Cesareo's younger brother, was killed in a most brutal manner. He was on his way to San Antonio to sell a herd of cattle. Six *vaqueros* and Luis, a young cousin, accompanied him. For five days they had fol-

---

[2]Major Heitzelman to General Lee. Executive documents. First Session of the Thirty-Sixth Congress. 1859, 1860.

[3]This bracketed passage, beginning "Then the Cortina incident occurred" is crossed out in the manuscript I restore it here for its historical significance. Cortina was one of the first Texas-Mexicans to offer organized resistance to the Anglo-Americans.

lowed the trail in a happy, care-free way. They sang their songs as they rode along and by night told their tales around the campfire. The afternoon of the sixth day Don Luis noticed they had lost the trail. Night was coming and just before dark they came to a ranch house. Here Don Juan stopped to ask for food and lodging for the night.

Too late he realized the place was owned by Americans and he had started to leave when the owner came out and asked him and the boy to come in and have supper with him. The *vaqueros*, the American told Don Juan, could camp out near the house. Just as they were beginning to eat, shots were heard. Don Juan ran to the door and what he saw made him realize he had been caught in a trap. The *vaqueros* lay dead on the ground.

"My men have given them a warm reception, my friend," his host told Juan. "I don't want to have to do the same with you but I shall be forced to unless you do as you are told. Hand over the cattle to me and I shall let you go."

"Kill me if you will," answered Don Juan, "but my brother's cattle are not mine to give away." No sooner were the words said then he was shot through the head.

"Go," the American told the boy. "Tell Don Cesareo what you have seen, tell him I have warned him enough, and that unless he leaves the land I shall treat him as I did his brother."

This incident, together with the constant warfare waged along the frontier, made Don Cesareo see that the turning point in his life had come. Two paths lay before him: leave Texas and return to the family estate in Mexico or join Cortina. The last he would not do, not that he considered him an outlaw as the *Americanos* did, but he thought enough blood had already been shed.

Like Boabdil the lesser who wept for his beloved Granada, he had not been strong enough to resist the onrush of the enemy, and like the Moorish monarch, he and his family were forced to abandon the land won by the sweat and blood of his ancestors.

The bitterness of defeat, the thought that he had lost the heritage of his ancestors, the very idea that he had been unfaithful to the sacred trust confided upon him crushed his proud spirit. He died a broken-hearted man leaving Doña Ramona, a spirited, arrogant woman to look after his possessions and their three orphaned children, Francisco, the oldest, a boy of twelve, Fernando aged ten, and María Rosa, the baby.

Doña Ramona's task was a difficult one. Not only did she have to look after the ranch and the welfare of the *peones*, but she had to be the guardian of the families who had been left fatherless by the Americans.

A woman of great strength and character, a woman who felt deeply, she could love and she could hate with equal vehemence. Her husband's name became a shrine of love and hate where she worshiped the memory of the man martyred by the hated foreigners.

Two things she kept before the minds of her children, particularly of Francisco; that they had been despoiled of their land and they must remain true to their traditions.

"My son," she often told Francisco, "later in life when you are a man you are bound to meet the enemies of your family. When that happens there is only one thing for you to do. Kill—and kill without compassion. Spare no one; if one of these foreigners should fall into your hands—kill him. If he should ask you for mercy, kill him; if he should kneel at your feet and beg for his life, kill him. Did they have mercy on your uncle Juan? Did they show mercy to your father? Did they have compassion on the hundreds they despoiled of their land? The blood of your father and of your uncle calls for vengeance!"

Time did not heal Doña Ramona's grief, neither did it soften her feelings for the people whom she believed had been the cause of her misfortunes.

The close of the American Civil War found her feeling as bitterly as she had ten years before. It was about this time that a new type of American came to the border. People from Virginia, Alabama, Kentucky, and the Carolinas, people of culture who had been impoverished by the Civil War. They did not come to profit by the spoils of war; they were the victims of war coming to look for peace and a new home. Carpetbag rules and the persecutions which they had gone through in their own homes made them have a kindly feeling for the *rancheros* who had undergone the same fate as a result of another war. They saw in the simple, easygoing life of the few remaining *rancheros* a similarity to the rural life they had been accustomed to and this, together with the fact that both had been unfortunate made them become friends.

One of these men, John Warren Preston Don Juan, as he came to be called married a cousin of Doña Ramona. And it was through him that the widow of Don Cesareo learned that not all Americans were cruel, heartless, avaricious men. This courteous, well-mannered man was much like her father had been. He had the same fine sentiments as her husband had had.

He and his wife often came to see Doña Ramona and both had invited her to visit them in Texas. But that she would not do.

"Why not let me take the boys?" Don Juan had once insisted. Perhaps something might be done someday about the ranch. And then the boys will have benefited by knowing what life in Texas is like."

He had also asked Doña Ramona to let him see the title to the grant deeded to Don Juan José and signed by Escandón and the Viceroy.

"Trust this document to me as you have your boys," Don Juan Preston told her. "I promise nothing but I'll do what I can."

Six months later he returned, the bearer of good news.

The State of Texas had recognized Doña Ramona's rights to the land where the Olivareño was located, sixty thousand acres in all; but the land on the Nueces was gone, he told her. It had been appropriated by a powerful man, a cattle baron of the state.[4]

This good action on the part of the American somewhat changed Doña Ramona's opinion. Perhaps she had misjudged these people, she thought; perhaps there were some who had a good heart and were not evil. The news of her good fortune spread through the Mexican towns and ranches, and many who had sworn never to go back, returned to their abandoned ranches across the river.

Again Don Juan acted, and again through his efforts many of the *rancheros* regained a part, if not all of their possessions in Texas.

Then there followed a return of the wealthy Texas-Mexican families. With them returned the culture of another race and another country. Again Mexico extended beyond the Río Grande; again the Mexican element, greater in number than the Americans, ruled the country that had once been explored by Escandón and settled by the early pioneers.

Interracial peace returned. In the towns, Americans, Germans, and French intermarried with the descendants of the old Mexican families, and Spanish became again the language of society.

Doña Ramona never returned to the Olivareño. She could not bear to set foot on territory tainted by the foreigners, but she commanded her sons, Francisco and Fernando to return. With them came their herds of cattle, the flocks of sheep and goats, and the *peones* who formed part of the Olivareño estate. Again the Olivares held dynastic sway over the land of their fathers and they were happy.

[4]A reference to the expansive King Ranch of this time and place? See Montejano (1987: 63-73).

# CHAPTER II
## The Stronghold of the Olivares[1]

In his spacious house in the center of the land he loved so well, Don Francisco de los Olivares lived like a feudal lord. Princely in generosity, but vindictive in revenge, he was ever in readiness to receive friends and foes, the former with open arms, the latter with ready arms. As head of his family, he led a patriarchal existence. His word was authority, no other law was needed, and there was no need of civil interference. Accustomed to command, he was master of everything, not only of the land he possessed but of the *peones* who worked the soil.

Proud, aristocratic, and a gentleman by inheritance, he retained those characteristics in the wilderness in which he lived. He was proud of two things, that he was a gentleman and that the land he possessed had been in the family for generations past. His one endeavor was to make his ranch a miniature Mexico. His family was encouraged and expected to keep intact the customs and traditions of the mother country; the servants and *peones* were commanded to follow in the footsteps of their equals in Mexico.

A tyrant by inheritance and breeding, Don Francisco was feared and respected by all who knew him. And whenever he appeared in the *corral* riding his powerful black horse, his eyebrows contracted in a frown, one higher than the other, the stoutest *vaquero* trembled in his boots. His expression was the sign of a tempest that would soon hurl itself with the fury of a tropical hurricane. As he rode through his possession, lashing

---

[1]The first nine pages of this chapter were stored separately but were marked as designated for Chapter II with no other direction. They seem to make the most narrative sense here. See footnote 3.

the *vaqueros* with his tongue and not seldom with his *riata,** no one dared utter a word.

But though he was the master of many he was the slave of one— Doña Margarita, his wife. And as he thundered through the rooms of the house, his spurs echoing through the tile floors, one look from his wife was sufficient to calm him. Often, when he was in one of his dark moods or when angered by the mismanagement of the *caporal,* she would come to him and say:

"Francisco, my Lamb, let me read to you a while." Then the lion, now a lamb indeed, sat by her while she read to him from the lives of the Saints, from a popular Spanish version of *Romeo and Juliet,* or from some romantic novel. When her reading was not sufficient to soothe him, she played melodies that both had loved in their youth. Doña Margarita was the undisputed mistress of her home, her eight children (all married now, save Rosita) and the women of the ranch. She had a maternal feeling for the poor whom she considered sent to her by Providence. Every evening, in the *patio,* while the warm weather lasted, and in the *sala,* during the winter, she gathered the women and children around her, instructed them in religion, told them stories, or played the harp. She always ended the gatherings with prayers, punctuated nearly always by commands or reproofs.

"Hail Mary, full of grace—Francisco, you are nodding, my Love, the Lord is with thee—Felipe, stop tickling your sister, Blessed art thou amongst women—Francisco, I heard you snore... Pray for us sinners, now and at the hour of our death."

In its simplicity, life at the Olivareño was like that of a small pastoral kingdom. The necessities of life were few; the government of the ranch, as understood by Don Francisco, was a paternal hierarchy with himself as absolute ruler.

With him he brought the system of peonage, perfected by centuries of existence and this he enforced at the ranch. As owner of the land he had certain duties toward his servants, and they in turn had specific obligations to perform. He was the protector in time of danger, the advisor and counselor, and not seldom the judge who tried the case and inflicted punishment. Besides these moral duties he had material obligations, toward his *peones* and their families. He furnished their living quarters and some articles of food besides payment of a small sum of money.

The servant class, as treated by Don Francisco, was composed of two distinct and separate groups: the cowboys and the *peones.* The for-

*Riata*—lariat.

mer, either *mestizos\** or *criollos* were fiery spirited men, wild and untamed, over whom Don Francisco had no control. A product of the frontier, they disliked law and restraint and hated innovations and new-comers. The open prairie, was their haven and as they galloped across the prairie both horse and rider appeared as one. They were the sons of the small landowners who did not have enough to occupy them at their own ranch.

The *peones*, on the other hand, led the same life of submission their brethren did in Mexico. Immigrants from that country, the Olivares had brought them to Texas to work. They had been with the family for gen-erations, obeyed the master's orders blindly and had no will of their own. They could never hope to rise to the dignity of being *vaqueros*, but became goatherds, worked the fields, performed all the menial and manual labor around the ranch, and sometimes became the personal ser-vants of the master and his sons.

A closer relationship existed between the *peones* and Don Francisco than between the *vaqueros* and the ranchmen. To the *peones*, the *amo* was master; to the *vaqueros*, the landlord was merely the owner of the cattle he punched. A social racial, and economic gulf separated the *peones* from the landowner, but the *vaquero* might some day rise to the level of his more fortunate associate. (9 cf. González 1927)

Since the *peones* received very small remuneration for their work they were always in debt to Don Francisco. In case of necessity, of sick-ness or death, he furnished the money and this formed a debt which the *peones* could never hope to pay. Besides debts similar to these, they were cursed with the debt was which was handed down from father to son, making the *peón* a serf to the land. The food debt accumulated year after year. Its existence dated back to colonial times when the landlords forced their Indians to buy at their own commissaries. Following this old custom Don Francisco had a general store at the ranch where the *peones* could buy all they needed, from patent medicines to calico. All goods were sold on credit and at a high price. An unfortunate situation resulted from this system; it gave Don Francisco absolute power over the *peones* and this control tended to convert them into a machine whom he could work at his will.

The *peones* often realized their position, grew pessimistic, and developed a spirit of hopelessness and despair. There was no incentive for them to save, since whatever they might economize went to pay for inherited debt. In this way the master, Don Francisco, exercised com-plete control over the *peones*, economically as well as socially. They

---

*\*Mestizo*—A person of mixed Indian and Spanish blood.

did not own any property. They might possessor of a goat, a few chickens and a pig, and these only if they were kept within their own enclosure. Neither did they cultivate any soil for themselves. In the backyard of the *jacal** their wife might plant a few rows of corn or beans and a few pumpkin vines. On the other hand, they were allowed the use or as many milk cows as they needed, and when Don Francisco butchered they were allotted a certain amount of meat.

The existence of such conditions does not imply that Don Francisco was cruel or unjust. The customs merely part of a system that had been inherited by both classes. Neither one nor the other knew of a better plan; the unfairness and injustice of it was never realized by the master and the *peones* looked upon it as a thing that had to be.

The living quarters of the *peones*, in keeping with their material position, consisted of a one-room, thatch-roof, dirt-floor *jacal*, which served as living room and bedroom as well. The kitchen was a still more miserable shack, often roofless, and many times without a fireplace.

[The furniture, which was of the most rudimentary type, was homemade. The bed simply consisted of four poles dug into the dirt-floor with boards across it, no springs, and a grass mattress. A few chairs, a table, and a small mirror hung on the white-washed wall, completed the furniture of the *peon's* home. But in all the homes, however humble they might be, a statue or an image of Our Lady of Guadalupe, enshrined in paper or natural flowers, occupied the place of honor.

Far different from the wretched existence of the *peones* was that of Don Francisco. His was a life of easy-going simplicity, not without its charms.][2]

Characteristically Spanish, he did not perform any of the manual work himself. He directed the farm work and rode out to the pasture with the *vaqueros*. During sheepshearing time when a thousand or more head of sheep were sheared or when the calves were marked and the cattle branded, he supervised the work.

Whereas Don Francisco was absolute master of the ranch, Doña Margarita had complete control in the management of the home. She was an excellent housekeeper and her home, which had all the comforts attainable in those days, was the center of border culture and hospitality.

---

*_Jacal_—thatch-roofed hut.

[2]Manuscript has what appear to be two cross-out marks over this bracketed passage. I restore it here for the focused ethnographic sense it gives us of a *peón* household.

Proud of her position as a leader in the rural society in which she lived, she had bought the best furniture that could be had. The bedrooms, almost luxurious in their equipment, had carved beds with tall canopies and draperies. Marble-top dressers, tables, and chests of drawers completed the furniture. Pictures drawn by the young ladies of the family, samplers, and tapestries decorated the walls.

The inside arrangement of the house, wherein reigned Doña Margarita Guerra de los Olivares, was typically Mexican. The principal room of the house was a big *sala*, the living room, where the family sat and talked in the evenings. Here, cane chairs, wide and low, and cushioned rockers with friendly arms extended, offered their welcome to friends and relatives. Deer, wildcat, and coyote skins took the place of rugs; mounted deer heads, powder horns and hunting guns added to the rustic simplicity and charm. And from a built-in niche, lit by crude, hand-made copper candlesticks smiled benignly the family Saint, a miraculous image of the Christ child.

Adjoining this *sala* was a smaller room, which Doña Margarita had furnished with all the feminine coquetry of her nature and where she entertained her friends. Only the daughters had their rooms in the house proper. When the sons came to be of age, their rooms were in the men's quarters in a nearby building.

The kitchen and dining room, which formed a separate establishment, were joined to the house by a long rambling *portal*. *Under its friendly shade hung Don Francisco's saddles, his spurs, the horse-hair lariats and the raw-hide braided quirts.

On the east side, an earthen pot *olla*, covered with canvas, which hung from one of the beams, was suspended from a hand-wrought iron hook. Two gourd dippers, mossy and dripping, hung by the side.

Perhaps the most interesting room of all was the kitchen with its enormous fireplace occupying one end of the room. It was about three feet from the floor and enabled the cook to do the work while standing. The iron and copper pots and skillets hung from nails on either side of the fireplace, and to prevent fires the kitchen had a dirt floor.

The dining room, inviting and cheerful with its huge beams across the roof, and its big home-made mesquite table and benches, was always ready to welcome the host of friends, travelers and transients who visited the ranch. Any traveler who passed by during meal hours was invited by Don Francisco to share the hospitality of the house.

*Portal—rambling porch, sometimes thatch-roofed.*

Proud of his position and wealth, twice a year, on Christmas Eve and Saint John's Day, he gave dances which were epoch-making in the border communities. To these he invited all the landed aristocracy from the surrounding country and from town. The ladies came in the family coach, escorted by mounted cavaliers who rode by the side of the carriage. A midnight supper was served and wine flowed freely.

On New Year's Day he took his family to town to share in the festivities of the season. The army camp stationed there, the nearness to the Mexican towns, the coming of officials from across the river added a touch of glamour and romance to this border town. Life was gay, exciting, at times even turbulent.

These dances, he often remarked, had made him lose his daughters. At one of them Ramona, the oldest, had met a Mexican officer, and one year later she left as a bride, to live in Mexico. At another, Dolores had fallen in love with a Frenchman, who according to Don Francisco, was a cross between a gentleman and a tradesman, for besides being consular agent for the French government, he was the leading merchant in town. María, now the wife of a German engineer at Monterrey, had also met "her carrot-headed glass-eyed" husband at another New Year's dance.

It was often said of Don Francisco that he was so busy being busy that he had no time for work. For when he was not riding with his *caporal*, he was arranging a hunt, a cockfight, a *rodeo* or attending the races in town. Thus lived Don Francisco, in the midst of this rural splendor, enjoying life to the fullest never realizing that he was a foreigner in his own land.[3]

It was August down in the Río Grande. The rays of the sun beat mercilessly upon the sandy stretches of yellow grass-covered prairie which glared angrily back at the sun. Gleamingly white, under the scorching sun, on a bend of *el Camino Real,* the king's highway, stood a pretentious house, rambling and flat roofed. Its grilled doors and windows and thick stone walls showed its Spanish or Mexican descendency. Stone benches, called *pollitos* because they were attached and formed part of the house, were on either side of the main door. Hackberry and cottonwood trees shaded the patio on the west side and a few pomegranate trees and oleanders in bloom added color to the landscape. A *maguey* fence surrounded the house; the iron-grilled gate swung from an ebony tree post and was latched to another by a handmade lock.

A man riding a spirited *potro\** galloped into view, dismounted at the gate with a leap, and not even glancing at a barefooted Indian boy

---

[3]End of inserted pages. Found separately.

who came running out to meet him, threw the reins at him. Banging the gate with a vicious clang, he stamped his way into the rambling portal which led to the *patio* of the house.

He was a picturesque figure, hardly conceivable in the United States, much more so in the year of Our Lord 1904—tight-fitting brown jacket, bell-shaped trousers and gay sarape over one shoulder, showed to advantage the slender body of the man who, although past his sixtieth year, was still in the prime of manhood. The lean face, with its pointed beard, clearcut features and deep-gray eyes, was contracted in a frown of anger, as he walked up and down clinking his silver spurs on the brick floor of the patio.

He stopped as though struck by a sudden thought; then cupping his hands in the manner of men used to speaking across the stretches of the Texas plains he called out:

"Marcos, Marcos."

Hurried footsteps were heard in answer, and an Indian *peón* stood before him hat in hand.

"Mande Vd. Don Francisco. Did you desire something?"

"Yes, you Indian bastard; have all the guests left?"

"Sí, my master."

"Tell your mistress I have returned."

"Yes, Don Francisco."

"And do it immediately, you son of ten thousand devils! Why do you stand there like a scarecrow staring at me?"

"For nothing master, for nothing," answered the *peón*, retreating as quickly as he could.

He continued pacing the patio with the steps of a caged mountain lion. What a fool he had been! He thought to himself, "an idiotic, doddering, spineless old fool too," emphasizing each discovery with a vindictive blow of his rawhide quirt on the helpless posts of the *portal*. Just that morning, armed with a pistol, knife, rope, and coyote poison, he had left the ranch suicide-bound, determined to end his life one way or another; and here he was back as usual, unharmed and very much alive, to face the scornful look on his wife's face. And all because he could not yield like any other father to the fact that his girls must marry. It wasn't that he wanted to keep them at home; but he was a father, he excused himself, and hated to see them leave the paternal roof. Fortunately, there was just one more, Rosita, his baby, and then he would be free from such scenes.

*Potro*—untamed horse.

"Why couldn't they have remained babies; we could have been so happy!" he mumbled, glaring angrily ahead.

"Francisco, my Love, you are an idiot," echoed a woman's voice. He whirled around. In the doorway stood Doña Margarita, his wife, stately and serene, still wearing the silk dress she had worn at her daughter's wedding. The look of anger faded and an ashamed expression suffused his handsome face.

"I know it, my Pearl," he replied meekly.

"You must be tired tonight," she continued, ignoring his behavior of the day. "Why not have Marcos bring your chair to the patio? It will be cool when the *lagueño** begins to blow, and from here you can watch the moon as it comes up. Do you remember that song we used to sing with the children when they were little?

> 'The lazy moon so full and red,
> Comes up surrounded by tinkling bells,
> Four pretty maids are playing a tune
> And Angels a lullaby croon.'

Do you remember, Francisco?"

"Yes, my Pearl."

"Here is your chair now," she added, seeing the *peón* approach. "Place it here, Marcos. What shall it be tonight? Shall I sing or play for you?"

"Whatever pleases you most, my Dove."

"Then it shall be both—Marcos, take off your master's shoes and make him comfortable."

"Sí, señora."

The precluding notes were played on a harp, and a song broke the peaceful stillness of the evening. The mistress of the house was singing what could only soothe the troubled, turbulent spirit of her husband – music of his native land.

The sun, a ball of orange pink, descended down the horizon at one stride and a soft cooling breeze, the pulmotor of the borderland, sprung from the east. Down in the *Cañada* (canebrake) which ran by the ranch, the doves were cooing and the redbirds in the cottonwood grove by the dirt 'tank' near the house began to sing. From the corrals came the voices of the *vaqueros* singing and jesting, and blended with the bleating of the goats and the sheep were the whistles and hisses of the pastor. The shrill, garrulous stridulations of the locusts completed the chorus of

---

*Lagueño—breeze from the Gulf of Mexico.

evening noises. Darkness subdued them; then as the moon came up, an unaccounted mob of mongrel curs set up a barking at it. [4]

As he sat there, listening to the soft notes of forgotten tunes, memories of the past, like flocks of returning swallows in spring, winged their way across his mind. He saw himself a child of twelve, at the bedside of a dying man; his mother kneeling at the foot of the bed, saying the De Profundis, the prayer for the dying; and the priest blessing the sick man. He could hear his gasping words, "Francisco, my son, soon you will be the head of the family; be the protector of your mother and the guardian of your sister and little brother. Remember yours is an honorable name, and above all, never forget the heroic deeds of your people. In time of trouble, in time of stress, let the motto of our family be your guide, 'Like an oak I may be bent but not broken.' My son," the dying man continued, "when you become a man take the cattle across the Bravo into Texas, to the land which the viceroy deeded my grandfather, Don Juan José. It is our heritage which I leave to you. And may God and His holy Mother be your guide."

He remembered how Don Cesareo, as was due one of his rank, was buried under the altar of the church, and how Doña Ramona, his widow, had become the mistress of her possessions. A tower of strength was she, and with an iron hand she ruled the *peones* who might have otherwise disregarded her position because she was a woman. He could see her, contrary to the custom of her time, riding with him and the *vaqueros* to the pastures whenever necessity required it of her. He remembered how once, her small, slender frame shaking with anger and indignation, she had slapped a *vaquero* who had dared to use an ugly word in her presence.

He could see her so distinctly even now as head of her household, stern and severe; her pale face, clearcut as an ivory cameo, contrasting with the snappy black eyes that saw everything and shone like burning coals when provoked to anger. And again her memory came to him, but in a different mood; not as the mistress to be feared, but as a mother, a Mater Dolorosa ever anxious for her children. Dressed in black, a mother-of-pearl and silver crucifix on her breast, lace mantilla covering the soft wavy hair, just turning gray, he remembered going to church with her; he could still hear her words, as she led him to that altar, "My child, pray for your father who lies buried here."

Grown to early manhood he remembered making love to the servant girls with the ardor and impetuousness of youth. He saw himself

---

[4]For another version of this character who laments the marriages of his daughters and is calmed by his wife, see Don José María in González (1932).

facing Doña Ramona in her room; her hair, almost white now, framed her deep-lined face. But the eyes had retained the fire and spirit of former times. Unable to stand the look of disgust and contempt in them, he had stopped to kiss her hand, but she had withdrawn it with violence."The kiss of one who is not a gentleman soils my hand," he heard her say. Another scene came to his mind; it was his wedding day. Contrary to tradition and his mother's wishes he was not wearing the black, formal suit. He was a *ranchero* and he preferred to dress like one. The finest buckskin suit trimmed in silver buttons had been brought from Saltillo for the occasion. Again he stood in his mother's room but this time for a mother's blessing. "Francisco, my first born," she had said, "dearer to me than life itself, tomorrow you will leave me to fulfill your father's wish. My heart bleeds for you when I see you go to another land. You will re-enter the heritage of your ancestors, it is true, yet you will be ruled by people who are the born enemies of your race. But remember, my boy, that wherever you may be, wherever you may go, you are the heir of a proud name and a prouder race. Keep your faith and be what God destined you to be, a Mexican and a gentleman."

The scene changed again. He could hear the cowboys urging and encouraging the frightened cattle to cross the river. He saw an oxcart loaded with household goods awaiting on the other side of the stream— a young girl, silent tears rolling down her face, stood by his side waving goodbye to those whom they had just left.

Trembling with joy and emotion he found himself again in his mother's presence, a newborn baby in his arms.

"He is yours, *mi madre*, hold him in your arms and bless him."

"Your first son and born in God's land."

"Of course, *mi madre*, did you think I'd ever want a child of mine to bear the traitor's brand?* I've already registered him in the *Palacio*, Francisco José de los Olivares, a proud name. No child of mine will ever be born in Texas."

That had been almost forty years before, and now his ranch, *El Olivareño*, The Stronghold of the Olivares, was one of the richest estates on the lower Río Grande. God had been good to him. He sighed contentedly, settled himself more comfortably in his chair and fell asleep.

In the afternoon of the following day Don Francisco, returning from a lonely ride in the pastures, was seen coming through the peons' quarters. He was in good humor, as always happened after a stormy

---

*Because a number of Mexicans fought on the side of the Texas Revolution against Mexico, the Mexicans of the lower Río Grande country called Texas a land of traitors.

scene at home, still felt remorseful but uncomfortable, conscience-stricken yet because of the bad behavior of the day before.

"*Ea muchachos*!" he called to a group of children, "What are you doing there? Why aren't you helping your mothers?"

"We are playing a game, señor."

"A very pretty one too, master; one that Rosita taught us," answered a bright-eyed little girl, "We'll play it for you too, Don Francisco, do you want to hear it?"

"*Excelente*! and if it is to my liking I'll give each one of you a '*gordo*'," he said, displaying before the astonished eyes of the children a handful of nickels.

"This is the way we do it, señor," continued the self-appointed speaker of the group, "We make a circle and the Golden Angel stands outside. Don't you want to be It? Please, *señor*, will you be the Golden Angel?"

"*¡Bueno! ¡Bueno!*" shouted the children dancing in glee as the newly-appointed Golden Angel dismounted from his horse.

The children's cries of merriment brought the women to the door of their *jacales*.

"*Válgame Dios.*\* Look, Mariana! Thirty years have I been at this ranch and never did I see what I behold now."

"I cannot believe what the eyes see," replied the old woman.

A strange sight it was indeed! In the center of the circle stood Don Francisco, bowing to the children and clapping his hands to keep time as they skipped and sang around him:

> "An angel of gold, am I this day,
> wearing a marquis brilliant crown,
> away from France have I come down
> in search of a Portuguese prince.

> "Good morning, my lady I wish to thee
> Good morning, my lady the Prince I see,
> Good morning, my lady I take him with me
> Dear lady, I take him to France, you see."

"Ah, these children!" he said sheepishly to the women who had assembled to see the strange spectacle. "No respect have they for my gray beard; at my age they make me do foolish things."

"Tonight we shell corn," he continued. "Ambrosio has prepared a barbecue. I want everyone to come. Tell the men. I shall expect every-

---

\**Valgame Dios*—May the Lord have mercy on me.

one as soon as the full moon comes up," he added, waving his hat as he galloped away.

Later in the evening, under the moonlit sky, the ranch hands, *peones,* and goatherds gathered at the Master's house. It was a merry crowd who joked and laughed with the boisterous, unrestrained animation of children.

A broad-shouldered, bowlegged *vaquero*, the self-appointed master of ceremonies, laughed loud and long as he greeted each guest.

"*Caramba, caramba,*" he shouted, slapping the side of his legs by way of emphasis. "Will you look and see who is coming?" he commanded, pointing to a thin, shriveled man who, followed by a brood of children, neared the group with a shamed expression and an apologetic look on his face.

"No other than Julianito with his flock of wild young ones. I have not told you his last adventure, have I?" he continued, ignoring the look of displeasure on the face of Alejo, the old white-haired fiddler of the ranch. "It is a very funny thing. Last Friday, when my wife was going to wash a pile of flour sacks she had been saving, much to her surprise she found them missing. I told her what everyone knows, that if she would offer what she had lost to an imp of Satan he would find it for her. And sure enough, an imp of Satan, in form of Julian there, did the trick. Much to everyone's amusement, the following Sunday, Tío Julianito's children appeared in uniforms of white, looking like sheeted ghosts. The funniest thing to see was the thick, floured, black little faces. In his hurry he had not bothered to wash the sacks but had merely made a hole at the end on either side."

"For shame, Martiniano," admonished the old fiddler again. "Laughing at motherless children. Your words do not surprise me though. 'He who keeps the company of wolves will learn to howl,' says the old proverb. You have learned that from Coyote. If there ever was a lowborn rascal, he is that."

"Was he not the one Don Francisco dismissed from the ranch?" queried one of the cowboys.

"And he deserved it too. He is the very same who humiliated Tío Patricio before the grand company one Christmas Eve."

"Ah, here comes Capul," cried Martiniano, not a bit abashed by the fiddler's reprimand.

Debonair and graceful in carriage, the new arrival joined them with a happy, broad grin. The name Capul, Blackberry, given him by popular consent, suited him well. Of an ebony-like blackness, his regular features, snappy black eyes, white flashing teeth and an exuberant good humor made him a unique, if somewhat strange-figure among the lean, wiry, bronzed cowboys and the squat, swarthy Indian *peones*. He was not a native of the border country. Many years before he had wandered into the ranch from no-one-knew-where, a ragged, hungry, black imp, guitar under arm. His ability to play that instrument and improvise songs often reminded Don Francisco of the singing mulattos he had seen and heard sing along the coast. But whatever his ancestry might have been, Capul had been adopted by the ranch people and was now the official singer at all the gatherings in the countryside.[5]

"Where is your guitar?" Don Francisco asked him.

"Close to my heart where it should be, Master," he answered with a happy grin.

"Fine, fine, things do improve when you give us music. What will you sing?"

To answer the black-faced Capul improvised,

> "Singing I hope to die
> Singing I want to be buried,
> And singing I'll go to heaven
> To face the eternal Father."

"Bravo, bravo, my boy," enthused the Master. Encouraged by Don Francisco's praise, Capul gave a yell of exhilaration, threw the guitar up into space, caught it in mid-air and began plucking the strings with sharp staccato notes as he sang again,

> "I like to sing of my freedom
> Like the birds that cross that sky,
> I do not nest on this earth
> But build on the mountains high."

"*Muy bueno muchacho*, very good, my boy," said Don Francisco, slapping him on the back by way of encouragement. "Your singing will always draw all like honey draws the bees."

In the meantime a big circular canvas had been stretched under the *portal* facing the kitchen. Rows of unshelled ears of corn, forming pyramids in the center, gleamed silvery white under the bright semi-tropical moon. Waiting neither for comment nor explanation, the Master's guests sat around the canvas within reach of the grain. Everyone knew what that meant. At a given signal the shellers began their task. "Swish, swish, swish," went the grains of corn as they hit the canvas with a soft whispering sound. Like the big clear drops of a summer shower the white grains slid from the brown fingers of the shellers. "Swish, swish,

[5]Here, González may be referencing the incorporating reception in Mexican South Texas of runaway black slaves from Anglo Central and East Texas.

swish," the sound became rhythmical as did the movements of the dark bodies silhouetted against the white light of the moon.[6]

"What a priceless privilege is mine," thought Don Francisco watching the silent figures at work, "to be the guardian of all these people, but what a heavy responsibility comes with it too, more so now than ever before. For I see the end of this peaceful happy existence. I can see my people scattered over the borderland like dry leaves driven by the autumn wind. The Americans are beginning to invade the stronghold of our people, and with that will begin the end of the *rancheros'* power, my power. Will the Olivares be again the exiles they have been before or will they be swept by the inevitable current of things?"

A shrill, strident whistle broke the tranquil stillness of night.

"The screech owl, the messenger of the Devil," shrieked one of the women. "May the saints have mercy on us."

"Calm yourself, Mariana," scolded Don Francisco. "Don't you know the Evil One has no power in Texas? Haven't you ever heard how Satan was fooled once here on earth and by a Texas *vaquero* at that? Since then he has had no desire to ever return here."

The astonished old woman, with a look of unbelief on her wrinkled bat-like face, could only shake her head on hearing the unheard-of statement.

"It is God's truth, Mariana, and I shall tell you about it. It is a tale which my grandfather told me on such a night as this, a story which he heard from his own grandfather, who got it from a wandering *vaquero* who might have been Pedro de Urdemañas himself. If you are ready, I shall begin now:

## The Devil in Texas[7]

It was an abnormally hot day in Hell. The big devils and the little devils were all busy feeding the fires, making final preparations to give a warm reception to a barber and a banker who had announced their arrival. A timid knock sounded on the door and Satan, who was sitting on a throne of flames, sent one of his henchmen to see who the arrivals might be. In walked three men. One with razor in hand, gave away his profession; the second held on to a wallet like Judas Iscariot to his. The two were abnormally terrified. The third did not seem a bit impressed

[6]The corn shelling account appears in a separate and abbreviated version in González (1932a).

[7]González published versions of these devil stories separately (1930a).

by the fiery reception awarded them, but with the coolness and noncha-
lance of one accustomed to such things glanced about with a look of
curiosity. He was an athletic sort of man, wore a five-gallon hat, chaps,
spurs, and played with a lariat he held in his hands. He seemed to be as
much at home as the others were terrified. Before he was assigned any
particular work, he walked to where a devil was shoveling coals, and
taking the shovel from his hands, began to work. Satan was so
impressed that he paid no attention to the others but went to where the
stranger was. He did not like this man's attitude at all. He liked to
watch the agony on the face of the condemned, but here was this man
as cool as a September morn. He went through the flames, over the
flames, into the flames-and did not mind the heat at all. This was more
than his Satanic Majesty could endure. Approaching the man he commanded him to stop and listen to what he had to say. But the man
would not stop and kept on working.

"Oh well," said Satan, "if that's the way you feel, keep it up, but I
really would like to know something about you and where you come
from."

"Then I feel I must satisfy your curiosity," the stranger replied. "I
am Pedro de Urdemañas by name.[8] I have lived through the ages
deceiving people, living at the expense of women who are foolish
enough to fall in love with me. Now as a beggar, now as a blind man I
have earned my living. As a gypsy and a horse trader in Spain, then as a
soldier of fortune in the new world, I have managed to live without
working. I have lived through the equatorial heat of South America,
through the cold of the Andes and desert heat of the Southwest. I am
immune to the heat and the cold, and really bask in the warmth of this
place."

The Devil was more impressed than ever and wanted to know
more of this strange personage.

"Where was your home before you came here?" he continued.

"Oh, in the most wonderful land of all. I am sure you would love
it. Have you ever been in Texas?"

The devil shook his head.

"Well, that's where I come from. It is a marvelous country."

"Indeed," said the Evil One, "and what is it like?"

---

[8]The well-known rogue-trickster figure of Spanish/Latin American tradition.

Pedro described the land in such glowing terms that the Devil was getting interested in reality. "And what's more," continued Pedro, "there is plenty of work for you down there."

At this Satan cocked his ears, for if there was one thing he liked better than anything else it was to get more workers for his shops.

"But, listen," he confided, "you say there are many cows there. Well you see, I have never seen one and would not know what to do were I to see one."

"You have nothing to fear about that. There is a marked similarity between you and a cow. Both have horns and a tail. I am sure you and the cows will become very good friends."

After this comparison, Satan was more anxious than ever to go to this strange land where cows lived.

So early the next day before the Hell fires were started, he set out earth-bound. Since his most productive work had been done in the cities and he knew nothing of ranch life, Satan left for Texas gaily appareled in the latest city styles. He knew how to dress and as he strolled through the earth seeking for Texas, he left many broken hearts in his path.

Finally, on an August day he set foot on a little prairie surrounded by thorny brush, near the lower Río Grande. It was a hot day indeed. The sand that flew in whirlwinds was hotter than the flames of the infernal region. It burned the Devil's face and scorched his throat. His tongue was swollen; his temples throbbed with the force of a hammer's beat. As he staggered panting under the noonday heat, he saw something that gladdened his eyes. A muddy stream glided its way lazily across a sandy bed. His eyes caught sight of a small plant bearing red berries and his heart gladdened at the sight of it. It was too good to be true. Here was what he most wished for—water and fresh berries to eat. He picked a handful of the ripest and freshest and with the greediness of the starved put them all into his mouth. With a cry like the bellow of a bull, he ducked his head in the stream. He was burning up. The fire that he was used to was nothing compared to the fire from the chile peppers that now devoured him.

But he went on, more determined than ever to know all about the land that he had come to see. That afternoon he saw something that, had he not been a devil, would have reminded him of heaven. The ripest of purple figs were growing on a plant that was not a fig tree.

"Here," thought Satan, "is something I can eat without any fear. I remember seeing figs like these in the Garden of Eden." Hungrily he reached for one, but at the first bite he threw it away with a cry of pain. His mouth and tongue were full of thorns. With an oath and a groan he turned from the prickly pear and continued his journey.

Late that same day just before sunset, he heard the barking of dogs. He continued in the direction from whence the sound came and soon arrived at a ranch house. A group of men, dressed like Pedro de Urdemañas—that new arrival in Hell who had sent him to Texas—ran here and there gesticulating on horses. The sight of them rather cheered Satan up.

And then he saw what Pedro told him he resembled—a cow. Here was a blow indeed. Could he, the king of Hell, look like one of those insipid creatures, devoid of all character and expression? Ah, he would get even with Pedro on his return and send him to the seventh hell, where the greatest sinners were and the fire burned the hottest. His reflections were interrupted by something that filled him with wonder. One of the mounted men threw a cow down by merely touching its tail. "How marvelous!" thought Satan. "I'll learn the trick so I can have fun with the other devils when I go back home."

He approached one of the *vaqueros* and in the suavest of tones said, "My friend, will you tell me what you did to make the lady cow fall?"

The cowboy looked at the city man in surprise and with a wink at those around him replied, "Sure, just squeeze its tail."

Satan gingerly approached the nearest cow—an old gentle milk cow— and squeezed its tail with all his might.

Now, as all of you know, no decent cow will allow anyone, even though it be the king of Devils, to take such familiarity with her. She ceased chewing her cud and gathering all her strength in her hind legs, shot out a kick that sent Satan whirling through the air.

Very much upset and chagrined, he got up. But what hurt more were the yells of derision that greeted him. Without even looking back, he ran hellbound and did not stop until he got home. The first thing he did on his arrival was to expel Pedro from the infernal region. He would have nothing to do with one who had been the cause of his humiliation. And since then Satan has never been in Texas and Pedro de Urdemañas still wanders through the Texas ranches always in the shape of some fun-loving *vaquero*.[9]

"Well, my father said, 'The Devil knows more because of his age than because he is the Devil,' and that brings to mind something that happened to him when he was a young man," added Martiniano. "Do you want to hear about it?"

"*Sí, sí,*" cried everyone in chorus.

"*Muy bien*, I'll tell it but don't blame me if you are frightened."

---

[9] Here, Don Francisco ends his narrative of The Devil in Texas.

It happened down in the Devil's River where the Evil One has been locked up in a cave. My father was a God-fearing, truth-loving man, and you can believe his word!

One evening as he was sitting on the porch of our house, smoking his after-dinner cigarette, a stranger called on him. He was a handsome man who looked like a Spanish gentleman. He showed a letter of intro-duction from friends. Being a very hospitable man, my father gave him lodging for as long as he wished to make our home his home.

He was a cattle buyer. He said he had come to Del Rio to buy stock and my father introduced him to the ranchmen in the vicinity. There was something strange and mysterious about him, something that made you shrink. As long as he stayed in our house he was never known to invoke the name of God or the saints, but as a host it was not my father's duty to question him about his religious convictions.

One morning, as usual, he rode away to a neighboring cattle ranch. At night he did not return. Two days passed and still he did not come back. Since everyone knew he had several thousand *pesos*, his disap-pearance was arousing great curiosity, and since he had been our guest, my father, fearing to arouse suspicion, organized a searching party.

As he knew every crag, thicket and cave in the Devil's river coun-try, he led the party. So engrossed was he in his reflections that he did not realize how far ahead of the others he was. So he stopped on the bank of the river to wait. Suddenly he heard groans coming from the direction of the opposite bank. He swam across and the moans sounded much nearer. Apparently someone was in great pain, for the groans were heart-rending and chilled his blood. He walked along the bank until he came upon a cave formed by the river. The moans were right at his back, and then he realized that someone was in the cave.

Crouching on all fours, he entered and what he saw was enough to make a stout man tremble. A man was buried up to his neck in the sand. His face was gashed and scratched horribly. One of his eyes was black and so swollen that it was closed. The other had the expression of an angry animal at bay. His mouth was open and the lips were swollen. His hair was standing on end. The beard was clotted with blood. The raw nose bone protruded above torn skin. It was the stranger. As soon as he saw my father, he cried out in a piercing voice:

"Don't come near me. The devil is here. Don't you see him there at the corner of the cave?"

My father moved nearer.

"Go back, I tell you. Do you want him to get you as he got me? See how he leers and jeers at me." And, saying this, the unfortunate stranger tried to bury his head in the sand.

My father, who had often heard of how the devil had attacked other people, was chilled with horror at what he heard. But he had a rosary in his pocket and taking it out, made the sign of the cross and demanded the Evil Spirit to depart. He must have left for the stranger gave a sigh of relief, saying:

"He has gone. Get me a drink of water."

My father left to get the water. When he returned, the Evil Spirit must have been there again for the man was shaking and trembling like one possessed and crying out, "He is there again. Take out your cross."

The sign of the cross was made and the man was again at peace.

He was taken out of the cave and placed on the bank of the river. While my father went to fetch a burro on which to carry him home, the man sat by the edge of the river holding the rosary in his hand.

Soon the searching party returned and as the man was lifted from the ground to the burrow, the rosary fell from his hands. Something like a whirlwind enveloped the group and to their consternation both the burro and rider were carried up in the air. The man screamed, the burro brayed, and the people, realizing the significance of the whole thing, said a prayer. A sound like the bellow of a bull was heard up in the air and beast and man fell to the ground.

For weeks the patient suffered. His physical injuries and the spiritual effects of the Devil's visitation had made a wreck of him. When he recovered, a priest was called. The priest heard his confession and gave him absolution. Then the man told my father what had happened. The morning he left home, as he came near the Devil's River-he was taken up into the air by what he thought was a whirlwind. However he noticed he was holding on to something slippery, long, and slimy. As he looked up he saw the awful face of the Devil. He tried to turn loose but the cloven hoofs of the Evil One beat him on the face and his hands were stuck to the tail. Satan took him over the whole town of Del Rio and the cemetery and finally dropped him in the cave. The Evil One then tortured him with his presence and because of that he had buried himself in the sand.

The stranger stayed until he regained his health and finally disappeared without any explanation. Whether he went home or was carried away by the Devil is a thing that has puzzled those who knew him.

"The sweet name of Jesus be our protection!" exclaimed old Mariana again, crossing herself.

"And music be our diversion!" added Don Francisco, "Capul, bring your guitar and while Alejo tunes his fiddle for the dance sing us a song."

"One of my own?"

"Whichever you please, but make it a gay one. Ambrosio will bring the food now."

The singing of the birds and the clucking of the hens as they jumped from the treetops were announcing the coming of another day, when the dancers left, not to go to bed, but to begin their daily chores.

# CHAPTER III
## Border Honor

In spite of his fourteen years there was something about Cristóbal that made him act and appear older. A certain sadness, a certain indescribable melancholy permeated a spirit which should have been young. His long, thin face, pale and sad, had the ascetic beauty of a medieval saint, and his black, haunting eyes had neither the light nor the sparkle of youth. He spoke in monosyllables, never laughed, and his smile, when he smiled, was bitter. It was the smile of a soul that weeps. He was a tragic figure on horseback as he rode by, usually seeking the loneliness of the pastures.

A group of women doing their weekly laundry at the creek stopped their work as they saw him approach.

"He is bewitched," whispered Juana, the oldest of the group.

"And possessed of an evil spirit besides," asserted another.

"They say he talks to the dead," added a girl who held a water jug on her shoulder.

"Yes, and at night he and three devils play ball with the eyes of sleeping children who have been naughty during the day,"cautioned a young mother pinching her seven-year-old boy in a warning manner.

Unconscious of all the comments he was creating, Cristóbal passed the women not seeing them at all.

"If I were his father I would whip the Devil out of him," commented old Juana.

"That's easier said than done. It has never been done, not that I know of anyway."

"That shows how little you know about it. His father whipped the Devil out of Doña Rita."

"That's strange, I have never heard such a thing before. Tell me about it," begged the girl putting down her water jar and sitting down on a big rock.

"Youth may have learning these days, but it does not have the wisdom that comes with gray hair," answered Juana, the old grandmother, rolling her corn-shuck cigarette. "This young generation is ignorant of many things; you go to school and the only thing you learn is to be ashamed of your beliefs, getting nothing in turn to replace them. This is the story, though. You may believe it and then you may not, just as you please.

When Cristóbal was little, eight years at the most, his mother took sick. It was a strange malady; she turned yellow and would neither sleep, talk, nor eat. She just laid in bed staring at the ceiling of the room. What she saw there, if she saw anything, must have been terrible for occasionally she screamed out fearful words and shook her fists at the beams. Don Ramón, her husband, who knew a great deal about home-doctoring thought at first it was her heart. He gave her a brew of *toronjil\** and powdered deer blood for nine consecutive mornings, but that did not cure her malady. This, he followed with *cenizo\*\** tea, which as you know, if left outdoors to be cooled by the night dew will cure any liver trouble. But even that did not make her feel any better. The poor man, not knowing what else to do, came to me for advice. Full well did I know what ailed Doña Rita; she was bewitched; but those things are better left unsaid, so I suggested that he go to Tío Anselmo, the witch healer. Well, he went," continued the old woman blowing rings of smoke as she spoke. "Tío Anselmo was no fool and he knew right away what to do. He told Don Ramón to go to the creek and gather all the chile peppers he could find; he was to make a fire with them, close all the doors and windows, and place Doña Rita by the open fireplace. The suffocating vapors would either choke or drive the evil spirits away. This done, he was to whip her with a rawhide rope folded three times, made from the hide of a black steer. Tío Anselmo told Ramón not to mind Rita's screams at all. He would be merely chastising the evil spirit that possessed her.

In the meantime, unseen by anyone, Cristóbal had entered the room, hidden by the darkness. His little pale face streaked with tears as he watched his mother writhe in agony under the cruel blows of his father. Her screams ceased; she fell in a merciful faint. For months she was more dead than alive. I think she would have died too, had it not been for young Cristóbal who, with the pale sorrowful face of the Crucified, sat by her bedside day and night and looked with eyes that saw nothing.

---

\**Toronjil*—sweet lemon.
\*\**Cenizo*—Texas shrub, silvery gray in color.

She recovered, but, and this is the thing that we dare not say," the grandmother finished in a confidential whisper, "it is thought that the evil spirit that left the mother took possession of the boy; for since then he goes about silent, looking at the world with the haunting eyes of the possessed. What is worse he shuns his father Don Ramón. Cristóbal hates his father."

[So engrossed were the women in the story that they did not hear the approaching hoofs of a rider.

"Good morning, *amigas\**," he cried to the women as he dismounted with the quickness of an expert horseman.]¹

"Don Ramón," whispered the old grandmother, "may the Lord have mercy upon our souls if he suspects we have been talking about him."

The women answered his salutation and went back to their forgotten washing.

He seemed to be in a hurry. While his horse drank at the stream he paced up and down under the shade of a gigantic mesquite tree. He gave a shrill whistle which was soon answered by the arrival of Cristóbal.

"Tell your mother," he said, "not to expect me early. I am going to *mi compadre\*\** Francisco's ranch and will not be home until dark."

In a few minutes he covered the distance that separated him from his friend's ranch. Don Ramón found him sitting in the *patio* smoking his after-*siesta* cigarette. In true Mexican fashion they embraced each other warmly and slapped each other on the shoulder with the vehemence of their race.

"*Bien, compadre*, sit down and tell me what you know. Where is that rascal Marcos? He was here a moment ago. Here, you good-for-nothing Indian, bring Don Ramón a chair. You simply cannot treat *peones* like human beings," he added turning to his friend. "As soon as you do, they think themselves better than their masters. Away with you," he said to the returning boy, "go water Don Ramón's horse, and see that you do it better than you did the last time. Now sit down, *amigo*."

They talked of trivial things, the *remuda\*\*\**, the approaching visit of the missionary priest, the love affairs of the servants. One thing led to

---

\**Amigas*—friends.

¹Inexplicably, this passage in brackets is marked out in the manuscript. Without it, what follows makes less narrative sense.

\*\**Compadre*—the godfather of a child and the father of the same become *compadres*.

\*\*\**Remuda*—relay of horses.

another until the conversation came to the thing nearest Don Ramón's heart, his oldest son, Carlos.

"He is the very devil, that boy is, just like Don Juan. Why *compadre*," he boasted proudly, "he can outdance and outdrink any young *caballero* in the community, and as to love affairs, all I can say is that I envy him."

"At your age, *compadre!*"

"Bah! you talk like an old woman."

"Merely like a gentleman."

"Where love affairs are concerned, who is a gentleman at Carlos' age? He is young, and youth, like birds, need wings. I often tell him, 'My boy, youth is a divine treasure that leaves us never to return; make the most of it, but never forget the honor of a man, and above all, keep your name above reproach.'"

"Right you are, Ramón, but remember one thing, youth, health, and money cannot be wasted ruthlessly."

"Pooh! pooh! again you talk like an old woman. Carlos will settle down and be a family man like all of us."

"And what nice girl will have him?"

"Any one; the more love affairs he has, the more acceptable he will be. A man has to have his escapades. Besides, what is a wife for, if not to be the depository of family honor? Do you know what the rascal is doing now?" he added, not noticing the frown of disgust on his friend's face, "making love to that pretty Carmela, old Juana's granddaughter. She came to me, the old woman did, to complain of Carlos' behavior towards the girl. 'Coop up your little chicken, for my rooster has the world to roam,' I told her. What are we coming to? In my day the daughter of a *peón* considered herself honored if the young master noticed her."

"That's a thing of the past, *compadre*. I can't condemn Carlos altogether, though. I also had those thoughts when I was young. But more fortunate than Carlos, I had a mother who made me see the shamefulness of such behavior. 'How disgusting it would be', she said to me, 'to see in low-born creatures the likeness of your ancestors.'"

"Perhaps you are right, my friend, but I did not come to speak to you about my boy. I came to consult you about more serious things."

"What can be more serious than your son's behavior?"

"Pshaw, *compadre*! The love affairs of youth are like the rosy clouds of dawn. They disappear with time."

"I shall make my daughter see it that way, and as for Carlos —"

"He will settle down when he marries Rosita and will be a better husband for his experiences."

The call to the *merienda** put an end to the conversation.

It was four o'clock by the kitchen clock and the shadow which the sundial projected. The meal was served to the two men under the *portal*, on a long, homemade, mesquite table covered with a red and white tablecloth. A neat brown-faced maid brought them platters of ranch delicacies–flour tortillas, pastry rich with powdered sugar and cinnamon, fresh corn muffins, cheese made that morning, pumpkin pies and newly roasted coffee with the fragrant flavor of the tropics. The meal ended, the two men resumed their conversation.

"Now what is it, *compadre*," urged Don Francisco. "I am sure you did not come to talk to me about Carlos' love affairs."

"Right you are. What I really came to see you about," said Don Ramón, "is to get your opinion about the stealing of cattle that's been worrying everyone. Have you lost any?"

"Fifty of the fattest and best of the herd."

"I have not lost that many; twenty at the most. The heaviest losers, I understand, are the people at the *Casa Verde* ranch. They are *gringos* though, it really does not matter."

"You shouldn't talk that way."

["Yes, a thousand devils take them, for like Cortina, the only *gringo* I like is one under seven feet of dirt. There was a man for you, *compadre*! Once he made up his mind, nothing ever made him retreat; he feared neither the living nor the dead. Seeing a *gringo*, he told me once, made his fingers itch and twitch for the feel of his pistol. And the next thing, he never knew how it happened, the man was dead at his feet. Times are changing, though. Things are not as they used to be. Too many Americans are moving in and I fear our children will be contaminated now. The other day I was telling Ramoncito, my grandson, about Cortina. My heart grows sad when I think of the answer the child gave me. 'He was a ruffian, was he not?' I shall get my revenge, though. When I am old I shall move to town, the largest American city I can find too. And this is what I am going to do; I'll buy a home near the cemetery—"

"What a strange desire!"

"Oh, it will be great, *compadre*! As far as the eye can see there will be thousands of graves. The very thought makes me happy. For in every one there will be a dead *gringo*. All dead, *compadre*."

---

**Merienda*—afternoon tea, usually served at four.

[2]This bracketed passage is marked out with a large X in the manuscript. I restore it here, again, for the historical value concerning Cortina.

"No one but you would think of such extravagant things."][2]

"This is what I think," continued Don Ramón, "but this I say to you alone. The cattle thieves are people who know us, and who know in what pastures we keep the best cattle."

"Impossible! What you say is absurd! Does that mean that it might be you or me?"

"Exactly."

"Do you realize you are accusing the whole community?"

"Yes, I do, but I also realize that the only way to find the thieves is to arouse the *rancheros* to action."

["I see the *caporal* coming this way, and he seems to be in a hurry too; perhaps he brings news. Well, what is it?" asked Don Francisco, as José entered, "have we lost more cattle?"

"No, *señor*, but the San Martín ranch was robbed last night; the thieves got away with five hundred *pesos* from the ranch store and the post office."

"That's an outrage, Francisco! And we stand here and allow this to happen?"

"Why not notify the rangers, *señor*?"

"How like one of your caste you talk," blurted out Don Ramón. "Keep this in your stupid mind; we, the Mexicans of the Texas ranches, have never needed the rangers and never shall. The rangers are not for men who are men. We can fight our own fights without the need of their interference. Do you understand that?"

"Yes, *señor*."

"If the cattle thieves are *gringos* as they may very well be, we can deal with them; if they are of 'ours', we can handle them too. It has been done before and it can be done again."

"Was I not right in saying we are not what we were once? Even the *peones* begin to doubt our strength. My theory is right, Francisco, they will take all that is ours, even our souls."][3]

"What do you say, Francisco, how shall we go about getting this thieving vermin?"

"The priest is coming Sunday and all the ranchmen will be here for the services. Suppose we leave it until then."

"Very well, until Sunday then, *compadre*. With the favor of God, *adiós*."

---

[3]Bracketed passage marked out with large X in manuscript. Again, I restore it for narrative coherence and sociological value concerning the Texas Rangers, *peons*, etc.

The pawing of a spirited horse was heard, followed by a swift gallop. From the distance came the echoes of a song:

> "With wounded soul and mournful thought,
> A fading face and wounded heart."

Don Ramón was going home.

Father José María, as Father Closs was lovingly called by his parishioners, was expected at the Olivareño. Since morning the children had been getting ready to meet him properly. There had been much scrubbing of faces and feet and much washing of dresses and shirts. And now they were all waiting in the *patio* of the master's house for the signal that would send them running and shouting to the *Camino Real*. The little girls, dressed in their Sunday calico dresses, faces aglow with excitement and an extra scrubbing of soap and water, pigtails, with bright, new ribbons, chatted, gossiped and wriggled like mischievous monkeys. More serious, more bashful, and certainly more ill at ease than their companions, the boys looked with resignation at their clean, bare feet, as though trying to solve the deepest mystery. One of them, bolder or less resigned than the rest, ran to the gate leading to the road.

"I see him coming—Father is coming," the boy shouted, pointing to a dim, white speck in the distance.

"Let's all run to meet him," suggested another.

"And we must not forget to scatter the flowers and greens on his path," added a third.

They fell upon him as an avalanche. He dismounted to greet them; they crowded around him kissing his hand and asking for his blessing. He laughed and talked with them pretending not to know the foremost thought in their minds. And when he saw their wide-opened eyes and the longing glances they cast upon his bulging saddlebags, he opened them with ceremonious precision. For these saddlebags contained all the mysterious wonders and riches of Alladin's cave. He brought bright-colored pictures which satisfied their love for the bizarre: Daniel in the lions' den; the young Tobias, a supposedly invisible angel traveling by his side; the adoration of the Magi-pictures of Saint Francis, gaunt and ethereal, a skull, at which the children shuddered, hanging from the rosary at his belt; Saint Cecilia, at the organ, a shower of roses falling on her hands; a guardian angel in blue, watching over two children dressed in purple and pink.

"See this medal," he said, holding it up beyond their reach. "I'd give it to the one who can say the Our Father best." They hesitated timidly at first, but encouraged by his friendly nods and smiles, he got the results he wanted. ["I see I must teach you, *Angelitos de Dios*, little Angels of God," he said. "What do you say if we sit here under this mesquite tree and talk a little."][4]

When at last he arrived at the ranch leading the horse with one hand, the flock of children were at his heels, some hanging from his cape and the youngest riding his mount. As he reached the *maguey* fence surrounding the ranch house, he noticed semi-hidden by olean-ders, the figure of a girl cutting the pink and white blossoms. Seeing the priest she rushed to him dropping the armful of flowers.

"Oh, *mi padre* José María," she cried joyously. "How late you are in coming, but blessed be this hour when you come to us."

She made a pretty picture as she knelt with bowed head before the white-haired priest. The soft brown hair which fell in two long braids down her back served as a frame for the olive-tinted face with its deli-cately arched eyebrows, severe patrician nose, and generous mouth, red as a pomegranate blossom. Her eyes now looking down in gentle sub-mission were the same color as the olives that had once grown in the *patio* of the Olivares house in Sevilla.

"Rosita, my child," smiled the priest, "I missed you among the children who came to meet me. I thought you might be ill. But now I see why you have not come," he added, stroking her hair. "Too old for childish things, eh? Of how many broken hearts do you boast? Ah, you little rogue," he continued teasingly, seeing the blushing face of the girl, "so we are a great lady now with love affairs and lovers who sigh for us. Where is your mother, where is everybody?" he added, changing the subject. *"Oye,* Francisco!" he called out, entering the *patio* arm in arm with the girl. "Since when is it customary for the priest to arrive unno-ticed to this ranch?"

*"Válgame Dios, Padre,* we did not even hear you come," exclaimed Don Francisco in surprise. "We waited all morning for you, even despaired of your coming, thinking you might have been detained at Roma. Let me ring this bell that all may know you have come. The men and women were here all afternoon in this very *patio* waiting for your coming." [Just watch them run, so anxious are they to see you.][5]

Due to the poor means of communication and the long distances he had to traverse, Father José María's visits to the ranches were not so frequent as he would have liked to make them. Yet, infrequent as they were, he brought much joy and consolation. This old priest was a man who understood the problems of the *rancheros*, the troubles and worries of the *peones* and the escapades and boisterous behavior of the *vaque-*

---

[5]Passage crossed out in the manuscript.

*ros.* In his zeal for service he had lost all idea of self; he had forgotten he was a Frenchman and had become as the humblest of his parishioners. His life became the life of those among whom he lived. He was young no more; he had given fifty years of his life to the border and its people. He had seen the *rancheros* dispossessed of their property, he had witnessed their return, and seeing them happy now, he was also happy.

This black-robed Oblate was a quaint figure as he rode through the country on his white horse, wearing deerskin leggings, a big cloak, and a broad-brimmed hat tied under the chin. Many were the stories that were told about him and his fortitude and nothing pleased his friends more than to tell the exploits of this, their *vaquero* priest. For Father José María was an expert horseman and could ride any beast that walked on four legs.[6]

One time, so the story went, he was called to pacify a *vaquero* who had been *with the grape* for a week, as is the polite border way of saying he was drunk. As days passed, the man got worse and worse. As is usually the way with such people, he felt braver and braver as *the grape* took a stronger hold of him. He now proposed to ride Lightning, the wildest *potro* on the ranch, who might have been the very Devil himself. Until now he had allowed no one to touch him. This was the horse the *vaquero in grape* proposed to ride. It meant certain death. The master was away and the *vaqueros*, always ready for excitement, encouraged him in his crazy whim. His wife was in distress and hearing that Father José María was at the Olivareño, she went to get him. They arrived just in time. The *potro*, pawing and foaming at the mouth, was already saddled.

"You are good, my children," said the priest to the group of men assembled there, "how did you know I needed a horse?"

And without another word, not even taking off his cassock, the priest mounted the *potro*. He took firm hold of the reins, lashed the horse with his quirt, punished him with the sharp spiked spurs and sat as firmly as though "he were sitting on a chair," as one of the *vaqueros* expressed it later. This incident won him the title of the cowboy priest.

It was also told of him that on a certain occasion as he was going from the seat of his parish to a ranch, he lost his way and was without food for three days. Yet when he arrived at his destination he would not touch the meal placed before him. The day was Friday and he had been

---

[6]An actual personage, Father Joseph Marie Closs (called José María), was a French missionary priest assigned to this area (González 1930: 66-67).

offered meat, the only food available at the ranch. "My food," he told the astonished people, "is to do the will of Him who sent me."

These and many other stories had endeared him to the *vaqueros* and *peones*. The former saw in him a fearless man, one after their own hearts and the latter loved him because he was humble and meek like they were.

His coming always created a stir. Among other things it meant that people would come to the ranch and Doña Margarita, who prided herself in her hospitality as a hostess, had been busy for many days making preparations. She and her maids had aired the unused quilts and mattresses and had prepared beds and cots in every possible place. In the kitchen all was bustle and stir. The women laughed and gossiped as they baked bread and cakes, and roasted cocoa beans that would soon be converted into foaming cups of spiced chocolate. The *metate* was kept busy grinding corn and the cook had counted twenty dozen *tortillas* she had already made. A cow butchered that morning was now being barbecued in two pits near the *corral*.

While supper was cooking, Rosita and the grown girls of the ranch made the altar—for background, a sheet hung on the wall was used and on it they constructed, with varicolored ribbons of red, yellow, orange, and blue, arches and arcades that would have made any architect blush with envy. Sprays of oleander and cedar, and artificial flowers were pinned here and there. Pictures of saints and angels formed a celestial host, and holy statues, some of wood and some of marble, were placed on the altar table.

At twilight while the people were still arriving, the priest prayed his beads as he walked up and down the patio under the stars. After supper Don Francisco, Doña Margarita, and their guests joined the priest at the improvised altar to recite the rosary and hear a sermon. After each decade of the rosary the hoarse voices of the *vaqueros* and *peones* mingled with the tenor of Capul and the voices of the women and children in praises to the Mother of God:

> Oh, Mary, my Mother
> Consolation of mortals,
> Protect us and guide us
> To our celestial home.

The unrest and excitement created by the coming of so many strangers subsided. By midnight all was quiet at the ranch. However, an occasional outburst of laughter coming from the quarters of the *vaqueros* showed that some were still awake. The morning star was already coming up the horizon when the stillness of night was broken by a rich voice singing somewhere near the cedars by the gate. It rose in the clear night air like the singing of a bird in mating time:

> "Awake, my beloved, awake
> Awake, it is already dawn,
> The birds are sweetly singing
> And the moon has gone to rest."

A figure slid noiselessly along the wall to one of the grilled windows and tapped gently on the window pane.

"Rosita, my love, come to the *reja*."*

A flitting shadow was seen at the window, a soft sound like the wind kissing a flower was heard, followed by whisperings and sighs. The morning light was dispelling the darkness of night when the figure was seen again; this time going to the men's quarters. It was Carlos who had been 'playing the bear'—making love—at Rosita's window.

After mass the priest left and while the women were gossiping and discussing the happenings at the ranches, Don Francisco and the *rancheros* met in the *sala* to discuss what concerned all so much—the stealing of their cattle. After a heated discussion it was decided to organize a party that would trail the thieves and shoot them down if they resisted arrest.

Don Ramón, considered the best *huellero*,** was selected to pursue the cattle thieves and fourteen men, selected because of their fearlessness, were appointed to go with him. The party left the next morning for the San Martín ranch, the seat of the cattle thieves' last exploit. Don Ramón found the trail without difficulty. He followed the tracks with such precision that he could tell the number of cattle they were taking. All day they rode in silence. Once Don Ramón broke the stillness to remark, "they have lost two head."

"How do you know?" asked one of the younger men.

"I was not born yesterday and fifty years of cattle raising have taught me much."

At dusk about half a mile from the Río Grande, they stopped to give the horses a rest and make some coffee.

"We are close to them," remarked Don Ramón, "the tracks are fresh but the darkness of night is against us; it will be difficult to find them."

After drinking a cup of coffee, they mounted again. The mockingbird was announcing the dawn when they saw, semi-hidden by the dark-

---

*Reja*—grilled window.

**Huellero*—a man who follows tracks.

ness, a herd of cattle. On the ground, heads pillowed on their saddles, rested some half dozen men. Noiselessly Don Ramón and his men surrounded them; then he shot into the air.

"Hands up," he shouted to those who were already his prisoners. "Boys," he continued, addressing his men, "bring a lariat with which to tie these shameless scoundrels," and he himself set the example by tying them elbow to elbow. His eagle-like look fixed itself on one who, covering his face with a handkerchief, tried to hide behind his companions.

"At least you are ashamed. How much better it would have been had you never been born. May God pity your parents whom you have so dishonored." And saying this he snatched away the handkerchief that hid the face of the thief.

With a cry like that of a wounded animal, Don Ramón leaped upon the thief with an oath.

"Carlos, my son," stammered Don Ramón. "My curse be upon you, and cursed be I who am the father of such a son."

"Friends," he said to his companions who witnessed the scene in astonishment, "you know what this means! You also know that I would prefer death to this. I do not kill this wretch because in my family there are no assassins. You also know that until now, my name was untarnished and beyond reproach. As your friend, I ask one thing of you. This unhappy father begs a favor from you; don't give up my son to be tried as a common criminal. He is a thief, I know, and my tongue burns when I say it. But don't allow his name which is mine to be dragged in the dust. Allow me to punish him as he deserves. I am his father, but I can forget it to become his judge. I do not need the interference of the authorities to inflict the punishment. I know how to deal with him."

"Your wish is granted," said the oldest of the group.

"Thanks, my friends; tomorrow at sunset I expect you at my ranch. Yesterday I called you to help in the pursuit of the criminals, little knowing the disgrace that awaited me; tomorrow you shall witness the fulfillment of a sacred duty. I expect you at sunset."

The other thieves were given up to the authorities; Carlos was taken home.

Late in the afternoon of the following day a group of men stood in the *patio* of Don Ramón's house. At the farthest corner three women in black sobbed. Close by was Cristóbal staring silently at the scene. In the center knelt Carlos, his breast and back bare. Above him towered a gray-headed giant, whip in hand.

"Carlos," the man said, "in the name of Heaven, I punish you for your sins." And he hurled upon the bare back of the boy lashes that cut the flesh like dagger thrusts. The blood burst like scarlet threads. The women wept. The scarlet threads became torrents, but Don Ramón neither saw nor heard anything. With a cry of anguish and pain the youth staggered from the ground only to fall back in a faint. Seeing this, Don Ramón dropped the whip, gathered the blood-covered form of the youth gently in his arms, took him indoors, and placed him on a cot. The oldest of the women fell on her knees before the cot, kissed the pale face of the boy, crying in an anguished tone, "Ramón, you have killed our son."

"No, Rita," replied the man proudly. "I have merely taught him not to steal cattle. Bring water and salve and I'll wash his wounds."

There were tears on the weatherbeaten faces of the men as Don Ramón gathered the bleeding body of his son. Don Francisco followed him into the house and he watched the tenderness with which the unhappy father bathed the wounds on the boy's back and chest. His task finished, Don Ramón stood at the foot of the bed with folded arms watching the unconscious form of his son. Then covering him, he leaned over and kissed Carlos' forehead.

"My God, forgive me this," he said in a choking voice, "and may He bless you, my son." He gazed lovingly on the pain-drawn face again and left the room. Once outside Don Francisco gripped Don Ramón's hand. "Always a man of honor, my friend. Courage would have failed me to do what you have done. Your sufferings are my sufferings."

"Yes, our poor Rosita, this will kill her."

"No, *compadre*, like the women of our race she will suffer but she will do her father's wishes."

"You mean?"

"I mean that the Olivares name stands for no dishonor. She will do as I command."

# CHAPTER IV

## Tío Patricio

Once a week at dusk, Tío Patricio was announced at the ranch by the bleating of his unruly flock which appeared enveloped in a cloud of dust. He was a giant dressed in a discarded soldier's uniform; however, his shoes and hat did not match his military array, for the former were rawhide *huaraches* and the latter, a high-pointed broad-brimmed Mexican *sombrero*.

His black patriarchal beard contrasted with his cheeks, rosy and firm like the girls'. In fact his complexion was the envy of all the marriageable girls of the countryside. When asked what he washed his face with, the reply was always the same, "God's water," meaning rainwater, and in that semi-arid part of the country, rain is very rare, three or four times a year at the most.

He was a wonderful storyteller, a mystic, a visionary, who saw in everything the handiwork of his Creator. All wonders of nature he attributed to a supernatural power. According to him all goodness and beauty was a gift of the Virgin Mary and was part of her. A beautiful sunset was her smile—the blue sky—the blue of her mantle; the rainbow was formed by the tears that she shed for sinners. His interpretation of the stars was accepted by the countryside. The Milky Way was the path through which the saints traversed the ethereal regions in summer and varied according to the month. In June it was the trail through which Saint John ascended to heaven; in July it was the path of the apostles Peter and Paul; in August it was Saint James who traversed the heavens on his white steed. Castor and Pollux were the eyes of Lucy, the little Roman maid who preferred blindness to man's love. The eyes which she lost in her struggle for chastity were up there in the southern sky to serve as a warning to frivolous maidens. Further down the Heavens, three bright stars, Orion, or the Three Marys; Mary the Mother, Mary Magdalene, and Mary, the sister of Martha, kept watch over Lucy's eyes;

**45**

Venus, the morning star, was the Virgin who wakes the shepherds at dawn.

[Many times the boy Cristóbal accompanied the old man who had no better friend than Cristóbal. The other children might sometimes make fun of his long beard; they might laugh at his stories, but the quiet little fellow always listened with his soul in his eyes.

On the day that Tío Patricio was here at the ranch, twilight found Cristóbal sitting on the corral fence waiting for the arrival of his friend, the goat herder. All day long the boy had wished for the comforting words and companionship of the old man. Carlos' incident the preceding afternoon had left him with a fear that gripped his heart. All day an atmosphere of gloom had permeated the place; his father, silent and sullen, Doña Rita weeping in her room, his sisters talking in whispers as they watched Don Ramón pacing the floor restlessly, Carlos moaning in bed.

A faint cry was heard in the distance. With a leap the boy stood up and listened attentively. Nearer and nearer it came. Soon he could make out the words, "*Arre, arre, cabra,*" accompanied by the bleating of the sheep and goats.

"*Arre, Arre,*" Cristóbal heard the *pastor* cry as he encouraged his flock to enter the corral.

"Guess what I have brought you this week?" cried the shepherd spying him. "Look in my bag."

"Oh, just what I like best, ripe *pitahayas,** where did you find them?"

"On the hills. I kept them fresh and cool in water for you. Why don't you eat them? Old Tío Patricio's heart will feel sad if you don't. Don't you like them anymore?"

"Of course I do, but I am going to give these to Carlos. Do you mind? Because," sobbed the boy, "he needs them more than I do."

"What is it now? Come, tell your old worthless Tío Patricio what has happened," encouraged the old man.

Between sobs, Cristóbal told him.

"*Dios de Dios,*** this old man is proud to serve such a master."

"Tío Patricio, you think my father was right?"

"Carlos did wrong, did he not?"

"But my father is cruel and I hate him."

"Your father is not; he knows what is good for his children!"

---

*\*Pitahayas*—cactus fruit.
\*\**Dios de Dios*—God of God. Such expressions are very common in Spanish.

"I saw him beat my mother the same way."

"Not your mother, but the evil spirit that possessed her. Your father is always right."

"Then he is not a bad man?"

"Of course not, you little mouse, Don Ramón is justice itself."

"But do you think he loves us?"

"He is your father."

"Let me whisper something in your ear, Tío; I love you more than I do him, and I am not afraid of you either."

"You mustn't say such wicked things, Cristóbal, the Virgin will punish you."

"Take me with you," begged the child, "I want to be in the pasture with the flocks where you can teach me all you know about the stars, and the birds, and the spirits that fly about at night."

"*Bueno, bueno*, that will be fine. Come, I have to see your father now." And hand in hand, the old shepherd and the boy walked towards the house.

Permission was given Cristóbal to stay with the old shepherd. At the crowing of the first rooster the two were ready to go. The flock, with the shepherd dogs in the vanguard, had already been let out.

The air, sweet with morning odors, opened new horizons of happiness and freedom to the boy, like an unrestrained colt that frisks in the prairie, his spirit free of the iron-bound chains of obedience which repressed his spirit, when at home. The beauty of the sage brush in bloom which covered the rounded domes of the hills invited him to sing.][1]

The sun came up as it ascended the heavens; a rainbow formed a perfect arc in the east.

> "Rainbow in the Orient at morn,
> unyoke the oxen; come home,"

chanted Tío Patricio. "That is a sure sign of rain, Cristóbal. The sky is clear now, but there will be a shower before night."

A soft mournful sound made Cristóbal stop to listen. "Do you hear that, Tío?"

"Yes, the turtledove calling his mate, listen how clearly it says, Coo-Coo.

[1]In the manuscript, the preceding bracketed passage is crossed out. For the sake of narrative sense and coherency, especially with regard to the Carlos incident, I have retained the original with minimal line editing.

Coo-Coo
What do you want, shepherd lad?
I want to eat tunas, eat tunas.
Good-bye, shepherd lad,
Good-bye, shepherd lad."

"Why does it say that, do you know?"

"Yes, once the turtledove was an Indian maiden. She was in love with a shepherd lad, but he wandered away with his flock and soon found another love. The lovesick girl mourned and wept many moons for her faithless lover. The Great Spirit took pity on her and changed her to a turtledove. And ever since then, when the dew is upon the earth or when the evening star makes her appearance in the twilight, the soft mournful cry of the dove is heard."[2]

"Tío Patricio, do you suppose Rosita will die too? And will her soul haunt the prairies like the doves? Will my mother's spirit haunt the prairies too?"

"Of course not; you have such fanciful thoughts."

"Last night I heard Don Francisco and father talking about her and father said, 'Poor Rosita, this will kill her.'"

"Fate and death descend from heaven, and no one, *hijito mío*,* dies unless the good God needs him."

"Do you think God will call her?"

"No one knows the just decisions of God. But this I know, He calls only those whom He needs. And whenever another angel is needed in heaven, He looks upon the earth and singles out some soul that wants to go. Have you ever seen a butterfly bursting out from the ugly cocoon that has held it prisoner? No? Its lovely wings flutter at first with uncertainty, but encouraged by the warmth of the sun it flies away triumphantly to more beautiful worlds. The soul goes like that and called away by God, flies to a better world than ours. When a good person dies one should never mourn for him. His going away only means there will be another angel in heaven."

"Will God make her an angel then?"

"Look at that red bird standing on that *huisache*," interrupted the old shepherd, hoping to divert the child from his morbid thoughts, "still

[2]Stith Thompson, *Motif-Index of Folk Literature: a Classification of Narrative Elements in Folktales, Ballads, Myths, Fables, Medieval Romanas, Exempla, Fabliaux, Just-Books and Local Legends.* 6 volumes (Bloomington: Indiana University Press, 1955-58), Motif-index number A 2426.2.8 Why dove coos.

*Hijito mío*—my little son.

fussing at his mate. Some day, and very soon too, I hope, he will be punished."

"Punished for what, Tío Patricio?"

"For fussing and scolding at his wife. He really shouldn't, you know. Where would he be now had it not been for her? Back in the plains, unknown and unheard, I suppose." And as they walked through the dew-covered brush, Tío Patricio told his story.

"Everyone regards the cardinal now for the brilliancy of his feathers and the sweetness of his voice. But once he was an insignificant, ash-gray, little person noticed by none until he met and spoke with the spirit of the plains. And this is the story as I learned it many years ago:

The singing birds were to have a concert in celebration of the arrival of spring. The mockingbirds, the thrushes, the doves, and even the magpies filled the air with their songs. With the blooming of the trees and flowers and the arrival of the butterflies, enthusiasm ran riot among the feathered creatures. Crazed with joy, they sang unceasingly. All were joyous except a little gray bird who, too sensitive at his inability to sing, stayed at home. He tried to sing but just a gruff, hoarse sound came from his throat. He tried again and again but with no success. And if birds can weep, he wept in despair.

'If I could sing just for once,' said the little bird, 'how happy I could be.'

'Why do you want to sing?' asked a voice.

'Why? Why? So I can sing a love song to my mate like all the other birds do, and praise the beauty of the world.'

'A wonderful thought indeed! I might help you, little bird, if I could but see your mate.'

So the lady bird came.

'You are not very pretty, my dear,' said the voice. 'And you cannot sing either?'

The little lady shook her head sorrowfully.

'Would you really want your husband to sing?'

'Oh, yes, yes,' said the little gray wife, clasping her little claws pathetically. 'We could be so happy.'

'I can give beauty and voice to only one of you. Which shall it be, you or your husband?'

'My husband, if you please,' said the little lady.

'Are you sure you will not regret it?' continued the voice.

'Yes, yes. You see he has to go out into the world while I stay at home and care for my babies.'

'And you,' said the voice, speaking to the male, 'will accept the sacrifice of your wife?'

'She has chosen well,' replied he in a pompous voice.

'Very well, tomorrow at dawn things will be as you wish.'

And when the sun tinted the horizon with red, both birds jumped from their bed in the treetop. The male was a brilliant red. They looked at each other, the female with a smile admiring the glory of her mate, the mate with a frown noticing for the first time the ugliness of his wife. Then, raising his crested head, he sang. The voice was clear and triumphant, and epic in song. He soon forgot his wife's sacrifice, grew overbearing and cruel, and scolded and pecked her because of her ugliness.

But the spirit of the Plains saw all and grew sorry for the little lady bird. He could not take away the gift he had so freely given to the male, and since he could give her just one gift, he made her a wonderful singer. Whereas her husband's song was one of triumph, hers became one of love and gratitude. Probably because of her unselfishness, the grayness of her dress has changed to a rosy tint. So now, whenever the male begins to fuss and scold, she, knowing the vanity of his sex, tosses her little head and flies off laughing at the stupidity of husbands, who like hers, are all woman-made and yet are proud of what they think is their own achievement."[3]

"He is very much like my father," sighed Cristóbal.

"*La Virgen de la Soledad*! Dear me, no, not at all! What things you can say," answered the old man, somewhat worried because he could not dislodge from the boy's mind the unpleasant thoughts about his father. Fortunately the whistling of the mockingbird in a nearby thicket distracted the boy's thoughts.

"Listen, Tío," he laughed, "the bird mocks you."

"So he does, the lazy vagabond. He listens to me during the noonday heat when I whistle to drown the noise of the locusts. There he goes, conceited creature that he is. Ah, *Señor Zenzontle*, don't forget your white feathers!"

"Why did you say that?"

"To remind him of something which makes him very ashamed."

"What is it, Tío," asked the boy eagerly.

"You are as curious as an old woman, my little mouse," he retorted playfully, "but if you must, you must, and if I must, I must, so here is the story. You listen, and I will tell it:

---

[3]Close versions of the dove and cardinal stories appear separately in González (1930a). Stith Thompson Motif Index number A 2313 Origins of bird's feathers.

There was a time when all the creatures of Nature talked a common language. This language was Spanish. *El zenzontle*, the mockingbird, had the sweetest voice of all. The other birds stopped their flight to listen to him; the Indian lover ceased his words of love; even the talkative *arroyo** hushed. He foretold the spring, and when the days grew short and his song was no longer heard, the north winds came. Although he was not a foolish bird, *el zenzontle* was getting conceited.

'I am great, indeed,' he said to his mate. 'All nature obeys me. When I sing, the blossoms hidden in the trees come forth; the prairie flowers put on their gayest garments at my call and the birds begin to mate; even man, the all wise, heeds my voice and dances with joy, for the happy season draws near.'

'Hush, you are foolish and conceited like all men,' replied his wife. 'They listen and wait for the voice of God and when He calls, even you sing.'

He did not answer his wife, for you must remember he was not so foolish after all, but in his heart he knew that she was right.

That night after kissing his wife goodnight, he said to her, 'Tomorrow I will give a concert to the flowers, and you shall see them sway and dance when they hear me.'

'*Con el favor de Dios*,'** she replied.

'Whether God wills it or not I shall sing,' he replied angrily. 'Have I not told you that the flowers obey me and not God?'

Early next morning, *el zenzontle* could be seen perched on the highest limb of a *huisache*. He cleared his throat, coughed, and opened his bill to sing, but no sound came. Then down with the force of a cyclone swooped a hawk and grabbed with his steel-like claws the slender body of the singer.

'*Con el favor de Dios*,' he cried in distress while he thought of his wise little wife. As he was being carried up in the air, he realized his foolishness, repented of it and said, 'Oh, God, it is you who makes the flowers bloom and the birds sing, not I.' As he thought this, he felt himself slipping and falling, falling, falling. He fell on a ploughed field, and what a fall it was! A white dove who had her nest nearby picked him up and comforted him.

'My wings,' he mourned, looking at them, 'how tattered and torn they look! Whatever shall I tell my wife?'

The dove took pity on him and plucking three of her feathers, mended his wings.

*Arroyo*—brook.
***Con el favor de Dios** If God wills it.

As a reminder of his foolish pride, the mockingbird to this day has the white feathers of the dove. And it is said by those who know that he begins to sing with saying, '*con el favor de Dios.*'"[4]

"Just like Don Francisco, always afraid of Doña Margarita," commented Cristóbal.

Tío Patricio's answer was a laugh.

"*Arre, Arre*, look where that Lucifer of a goat is now. Ten thousand devils on horseback take her there, Cristóbal, see if you can head her. That's a good boy."

Dusk was gathering. Heavy dark clouds were massing in the north.

"Another sign of rain, Cristóbal," said Tío Patricio, looking at the sky. "If we hurry, we might reach the *jacal* before it strikes us."

Lightning zigzagged across the sky and drops of rain were beginning to fall when they saw a man plodding his way through the now gray *chaparral*. Undoubtedly he was lost, for once in a while he stopped and looked around as if wishing to guide himself by some sign of nature. Lobo, the shepherd dog, saw him too and gave a bark followed by a growl of warning.

"Hush, Lobo, hush," cried Tío Patricio.

The stranger answered the bark by an '*Ave María*'* and would have come nearer but for Lobo's growls of warning.

"*En gracia concebida*,** excuse my Lobo, *señor*," responded Tío Patricio, finishing the angelic salutation, "he never sees anyone but your most humble servant, and considers everyone else, except Cristóbal and I, the enemy of his flock. Hush, Lobo, the *señor* is a friend." The dog probably understood for he wagged his tail in sign of friendship.

"Can I be of any help, *señor*?"

"I am lost," the stranger said. "I left camp this morning and got turned around looking for deer tracks. I am hungry and I am tired; something to eat and a bed will be all I need. Could you guide me to a ranch house where I can spend the night?"

"The nearest one is some miles off," the shepherd replied, "but if the *señor* wishes to share the humble home of a poor man, this child and I will be very proud indeed." The man nodded in silent assent and prepared to follow.

"This way, *señor.*"

---

[4]The *zenzontle* story appears separately in González (1927). Stith Thompson Motif-Index number A 1915 The creation of the mockingbird.

*Ave María*—Hail Mary. This salutation is still used in the rural communities.

**En gracia concebida*—Conceived in grace.

Night was swiftly descending, and what had been intermittent drops was changing to rain. At a turn in the trail they were following, silhouetted against the darkness of the *chaparral* was faintly discerned a white mass. As the three approached, the stranger discovered it to be a white stone house semi-hidden by shrubs and *nopal*.*

"Didn't you tell me there were no ranch houses near here?" asked the stranger. "What do you call that?"

"Oh, *señor*," replied the *pastor*, "hush! Do not ask me, *Por la Virgen Santa*,* and above all, do not go in."

"Do you mean I should stay out in the rain when I could have shelter? Ridiculous!" And with these words the brusque stranger walked towards the house.

"*Señor, señor*, but you'll come to harm."

"But what is wrong with the house?"

"It is accursed, *señor*," said the *pastor* crossing himself reverently. "The spirits of the dead live there."

"Indeed!" the stranger replied with a smile of incredulity. "Have your way about it. I will not go in, but you'll have to tell me the story of that house."

"The ghosts do not like the living to speak of them. It molests them, *señor*, and I do not like to do it, but to keep you from harm I will gladly do that and more. Now, *vámonos, señor*."

Soon they came to a thatch-roofed *jacal* built at the foot of a large mesquite.

"This is your home and mine, *señor*. Let me build a fire and you will be as comfortable as a king."

After supper, as the fire blazed, the stranger said to the goat herder, "I want to hear that story now, *amigo*."

"*Bien*, it is a long story, *señor*. That house we passed was built by an old Spanish family, los Vegas by name, many years ago when the Spaniards ruled the land. They built the house well and strong, out of solid rock. In time of danger it was used as a fort, for you can still see the loopholes on the walls. Some dreadful calamity must have befallen los Vegas, for they disappeared as mysteriously as they came. Some say they were carried away by the Indians; others, that they were killed by enemies, probably Spaniards. Their blood stains the floors yet. And, because there is a fireplace in nearly every room we call the house Las Chimeneas.

*Prickly pear
**Por la Virgen Santa*—In the name of the holy Virgin.

The spirits of los Vegas wander at night. They look for the gold they buried. The *vaqueros* here call it a shepherd's superstition, but I swear to you that strange things do happen there, *señor.*

One evening at sundown, as I was returning home with my flock, I heard voices inside of the house. Thinking that some of my friends were there, I stopped. They were talking of something that I did not quite understand; of a duel fought with swords, a murder, a proposed vengeance, and of money buried under a certain tree. Then I realized that I had been listening to the voices of the dead. I hurriedly gathered my flock and left.

Just then Coyote, that worthless *vaquero* of Don Francisco, caught up with me and said meaningfully, 'You'll soon be rich, won't you, Tío?'

'No,' I answered, 'there is not much money in herding goats.'

'Don't be so sly, Tío. What about the legacy of los Vegas?'

He had also heard, the scoundrel. *Bien, señor,* the next day, taking a pick, I went to the place where I thought the money would be. But I was too late. Coyote had been there before. Queer things happen there, *señor.*

My wife, Juanita—may her soul rest in peace!—saw an apparition once. She was outside of this very *jacal* watering her flowers. She felt a presence near her; looking up, she saw a beautiful Spanish lady, all dressed in black. She wore a dress like the one *mi señora's* great-grand-mother wore when she was presented to the viceroy in Mexico. She smiled at Juanita. My wife asked her what she wanted, but her only reply was a smile; and she faded away. Juanita never forgot that lovely face and smile; she was haunted by it day and night, and like her, she faded away. I buried her on the hilltop; from here I can see her grave and I often say an *Ave* for the repose of her soul. Believe me or not, it is the truth.

That you may be fully convinced, I am going to tell you what happened to some *vaqueros.* They were regular daredevils fearing neither the dead nor the living. They boasted that they would spend a whole night at Las Chimeneas. Everybody was anxious, of course, to see what the outcome of it would be. They made their preparations in true *vaquero* fashion. Got their six-shooters in readiness, took enough tobacco to last them a week, and provided themselves with a deck of cards to play poker.

All went well until midnight, the hour when the spirits of the dead wander about. All of a sudden the light went out. Footsteps of someone wearing spurs were heard coming into the room. Of course they said it was the wind—as if the wind could wear spurs. One of them got up, lit the lamp, and the game went on. Again they heard footsteps, and this time they heard the clashing of swords as if combatants were fighting a duel. What else happened that night I never knew. Of one thing I am certain. By 4 o'clock that morning the *vaqueros* were camping a mile from the house. Another thing I have noticed is that they do not make fun of me anymore, and when I mention las Chimeneas, they talk of something else or look at each other with a look of alarm.[5]

"It is time to go to bed, *señor*. I hope the ghosts will not molest you. You and the boy sleep inside. The rain has stopped and I will keep watch. '*Hasta mañana,* * *señor*,' may the Virgin protect you from all evil spirits."

The barking of Lobo and the bleating of the flock awoke the stranger the next morning. Tío Patricio and Cristóbal, who had been up since daybreak, were in the *corral* helping the new-born lambs find their mothers and milking the goats.

"God has given the prairie a bath," said Tío Patricio, "and it is now stretching its limbs and smiling like a baby after a nap."

"He has also given you water. Have you washed your face and beard yet?"

"Early this morning I bathed it in dew," answered the old man. "Ah, good morning, my friend," he added, seeing the stranger approaching. "I hope you slept well; the spirits did not trouble you, *señor*?"

"Not the spirits of the dead," but he added, smiling, "hunger is making me somewhat uncomfortable though; you know the proverb 'A full stomach and a happy heart.'"

"If you'll share our humble breakfast, we shall be very happy, *Señor*. Cristóbal, go stir the embers and start a fire; the *señor* will eat with us."

"A fine boy," remarked the stranger as Cristóbal left, "your son?"

"Oh, no, *señor*, the master's, but he likes to be with me in the pasture and we both enjoy it together. He is my one lamb that worries me at times. I see him calling us now, breakfast must be ready."

While they ate their breakfast of goat's milk and newly made corn bread, the stranger talked to the shepherd about his life in the plains.

"Do you ever get lonely here?" he asked.

"Lonely! Never, *señor*!"

---

*\*Hasta mañana*—until tomorrow.

[5]Stith Thompson Motif-Index no. N 572 Woman as guardian of treasure and N 576.3 Ghost of treasure's human owner as guardian.

"I do not even know the meaning of the word. At night the stars keep me company; I love to watch them wink at me. Do you know what they are? I like to think they are the eyes of the dead that have purged their sins and are now happy in heaven. I enjoy the sweet contentment of our life here; the flowering trees in spring, the singing of the birds and the murmuring of the wind among the leaves makes this an enchanted place."

"And you never miss the company of people?"

"No, I do not like them, they talk too much. Once the master took me to town to buy me a pair of shoes. I did not want to go. I do not need shoes, *señor*, this," he said, pointing to his handmade *huaraches*, "is all I need, but he is the master; he commands and I obey. I did not like the city, *señor*. The sky was hidden away from my sight and at night I had to sleep in a house. I missed the breeze caressing my face and the bleating of my sheep. When I die I want to be buried here in the open plain, under the stars I know so well, and by the side of my wife. I want to be here, *señor*, so that if my spirit in heaven should ever get lonesome for the things I love, I can look down and see the *cenizo* in bloom and the prairies covered with flowers."

"I envy your faith; would I but had your beautiful beliefs! But I must go now," he added, getting up, "the men at camp are no doubt worrying about my disappearance. But before leaving I must ask one more favor of you. Will you show me the way out of here?"

"*Con mucho gusto, señor*, certainly. Cristóbal, you and Lobo stay here while I go with this, our *amigo. Bien señor*, whenever you say, *¿Listo?*"

The two men walked in silence, the old shepherd buried in his thoughts; the stranger wondering about the strange child with the haunting face who preferred living with an old shepherd in the pasture to life at home.

"Have you been long with the boy's family?" queried the stranger, breaking the long silence.

"*¿Qué dice, señor?*"

"How long have you served your master?"

"All my life, *señor*. My father worked for my master's father, and I was born at the ranch. As a boy I served the master as I still do. I was his personal servant in those days. He was a young fellow and had more love affairs than any other young fellow. I remember how he made love to all of the marriageable girls, whether they belonged to his class or were the daughters of *peones*. I was kept busy delivering love messages which he sent to them; and when I was not doing that I was accompanying him to keep some love tryst. He was not bad, my master; he merely wanted to live and enjoy himself while he could. His father had arranged a marriage for him with Rita, a neighbor's daughter whom he did not love at all. She was a nice girl, but somewhat queer; she would go into trances and was supposed to have been bewitched. My master tried to argue with his father about the match, but with no success. 'Beauty is not essential in marriage, it soon fades away, but virtue remains,' the old gentleman would say, but my master who always had a ready answer replied, 'Yes, my father, but think how long ugliness lasts!'

Neither one nor the other was convinced, but the marriage took place all the same. My master, who was a gentleman above all things, realized he must change his mode of living. Ah, *señor*, it breaks my heart to see him now. The quick change soured his character and embittered his spirit. A loveless marriage has the curse of Heaven. Why, *señor*, even the creatures of the woods mate only when they are in love! And there was my master's wife bearing a child every year just because it was her duty to do so. That is terrible, *señor*! Only the children of love can be happy. The one spark of joy in his life was his oldest son, Carlos, in whose escapades he lived his life again, but even that is now gone. His two daughters are like mournful doves; they are always sad and the youngest child, my little mouse, has inherited his mother's illness. Doña Rita was once possessed of an evil spirit, but my master whipped it out of her. That was five years ago and Cristóbal saw it done. Since then he cannot stand to be near his father. Whenever Don Ramón approaches him, the child turns pale and begins to tremble like a leaf shaken by the wind. It might be fear, and it might be hate. But he worships Doña Rita and whenever she is not well the child sits by her bedside and will neither eat nor sleep. Don Ramón has brought the doctor to see him, but the child has remained the same. The women at the ranch wag their tongues and say that the evil spirit that left Doña Rita possesses the child now, but that's all nonsense, *señor*. I think he merely has a *susto*.* Don't you know what a *susto* is," asked Tío Patricio in a pitying voice, seeing the perplexed look in his companion's face, "*Madre de Dios*, people in the cities are ignorant, are they not? Everyone," continued the old man, "suffers from *susto* at one time or another. I understand now why so many people die in town. People get a *susto*," explained the shepherd, "when they have been terribly frightened, or when they have had a shock. At times when the shock is very great the spirit always leaves the body. I know this is what troubles my

---

*_Susto_—Fright; shock.

Little Mouse. He has all the symptoms. He is pale, he does not talk much and at night has terrible dreams of spirits and ghosts. He lives in constant dread of being bewitched."

"Is there a *cura** for that strange illness, my friend?"

"Yes, a very simple one. The patient is laid with outstretched arms at a crossroads and with a broom he is swept up and down and then sideways always making the good sign. While doing this the Our Father and the *Credo* are repeated three times. This done the patient is given a cup of tea made from the brewing of a piece of red ribbon, a cross of holy palm, a wedding ring and anise seeds. The remaining tea is poured into an iron pot that has been heating over the fire. The hissing sound of the water frightens the spirit of *susto* away and after a nap the patient recovers. You see how simple it is. Here we are at the gate. This is the path that will lead you to Don Ramón's house."

"I have heard you refer to your master as Don Ramón, can he be Don Ramón Aguilar?"

"Do you know my master?" asked Tío Patricio in surprise.

"I have not had the honor yet, but he is the man I came out here to see. I am Ignacio Amonte and have come here to consult him about a cattle trail I want to find. Our camp is just a few miles from here, but yesterday, as you know, I foolishly lost my way. But I really must go now. Don Ramón is expecting me and I must not keep him waiting. *Muchas gracias, amigo*, and *adiós*."

"*Adiós señor*, may you go with God. And now," thought the shepherd, "back to the goats and sheep. I must go *aprisa*.** I have a feeling something unpleasant has happened."

"Tío Patricio, Tío Patricio," cried Cristóbal seeing him approach, "Carlos has been here and he wants to see you."

"*Madre de Dios*," exclaimed the old man in surprise, "Where is he?"

"Hiding in the *mota*. He told me to ask you to come right away."

"Why can't people be like goats," muttered the old man. "They may have no sense, but at least they never get themselves or anyone else into serious trouble."

"That's the place where he is, Tío," said Cristóbal pointing to a motte of trees, "we have to go to him though. He says he is running away and does not want anyone to see him."

"*Madre de Dios*, who is he running away from?"

"Father and everyone else."

---

*Cura*—Cure.

**Aprisa*—In a hurry.

"A nice business indeed," grumbled the old shepherd as he worked his way through the thorny thick brush, "but what must be, must be, I suppose."

They found Carlos standing by his horse. His face revealed the crushed spirit of one who in a short time has suffered and thought much. Seeing him standing there so much like his master, the old shepherd dropped on his knees before the lad, crying out:

"*Pobrecito Mío. Pobrecito angel de Dios.*"*

"Get up, Tío. I am not worthy of your love," sobbed the boy. "I am a thief, do you hear me? A common cattle thief."

"You are my Carlitos whom I carried and rocked to sleep in my arms. You did not do this terrible thing, my master's son could not have done it."

"I am leaving, Tío"—interrupted the boy brusquely, "I am going to Mexico."

"But your father—?"

"I have disgraced him and my presence would be a constant reminder of our shame."

"Think of your mother and Rosita."

"I have; my mother will weep and pray for me; Rosita will forget me; perhaps she already hates me as I well deserve to be. If she does, it will be easier for her; if she still loves me, her suffering will increase mine. This is what I want you to do, Tío. Take this letter to her but see that no one knows about it. Cristóbal will look after the flock while you are gone. I shall be here in the thicket watching and if anything goes wrong, I am here to help him."

It was a good three hour walk to the Olivareño ranch, and when Tío Patricio arrived there, Don Francisco and Doña Margarita were still sleeping their *siesta*. He hid behind the fence in a nook formed by *maguey* and cactus and from his hiding place could see every move at the ranch. Fortunately for him the cowboys were all in the pasture, but he had to watch out for the eagle eyes of Ambrosio, the Indian cook. On this particular day he was in the kitchen sucking the raw marrow from a pile of fresh bones and singing his wild Indian songs.

"Plague take the heathen Indian," thought Tío Patricio, "why can't he take a nap like a well-behaved Christian should? If he would only go, I could get to Rosita's window without being seen."

As though evoked by the old man's thoughts, the girl came into the patio. She looked around and seeing herself alone walked deliberately to a cage hanging from a hook. She opened the door, took the bird out,

*\*Pobrecito angel de Dios*—My poor little angel.

and stroking its head murmured softly, "You have also been torn from your lover, but you shall be more fortunate. I will set you free and you can go back to him." The bird stood on the palm of her hand and with a timid flutter of wings flew away to the *cañada*. The girl looked at the empty cage and with a heartrending sob turned to go into the house. Realizing that this was his one chance to see her, Tío Patricio came out from his hiding place.

"Don't be frightened, Rosita," he said, seeing the look of alarm on her face, "it is just Tío Patricio who brings you news from Carlos."

"Oh, Tío," sobbed the girl flying to the old man's arms.

"There, there, my little lamb, cry all you need to cry in the arms of this worthless old man."

"My father commands me to forget him," she sobbed, "as though love could be ordered away. He told me that Carlos had disgraced himself and his family and that I must never think of him again. What have they done to him now? Where is he?"

"He is with us in the pasture," whispered the old man. "But my little Rosita, he must go away, for a while anyway."

"And he will leave me?"

"Oh, just for *un tiempecito*, a very short time. He is going to Mexico and in less time than it takes a rooster to crow, we shall see him coming back, his saddlebags filled with gold coins. And then we shall have a gay wedding and Doña Rosita will be a very happy and a very grand lady. Let me wipe your tears; you must smile so I can take that smile back to Carlos. Now that's much better, and it will be nicer yet when I repeat his very words to you, 'Tío, he said, 'tell her that I am going away to erase the blot that has been cast upon my father's name; tell her that though in disgrace now, I am not as guilty as I seem to be, and that some day I shall return to claim her and to clear my name.'"

"Let me go with you, Tío, take me to him, please?"

"No, *mi palomita*,* that cannot be. What would your father say if he ever found out? Besides the way is long, and you could not return before night. What shall I tell Carlos for you?"

"Give him this medal of *La Dolorosa*, Our Lady of Sorrows, that I have always worn around my neck; tell him that my love is as lasting as the love of the Blessed Mother and that I shall pray and wait for him."

"That I shall and very glad will I be to take him such a good message. May the good God bless you and may His holy Saints help you to be brave."

---

*Mi palomita*—My little dove.

Carlos left at dusk. There were tears in the old man's eyes as he saw the young man disappear into the night.

"He has gone, little mouse, may the Archangel Raphael and Saint Christopher, patrons of travelers that they are, bring him back to us."

# CHAPTER V

## The Unwelcomed Guest

Fall came bringing no relief from the summer heat that had scorched the prairie grass an amber yellow. Occasionally, winds from the north brought hopes of cooler days that never came. The sand, a golden glass, reflected a copper colored sky; while the sun, an opaque, jaundiced disk wearily ascended its daily path. One sandstorm after another had killed the last vestige of vegetation; and the wind blew across the land hurling clouds of yellow sand, every grain of which pricked and burned like so many needles.

Ill days had come to the Olivareño. The cattle were dying from starvation and thirst; the flocks of sheep and goats once so plentiful were fast decreasing in number. Worst of all, Rosita was ill. Carlos' disgrace and his sudden departure had done something to the girl's sensitive nature. She was a mere shadow of the once carefree girl whose song had echoed through the house as she went about helping her mother.

Doña Margarita's heart bled for the girl. "Like a dove she mourns for her lover," she often said to herself as she watched the girl sitting listlessly in the *patio*, neither seeing nor hearing what went about her.

"It's all a result of the evil days in which we live," raged the patriarch of The Olivareño. "In my time no girl would have fallen in love without first consulting her father and mother. She would have married the one chosen for her."

The doctor was called, but he had nothing to prescribe.

"At her age," he advised them, "such illness is only cured by the curate."

Don Francisco could have cursed him for his stupidity. Did he suppose that he, her father, did not realize that? But all the doctors were the same; mere charlatans who spoke many idle words but said nothing.

"Seriously speaking," the doctor told him later, "due to her delicately nervous constitution and the great love she bears the young man, unless she is made to feel the possibility of her marriage, I fear she will not recover."

After the doctor's verdict, Doña Margarita pleaded with Don Francisco, but he remained adamant in his decision. He could not and would not tolerate the marriage of his daughter to one who had brought shame to his family and to his name.

"What is a name to the life of a daughter?" argued the mother.

"A name is family honor, honor comes from the soul, and the soul belongs to God."

"How like a man you reason! I can forget family honor, I can forget all, all, to save the life of my daughter. What is a name? A hollow sound easily carried away by the wind. Something that passes; but a daughter, ah, Francisco! A daughter," she continued softly, "is a being so tender and so loving; someone created from our very selves and sent to us by God. Would you sacrifice her? Would you break her heart with your harsh actions and words?"

All of Doña Margarita's eloquence fell on barren soil. With the firmness of conviction that characterized him, Don Francisco vowed he preferred to mourn for a dead daughter than for one living in disgrace.

Then Antonio Traga-Balas, a local *ranchero*, came. He arrived late one afternoon and unnoticed by everyone at the ranch had managed to speak to Rosita alone. He had many things to tell her. That summer he had crossed the river into Mexico and had followed the villages and ranches along the Rio Grande buying and selling cattle. One afternoon while in a saloon drinking a *copita**, he had seen a dust-covered rider gallop by. This was not at all unusual, but this time the fact that the man's shirt was blood-stained caused everyone to notice him. The stranger had dismounted and had been immediately surrounded by the many idlers gathered there. But he had walked past them without as much as a glance. He returned sometime later dressed as a *ranchero*, and it was then that he had recognized Carlos. They had been together two days, at the end of which Carlos had told him he was going to the mines of Mapimí. "I then told him I was coming to Texas and he asked me to bring you this."

"For me, Carlos sends this to me? I cannot believe it," sobbed the girl. Grabbing the package from the astonished messenger she ran into the house looking for her mother. Thrusting the package into Doña Margarita's hands she cried out, "Look, *mi madre*, a gift from him. Open it! I cannot, my hands shake so and I cannot see for the tears of joy."

*Copita—a drink.

"Oh, *mi madre*," she cried again seeing the contents, "a crucifix. See again, perhaps there is a message."

"Yes, my daughter, there is. Pray for me. By this Cross I promise to return and prove my innocence."

"I knew it, *madre*! My heart could not love him otherwise."

"Let us pray it be so, and let us hope he will return soon to explain this dreadful thing. But until then, my daughter, your father must not know. Keep your cross and keep your message. You will need the comfort of both," added her mother kissing the girl. "May God forgive me! Never until now have I kept a secret from your father. It is for her happiness," she explained to the messenger who had followed Rosita into the room. "Francisco must never know, Antonio, understand, never. And above all things he must never know you have been here. I forgive you for the good you have done my daughter, but go before he comes."

"He is a hard man, Margarita. Does he ever forgive?"

"Those who have offended him as you have, never. You, his cousin, did something dishonorable, unworthy of the name of the Olivares, and that he will neither forget nor forgive. Go with God, Antonio, and may he guard your steps."

"You will not drive me away without food, Margarita! I am hungry. I've ridden all day and the old wound in my neck will not stand a thirty mile ride back to the river."

"Hide in the pasture and after dark come to the *vaqueros'* house. Tell them I sent you, and you will be given all you need. Go now, Antonio, and may your Guardian Angel protect you."

"I am afraid he does not claim me anymore," he laughed, "but thanks all the same for your good wishes. *Adiós*."

## Antonio Traga-Balas

That evening Antonio Traga-Balas was in his element, smoking, drinking black coffee and telling the *vaqueros* incidents from his adventurous life.

He was a wiry little man, a bundle of nerves in perpetual motion. Quicksilver might have run through his veins instead of blood. His right arm, partly paralyzed as a result of a *machete** cut he had received in a saloon brawl, terminated in stiff claw-like dirty-nailed fingers. One eye was partly closed; a knife cut had done that, but the other, amber in color, had the alertness and quickness of a hawk's. Chairs were not

*Machete*—a big knife with a straight long blade.

made for him. Now squatting on the floor, now sitting on one heel, he told interminable stories of border feuds, bandit raids, and smuggler fights, as he fingered a murderous knife which ended in three inches of zigzag, jagged steel. "No one has ever escaped this," he said caressing it, "sticking it into a man might not have finished him, but getting it out, ah, my friends!, that did the work. It's a very old one, brought from Spain, I guess," he added in an unconcerned voice, "here is the date, 1830."

A landowner by inheritance, a trail driver by necessity, and a smuggler and gambler by choice, he had given up the traditions of his family, to be and do that which pleased him most. Through some freakish mistake of nature he had been born three centuries too late. He might have been an adventurous, fearless *conquistador* or he might have been a chivalrous knight of the Rodrigo de Narváez* type, fighting the infidels along the Moorish frontier. A tireless rider, a man of *pelo en pecho*,* as he braggingly called himself, he was afraid of nothing.

"The men of my time were not lily-livered, white-gizzarded creatures." He told the admiring group, "we fought for the thrill of it and the sight of blood maddened us as it does a bull. Did we get a gash in the stomach? Did the guts come out? What of it? We tightened the sash and continued the fray. See this arm? Ah, could it but talk! It could tell you how many it sent to Purgatory, but none I am sure to heaven. The men I associated with were neither sissies nor saints. Often at night when I cannot sleep because of these accursed sounds I often say a prayer, in my way, for the repose of their souls, in case my prayers should reach the good God.

People call me Traga-Balas, bullet swallower, Antonio Traga-Ballas to be more exact. Ay! were I as young as I was when the incident that gave me that name happened!

We were bringing several cartloads of smuggled goods to be delivered at once and in safety to the owner. Oh, no, it was not ours. But we would have fought for it with our life's blood. We had dodged the Mexican officials and now we had to deal with the Rangers. They must have been tipped, because they knew the exact hour we were going to cross the river. We swam in safety. The pack mules, loaded with packages wrapped in tanned hides, we led by the bridles. We hid them in a clump of trees and were just beginning to dress when the Rangers fell upon us. Of course we did not have a stitch of clothes on! Did you think we were fully dressed? Had we but had our guns in readiness they might have had another story to tell. We would have fought like wild cats to keep

*Rodrigo de Narváez, celebrated Spanish warrior, surnamed the Good.
**Pelo en pecho* means hair on chest, manly.

the goods from falling into their hands. It is not ethical among border smugglers to lose the property of a Mexican to an American, and as to falling into their hands, we preferred death a thousand times. It is neither a disgrace nor dishonor to die like men, but it is to die like a rat. Only canaries sing; men never tell, however tortured they might be. But that is another story. I have seen the Rangers pumping water into the mouth of an innocent man because he would not confess to something which he had not done. And of course we did not want to run the same risk.

I ran to where the packmules were, to get my gun. Like a fool that I was I kept yelling at the top of my voice, 'You so-and-so *gringo* cowards, why don't you attack men like men? Why do you wait until you see them undressed and unarmed?'

I must have said some very insulting things for one of them shot at me right in the mouth. The bullet knocked my front teeth, grazed my tongue and went right through the back of my neck. Didn't kill me though. It takes more than bullets to kill Antonio Traga-Balas!" he added boastfully.

"The next thing I knew I found myself in a shepherd's hut. I had been left for dead no doubt, and I had been found by the goat herder. The others were sent to the penitentiary. After I recovered I remained in hiding for a year or so; and when I showed myself, all thought it a miracle that I had lived through it. That's how I was rechristened Traga-Balas. That confounded bullet did leave my neck a little stiff though; can't turn around as easily as I should; but outside of that I am fit as though the accident, I like to call it that, had never happened. It takes a lot to kill a man, at least one who can swallow and spit bullets.[1]

I've seen and done many strange things in my life and I can truthfully say that I have never been afraid but once. What are bullets and knife thrusts to seeing a corpse arise from its coffin? Bullets can be dodged and dagger cuts are harmless unless they hit a vital spot. But a dead man, staring at you with lifeless open eyes, and gaping mouth is enough to make a man tremble in his boots. And mind you, I am no coward; never have been. Is there anyone among you here who thinks Antonio Traga-Balas is one?" he asked taking the knife from its cover and fingering it in a way that made the *vaqueros* feel a queer empty spot in their stomachs.

This incident happened at Roma some years ago. I was at home alone. My wife and children were visiting in another town. I remember it was a windy night in December. The evening was cold, and not

---

[1]Stith Thompson motif-index number F615—strong man evades death.

knowing what else to do, I decided to go to bed early. I was not asleep yet when someone began pounding at my door.

'Open the door, Don Antonio, please let me in!' said a woman's voice. I got up and recognized the woman before me, one of our new neighbors. They had just moved into a deserted *jacal* in the alley back of our house.

'My husband is very sick,' she explained, 'he is dying and wants to see you. He says he must speak to you before he dies.'

I dressed and went with her wondering all the time what this unknown man wanted to see me about. I found him in a miserable hovel on a more miserable pallet on the dirt floor; I could see by the sunken cheeks and the fire that burned in his eyes that he was really dying, and of consumption too. With mumbled words he dismissed the woman from the room and once she had gone asked me to help him sit up. I propped him on the pillows the best I could. He was seized by a fit of coughing followed by a hemorrhage and I was almost sure that he would die before he had time to say anything. I brought him some water and poured a little *tequila** from a half empty bottle that was at the head of the pallet. After drinking it he gave me a sigh of relief.

'I am much better now,' he whispered. I could see that his voice was already failing, 'my friend,' he said, 'excuse my calling you, an utter stranger, friend; but I have heard you are a man of courage and honor and will understand what I have to say to you. That woman you saw here is not my wife; but I have lived with her in sin for the last twenty years. It weighs upon my conscience and I want to right the wrong I did her once!'

I could not help but think of the changes that are brought about by the mere thought of facing eternity. I thought it very strange indeed that after so long a time he should have qualms of conscience now, but I imagine death is a fearful thing; and never having died myself I could not judge what the dying man before me was feeling. So I decided to do what I would have expected others to do for me and asked him if there was anything that I might do for him.

'Call a priest, I want to marry her,' he whispered.

I did as he commanded and went to the rectory. Father José María was still saying his prayers and when I told him that I had come to get him to marry a dying man, he looked at me in a way he had of doing whenever he doubted anyone; with one eye half closed and out of one corner of the other. As I had played him many pranks before, no doubt he thought I was doing it again. He somewhat hesitated at first and then

---

*Tequila*—An intoxicating drink made from the *maguey*.

got up somewhat convinced. 'I'll take my chance with you again, you son of Barabbas,' he said, 'I'll go. Some poor soul may want to reconcile himself with his Creator.' He put on his black cape and took the little bag he always carried on such occasions. The night was as black as the mouth of a wolf and the wind was getting colder and stronger.

'A bad time for anyone to want a priest, eh, Father?' I said in an effort to make conversation, not knowing what else to say.

'The hour of repentance is a blessed moment at whatever time it comes,' he replied in a tone that I thought was reprimanding.

On entering the house we found the man alone. The woman was in the kitchen he told us. I joined her there, and what do you suppose the shameless creature was doing? Drinking *tequila*, getting courage she told me for the ordeal ahead of her. After about half an hour, we were called into the sickroom. The man looked much better. Unburdening his soul had given him that peaceful look you sometimes see on the face of the dead who die while smiling. I was told that I was to be witness to the holy Sacrament of Matrimony. The woman was so drunk by now, she could hardly stand up and between hiccoughs she promised to honor and love the man who was more fit to be food for worms than for life in this valley of tears. I'd never seen a man so strong for receiving Sacraments as that one was! He had received the Sacrament of Penance, of Matrimony, and could see no greater penance than marrying such a woman, and he was to receive Extreme Unction, the Sacrament for the dying. The drunken woman and I held the candles as Father José María anointed him with Holy Oil. And when we had to join him in prayer I was ashamed that I could not repeat the Lord's prayer with him. That scene will always live in my mind; and when I die may I have as holy a man as Father José María to pray for me! The priest lingered a few moments and seeing there was nothing else to do said he would go back. I went with him under the pretext of getting something or other for the dying man; but in reality I wanted to see him safe at home. On the way back I stopped at the saloon for another bottle of *tequila*. The dying man might need, I thought, a few drops to give him courage to start on his journey to the unknown; although from what I had seen, the priest had given him all he needed.

When I returned the death agony was upon him. The drunken woman was snoring in the kitchen; and I saw it was up to me to see that the man did not die like a dog. I wet his cracked lips with a piece of cloth moistened in *tequila*. I watched all night. The howling of the wind and the death rattle of the consumptive made the night a veritable Hell for me. With the coming of dawn, his soul, now pure from sin, left the miserable carcass that had given it lodging through life. I folded his arms over his chest and covered his face with a cloth. There was no use in calling the woman. She lay on the dirt floor snoring like a trumpet. I closed the door and went out to see what arrangements could be done for the funeral. I went home and got a little money to buy boards for the coffin and black calico for the bride, now a widow. I realized she did not deserve it but appearances must be kept. I also bought a few candles.

I made the coffin and when all was done and finished, went back to the house. The woman was still snoring, her half opened mouth filled with buzzing flies. The corpse was as I had left it. I called some of the neighbors to help me dress the dead man in my one black suit. But he was stiff already and we had to lay him in the coffin as he was, unwashed and dirty. If it is true that we wear white raiments in Heaven, I hope the good Saint Peter gave him one at the gate, before the other blessed spirits got to see the pitiful things he wore. I watched the body all day. He was to be buried early the following day. Father José María had told me he would say mass for him. The old woman, may the curse of Heaven be upon her black soul, had gotten hold of the other bottle of *tequila* and continued bottling up courage for the ordeal that she said she had to go through.

The wind that had started the night before did not let down. In fact it was getting stronger. Several times the candles had been put out and the corpse and I had been left in utter darkness. To avoid the repetition of such a thing I went to the kitchen and got some empty fruit cans very much prized by the old woman. In fact she did not want to let me use them at first; because, she said, the fruit on the paper wrapping looked so natural and it was the only fruit she had ever owned. I got them anyway, filled them with corn and stuck the candles there.

Early in the evening about nine or thereabouts, I decided to get out again and ask some people to come and watch part of the night with me. Not that I was afraid to stay alone with the corpse; one might fear the spirit of those who die in sin, but certainly not this one who had left the world the way a Christian should. I left, somewhat regretfully for I was beginning to have a kindly feeling towards the dead man. I felt towards him as I would towards a friend; no doubt because I had helped him to transform himself from a sickly human being to a nice Christian corpse.

As I went from house to house asking people to watch with me that night, I thought of a story that the priest had told us once; and by the time I had gone half through the town I knew very well how the man who was inviting guests to the wedding feast must have felt. All had some good excuse to give but no one could come. To make a long story short I returned alone to spend the last watch with my friend, the corpse.

As I neared the house I noticed it was very well lighted and I thought perhaps someone had taken pity upon the poor unfortunate and had gone there with more candles to light the place. But soon I realized what was really happening. The place was on fire. I ran into the house and the sight that met my eyes is one that I will ever see. The corpse, its hair a flaming mass, was sitting up in the coffin where he had so peacefully lain all day. The glassy, opaque eyes stared into space with a look that saw nothing and its mouth was convulsed into the most horrible grin. I stood there paralyzed by such horror. To make matters worse, the drunken woman reeled into the room yelling, 'He is burning before he gets to Hell.'

Two thoughts ran simultaneously in my mind, to get her out of the room and to extinguish the fire. I pushed the screaming woman out into the darkness and arming myself with courage, re-entered the room. I was wearing cowboy boots and my feet were the only part of my body that was well protected. Closing my eyes I kicked the table and I heard the thud of the burning body as it hit the floor. I became crazy then.

With my booted feet I trampled upon and kicked the corpse until I thought the fire was extinguished. I dared not open my eyes for fear of what I might see; and with eyes still closed I ran out of the house. I did not stop until I reached the rectory. Like a madman I pounded upon the door and when the priest opened it and saw me standing there, looking more like a ghost than a living person, he could not help but make the sign of the Cross. It was only after I had taken a drink or two, may God forgive me for having done it in the presence of the holy man, that I could tell him what had happened.

He went back with me and with eyes still closed I helped him place the poor dead man in his coffin. Father José María prayed all night. As for me I sat staring at the wall not daring to look at the casket, much less at the charred corpse. That was the longest watch I ever kept. At five o'clock, with no one to help us, we carried the coffin to the church where the promised Mass was said for him. We hired a donkey cart to take him to the cemetery and as the sun was coming up Father José María, that man of God, and I, an impenitent sinner, laid the dead man in his final resting place.[2]"

"No, don't trouble about giving me a bed," Traga-Balas told Matiniano, seeing the *vaquero* was making preparations for him. "I'll close my eyes for a few minutes, and leave. The river must be crossed before the buzzards smell their prey."

---

[2]González published the Traga-Balas stories separately in González (1935).

December and the drizzling rains came bringing temporary relief. The cool, gray foggy days were a benediction that quenched the thirst of the prairie and promised a fruitful spring.

Two weeks before Christmas, Eli made his annual visit to the ranch. Since the women could not go to town, this good-natured Syrian peddler brought town to them in the many bundles and suitcases he brought with him. Of late Eli's visits had not been very profitable. He had one unseen competitor whom he hated with oriental vehemence— Sears Roebuck! Even Doña Margarita, whose boast had been that after Eli came to the Olivareño there was no need for him to go anywhere else, could not buy much this year. The wool had brought very little; no cattle had been sold in the fall and her purse could not meet his prices. Much to her sorrow and regret her purchases were limited to a dress and a few trinkets for Rosita.

Disgusted with the small sales he had made, the Syrian wrapped his bundles viciously, vowing never to return.

"But you will have supper with us, of course," invited Doña Margarita.

"If the *señora* commands, I cannot but obey," replied Eli with his accustomed exaggeration.

The night promised to be cold and damp. A big fire, which crackled and sputtered in the dining room fireplace revealed a big room furnished with the simplicity and taste of its owners. A long table made of ebony wood occupied the center. At the head was the Master's seat, a roomy high-backed chair made of rawhide leather. On either side, long benches with curved backs served as seats for the family and guests. On the left wall stood a hand-hewn cupboard made from mesquite wood. On it was placed the family silver, hammered goblets and plates, spoons and big water pitcher. In a niche on the opposite wall garlanded with paper flowers, a statue of the Virgin kept watch. Under it, on a hand-carved stand, a lighted candle on a brass candlestick cast a glow on the downcast face of the Immaculate.

Once the family was gathered for the evening meal, Don Francisco lit the big lantern hanging from the *Viga Madre*, the main beam. The rays of light revealed the Gothic lettering of one family motto, "Like an oak I may be bent, but not broken." His eyes traveled from it to the pale, but now animated face of Rosita. "The wise words of an ancient family are consoling," he said to himself, "and like a true daughter of that family, mine is living it though it breaks her heart."

Ambrosio, the ranch Indian cook, served supper with the resigned expression of a martyr. He hated Eli, whom he suspected of being a child of the Devil, because he looked like a Jew. Much to Don Francisco's amusement, he crossed himself everytime he served the unsuspecting Syrian.

After the meal, as was customary during the long winter evenings, the *caporal* and the *vaqueros* came to talk and discuss the affairs of the ranch. The conversation was becoming general when a whistle was heard over the house. With a cry of fear, Ambrosio ran into the dining room crying excitedly, "I told you he was the Devil, *Señora*," he cried out pointing to Eli. "He brings the screech owl."

Eli, not knowing what it was all about, but hearing himself called a devil, and by an Indian at that, got up from his chair determined to avenge the insult with his fists. Don Francisco, however, was too quick for him. Holding him by the arm he pacified his ruffled spirits apologizing for Ambrosio.

"Maybe he is not the Devil," muttered the cook dubiously, "but the screech owl is and he brought him here. But owl can do us no harm now. I have told him to come for holy water tomorrow, and he will not return for fear of being baptized. He is afraid of holy things."

"Nonsense, nonsense, Ambrosio, the poor harmless bird is merely looking for food," explained Don Francisco.

"I am not so sure of that, Master," interrupted one of the cowboys. "Queer things have happened to me. I know, for was I not bewitched once? If you will allow me, Don Francisco, I can tell you how it came about."

"Certainly, go ahead."

"With your permission then, I will begin. When I first came to work for Don Ramón, I was a young man. And the first thing I did after getting a job was to fall in love. She was Doña Rita's maid and a prettier and sweeter girl has never lived than my Lupita. I saved all I could and before the year was out I asked Don Ramón's permission to marry. He liked my plans and because Doña Rita could not live without Lupita, Don Ramón suggested we live close by, in one of the unoccupied *jacales*. Everyone was pleased with this, except Tía Saturnina. She had wanted me to marry her daughter and when she heard of our marriage she vowed we would never be happy. We were married in the Master's house. There was no happiness like ours. Lupita sang as she went about her work. And in the evening, when I returned from the pasture, she waited for me at the gate. However, I noticed a change in her. She was pale and even though she did not complain I was afraid for her. One night as we sat outside watching the moon, a most horrible screech was heard. Lupita crossed herself and I clasped her closely in my arms. It was the screech owl; just as we heard it tonight. I remembered Tía Saturnina's threat and my heart grew heavy. Lupita got worse after this and she took to her bed. A doctor was brought from town, but could find nothing wrong with her. How could he when the darling of my soul was bewitched? I also took sick, rheumatism in the left foot and I could not even walk. Lupita wasted away and one stormy night she died. A few days later, lonely and sick as I was, I dragged myself out and sat by a *maguey* fence in front of the house. I was making figures on the sand with my stick to amuse myself when accidentally I struck something hard. My curiosity was aroused and I continued digging. A small tin box was buried there. I dug it out and opened it. Holy Virgin! What I saw there made me turn cold. Two rag dolls, one dressed as a bride, a pin thrust through the left side where the heart would be. The other, a man, had another stuck in his left foot. I realized then the meaning of it, Lupita and I; she, already dead, I, suffering the curse of the old woman. With a cry of rage I pulled the pin from Lupita's heart, and believe me when I tell you that I heard something like a sigh of relief and something soft like the wing of a dove brushed my cheek. It was Lupita's soul free at last. I then pulled the other pin out. I was able to walk back to the house, the pain gone."[3]

"Did that really happen to you?" queried one of the listeners.

"May the Virgin punish me if I am not telling the truth."

"A very strange tale indeed."

"Not so strange, Master, if you realize there are evil spirits floating in the air to harm you. Have you ever seen them? Well, I have and the very thought makes me shudder. My father was once accosted by one. He was a young man and was returning from a dance. It was after midnight; no thought of evil disturbed his mind and he whistled to himself as he remembered the pleasures of the dance. All of a sudden his horse reared and snorted as if frightened. And a good reason the poor beast had to be so terrified. For there in the middle of the road, stood a woman dressed in white, her hair hanging down her back. Giving a sudden leap, she grabbed the reins of the horse. My father, as you may very well imagine, was greatly frightened, but he had enough presence of mind to ask,

'Are you from this world or the other?'

'From the other,' the ghost replied. For a time which seemed an eternity, my father and the ghost struggled. Finally, arming himself with courage, my father took out his pistol and shot once, twice, but the ghost held a firm grasp on the reins. About this time the moon came out from behind a cloud and my father saw the fleshless face of the ghost.

---

[3]Motif-Index number E 411.10—Persons who die violent or accidental deaths cannot rest in grave.

As soon as he saw her face to face, the spirit dropped the reins and faded away. Another *vaquero* told him later that on passing by the same place one dark night, his horse had begun to limp. He would not stop, but kept on moving. He passed by two ranches which he knew were on the way. In fact he traveled all night, yet found himself at dawn at the same place."⁴

"When we were children," added Don Francisco, "my old nurse, Nana Chita would often tell us a story, the mere thought of which still sends chills running up and down my spine."

"Tell it, tell it," begged the *vaqueros*, getting close to each other.

"She would tell it on dark nights when the wind howled over the housetops, and when she had us in the proper mood would begin:

The night was dark and gloomy, the wind moaned over the tree-tops and the coyotes howled all around. A knock was heard. The only occupant of the room limped across the floor and opened the door. A blast of cold wind put out the candles.

'Who is there?' he asked looking out into the darkness.

'Just a lost hermit,' answered a wailing voice, 'will you give a stranger lodging for the night?'

A figure wrapped in a black cape entered, and as he entered a tomb-like darkness and coldness filled the room.

'Will you take off your hat and cape?' the host asked solicitously of his mysterious guest.

'No—but—I—shall take off my head,' and saying this the strange personage placed his skull on the table nearby.'"⁵

The last story proved too much for Ambrosio, "M-m-m-aster, he stammered—"G-g-good n-n-night, b-b-but I a-am a-afraid t-to g-go alone."

"Come with me, you cowardly Indian," said Martiniano, "I'll take you."

"I had to look under his cot," laughed the *vaquero* when he returned. "At first I thought he was pretending, but no sir, Don Francisco, his teeth were really chattering with fear."

Hardly had Martiniano taken his seat when a bloodcurdling scream was heard, "Sounds like the bleating of a goat when a knife is stuck in her heart," suggested Martiniano. "I bet it is Ambrosio."

Led by the men in the dining room, Don Francisco, lantern in hand, ran out to the bunkhouse. In the middle of the room was Ambrosio, face

⁴Motif-Index number E 425.1.1—Revenant as lady in white.
⁵Motif-Index number E 422.1.1—Headless revenant.

distorted with fear and eyes popping out of their orbit. He could not speak. With a trembling finger he pointed towards the bed.

"The Devil there, horns prick here," he stammered touching his side. Holding the lantern on high Don Francisco examined the bed. Snuggling close to the blanket was Rosita's pet goat.

"The Devil indeed," laughed Don Francisco. Ambrosio looked around him and seeing Eli among the group could not understand what had really occurred.

"Goat in bed, Eli here—Then he is not the Devil," was his conclusion. Then throwing his apron over his head he doubled up with laughter much to the amusement of all. Approaching the peddler he said in a conciliatory voice, "Sorry, *señor* Eli, tomorrow I buy red handkerchief."

Late that night in their room, Don Francisco said to his wife, "I am glad you bought Rosita a new dress. It is surprising how a gift can make a girl forget so much! Did you notice her tonight? I believe she is forgetting."

"Yes, I noticed. A little gift has done it; she is happy now."

# CHAPTER VI

## They Toiled Not

Pedro was a hunter, the best *venadero*,* of the border country. But he was lazy and he was shiftless; a happy-go-lucky lovable vagabond who was neither a *vaquero* nor a *peon* nor a tiller of the land. The thatch-roofed *jacal* in which he and his mother lived, leaked like a sieve and the mesquite logs which formed the logs of the kitchen went up and down according to his mood and the hunting season. As fall approached and he began oiling his rifles, his mother was forced to use the wooden walls of the kitchen for fuel and when the north winds came again, Pedro found it necessary to go to the pasture for more wood with which to rebuild the walls.

Don Francisco[1] had given him a piece of land, but Pedro took neither the time nor the trouble to plant anything on it; and if by chance he did, the cows and pigs were allowed to roam at will through the field. He depended upon nature for his maintenance, and when hungry, merely tightened his belt a notch or two. But he enjoyed life to the fullest, wandering through the pastures and living on the things which nature provided for him, prickly pear and mesquite beans in the summer; venison, turkey, and *javalinas* in the fall and winter. In the spring he usually fasted, but when he ate, he ate, as a snake which devours a rabbit whole. Whenever he killed a deer he and his friends ate it at one sitting, all but the horns, skin, and bones.

*Venadero*—dear killer

[1] In this chapter, the manuscript originally had "Don Francisco" in this and subsequent sentences; it is scratched out every time and "Grandfather" is substituted. I cannot account for this autobiographical intervention except that clearly González is drawing on her own family history and may, at one time, have contemplated writing an extended autobiography fictionalizing this material.

His mother, old Nana Chita, had been Don Francisco's nurse and that alone sufficed to make him inviolable. For to dislike or hurt him in any way was torture to the old nurse and whatever caused her suffering provoked Don Francisco's displeasure and anger.

The Master's tolerance made him conscious of his superiority and he strutted about like an only rooster in a small barnyard. But in spite of that and his shiftlessness he was not disliked. For he was a traveled man, had seen the world, spoke English, and knew many stories with which he entertained his listeners on winter nights.

He was the Pied Piper of the ranch and when not hunting or visiting, he was followed by a troop of children whom he charmed, not with mysterious music, but with tales and adventures of his travels which he recited sitting on one heel and always handling one of his hunting guns. Only once had he ever disappointed [us],[2] and that had been when an American peddler came to the ranch selling tin cups. Pedro had been unable to understand him, but that, he explained, was because the man did not speak the same English as he had learned. And his worshipers were well satisfied with the explanation.

Yes, Pedro was a traveled man. He had been as far as Sugar Land and had worked on the sugar plantations. He had seen how the convicts were worked in the fields and were whipped for the least offense. Yes, he, Pedro, had seen that with his very eyes.

There was something strange, he said, that he could not understand. Not all Americans were white. He had seen some black as coal who had wool for hair and big, thick, purple lips. He had gone to one of their dances; but had not been able to stay long. They smelled like buzzards after they had been feasting on a carcass and the odor was so strong he could hear it. No, he was not mistaken. He was sure they were Americans. Did they not speak English? He had not stayed long at Sugar Land. The dampness was making him have chills. So he had hired himself as a section hand.

"You should have seen that big monster, *El Tren Volador*, The Flyer. It roared and whistled and belched fire and smoke as it flew over the land," he told his listeners. He would have liked being a section hand had it not been for the food—corn bread and salt pork. He had been told that if he ate salt pork he would soon learn to speak English. Bah! What a lie! He had eaten it three times a day and had only learned to say "Yes." There was even a song about it. And dropping his gun for

---

[2]Again, the autobiographical mode continues as the word "us" has been inserted here in the manuscript.

a few moments he extended his arm as though holding a guitar; while with the other he strummed across his vest singing the song.[3]

However he had soon tired of that life and being anxious to see the city, he moved on to Houston where he met with a very strange adventure. One Saturday evening while walking through the downtown streets, he saw some beautiful American ladies singing at a street corner. What had attracted his attention more than anything else was that they played the guitar. And that had made him so lonesome for the ranch. He stopped to listen and before he knew what was happening the tears were rolling down his cheeks. One of the beautiful ladies patted him on the back and talked to him. He did not know what she was saying, but he answered "yes" to everything she said, that being the only English word he knew. The kind ladies took him home that night and let him sleep in a room next to the garage. He could not understand what they said, but they were very kind and taught him to play the drum; and every evening the ladies, after putting on their funny hats, took the guitars and he, the drum, and they went to town. They sang beautifully and he beat the drum in a way that must have caused the envy of passers-by; and when he passed a plate, many people put money in it. During the winter he learned English. But with the coming of spring he got homesick for the *mesquitales** the fragrant smell of the *huisaches*, the lowing of the cattle at sundown, and above all for the mellow, rank smell of the *corral*. What would he not have given then for a cup of good, black, strong ranch coffee and a piece of jerky broiled over the fire and wrapped in a *tortilla*! And so one night with his belongings wrapped in a blanket, he left south for the land of his youth. And here he was again, a man who had seen the world, but who was content to remain at home.[4]

If Pedro was thought to be a great man, his mother was considered even greater. Nana Chita, as she was called, was a small, agile, old

[3]The well-known traditional association of Anglos and pork consumption in Mexican-American south Texas. Cf. Américo Paredes, *With His Pistol in His Hand": A Border Ballad and Its Hero* (Austin: University of Texas Press, 1971)36. The song is probably "El Corrido de Jacinto Treviño" with this verse: "Entrenle, rinches cobardes/validos de la ocasíon, / no van a comer pan blanco / con tajadas de jamón."(Come on you cowardly rinches you always like to take advantage; this is not like eating white bread with slices of ham.) Américo Paredes, *A Texas Mexican Cancionero: Folksongs of the Lower Border* (Urbana: University of Illinois Press, 1976) :70)

**Mesquitales*—Mesquite growth.

[4]The story of Pedro, hunter and traveler, appears separately in González (1932a).

woman who, whether walking sprightly or talking tartly with a ready comeback, resembled a little brown bird. Besides being the mother of Pedro, and Don Francisco's old nurse, she was the weaver of fanciful tales. She worshiped her husky, lazy son, and whenever anyone said anything about his carelessness as a provider she would say,

"Ah! Mi Pedro! Not because he is my son—but he is a good son."

But there was something else that made Nana Chita more interesting and more fascinating than being either Pedro's mother or a wonderful storyteller—she baked the flour *tortillas* on the coals of the open fireplace in her roofless kitchen. It was fascinating to see the round, flat cakes puff up and more fascinating still to see her break the air bubbles with a black hairpin she used for the threefold purpose of pinning her hair, picking her one tooth, and pricking the air bubbles on the flour *tortillas*.

"I do that so they won't get puffed up and spongy," she would explain sticking the hairpin into the flat cake. "Many people are like that, get big and puffed up about nothing, but of course you can't prick them up like you can a *tortilla*." [The] children who loved her naturally agreed to that.[5] Another source of attraction was the fact that she always kept dry venison hanging on a long, wire line in their one-room *jacal*. And after the *tortillas* were baked, she threw a piece of jerky into the coals. It was wonderful to see it curl around the edges as it got brown and crispy, but more wonderful still was it to inhale the fragrant pungent aroma as it cooked. After it was well done she jerked it out of the coals with fingers now immune to the heat from constant handling of the coals. While still hot and while the fat was still dripping from it, she cut the meat into small pieces, wrapped one of her half burnt *tortillas* around it and with a chirp and a grin distributed it around. That was the official dismissal.

There was charm and poetry in the stories which she said she had…[6]

[5] Editorial change. Original manuscript says, "we who as…", again suggesting that González was, at one moment, writing this material as autobiography.

[6] Here some five pages of the manuscript are missing, probably containing a narrative transition and probably another one or two stories from Nana Chita like those that follow as the manuscript continues from this break point. Perhaps it is also in these missing pages that the story of Carlos and Rosita is continued.

"There were good souls and there are bad souls and they wander through space doing good and doing ill to people," said Nana Chita to her *comadre* María as they sat on cane rocking chairs on the cool, shady porch of a white-washed adobe *jacal*. "I believe they exist, I am as sure of that as I know I am sitting here under the shade of this *huisache* tree, as sure as I know I smell its blossoms, and as sure as you know you are sitting opposite me, sewing on your daughter's wedding dress."

"May God pity them, poor wandering souls!"

"God have mercy on the evil ones; but may the good remain with us."

"Sometimes I wonder where they keep themselves when they are not in the presence of people."

"How you talk, *comadre* María! Even a child can answer that. They are everywhere. If they are good spirits they select pleasant places, the *cenizo* in bloom, a grass-covered *llano*,* a flower-scented prairie. Have you ever heard the rustling sound that comes from a corn-field? Sometimes it is soft like the sigh of a sleeping child; again it sounds like the echo of distant voices. Did you think it was merely the wind? No, *comadre*, that was the good spirits conversing with each other. Sometimes they prefer the room where a baby sleeps. Many times when my Pedro was a baby did I see him smiling in his sleep. No doubt he was playing with the spirit of a good soul."

"But the evil ones. Where do they go?" shuddered *comadre* María.

"The evil ones," interrupted Nana Chita in an important, knowing voice, "haunt the dark silent places. They abhor the light and run away from good people; that is, unless they can get them unaware to do them harm. I have seen them, *comadre*, like balls of fire arising from bone yards and cemeteries, as big bat-like birds which have no place to go, and again as toads that hop about in damp cold places."

"O-o-o- if it were not the middle of the afternoon, I would be too frightened to move. Just feel my hands, like ice they are. The thought of such things turns me cold and makes my hair stand on end."

"Hog lard will keep your hair down, however frightened you may be."

"In that case, *comadre*, let me have a little. I already feel itching at the root of my hair."

"Holy Angels of the Celestial Court! María, you have the heart of a hummingbird without the beauty of one."

*\*Llano*—plain.

"Everyone is as good as the Lord makes her, *comadre*. It pleased Him to make me the way I am and it pleased Him to make you the way you are, blessed be His name. Hog lard or no hog lard, you can continue and I shall say a prayer and be brave while you talk."

"You don't have to be so frightened. My family has never been acquainted with evil spirits."

"My grandmother, as you know, lived in this very house where we are now. As a girl she was very fond of flowers and birds. When she was not cultivating or watering her pot plants, she was taming baby mockingbirds and cardinals. One morning having gotten up late, she had gone to a dance the night before, much to her surprise she found the garden watered and the birds fed. She knew her mother had not done it because she could not carry water from the well. She asked her father but he knew nothing about it. Perhaps Felipe had done it she thought blushingly; she married him later, you know. But when he was asked he stammered a denial. She gave it no more thought. The following morning however, not only had the birds been fed and the garden watered, but the *patio* was well swept and sprinkled. She inquired among all the neighbors. No one knew anything about it. As this continued indefinitely her father and mother became alarmed; as to my grandmother, she knew she was under a spell and began to lose weight and sleep. An old woman who knew all about the things of this world and of the other as well, was consulted.

'Some spirit is doing your work,' she said, 'wait until the moon is on the wane and get up at midnight. Go to the garden and wait. Do not be afraid of anything but say to whoever you see there,'

> Come out, come forth, come out,
> Soul that suffers pains,
> A Rosary will I repeat
> To break away your chains.

She did as she was told. She went to the window just as the moon, a mere crescent, was coming up. By the dim light she saw a black figure, small, and stoop-shouldered, busily sweeping. Making the sign of the cross my grandmother called out, 'In the name of the holy souls of Purgatory, tell me who you are and what you want?'

Hearing this the ghost stopped for a brief moment, looked her in the face, and again went on with her sweeping.

'Stop your work and tell me who you are?' She called again. The old woman stopped. She was a frail, little woman and her face was so lined and weary, it made you want to cry. Again my grandmother asked her the same question.'

'I was your grandmother's friend' she said, 'and have been dead these many years. Just before my marriage I gave her some wool to card and because I was vain and wanted a foolish piece of red ribbon, I used the money which would have paid her. I died and my soul can find no rest until the debt is paid. I have plowed fields, ground corn; I have carried water, but no one until now had ever noticed me. And I am so tired and in so much need of rest.'

'What can I do for you?' my grandmother asked somewhat frightened.

'Forgive the debt that I may rest.'

She made the good sign and the little old woman faded away."

"Saint Barbara and our Lady of Guadalupe preserve me from a thing like that! Do you suppose your grandmother really saw what she thinks she saw?"

"She was a saintly woman, my grandmother, and forever spoke the truth. There is no doubt but that the spirit of those who loved us while on earth remain near us after death and help us in time of distress. Do you remember old Candelaria?"

"You are not going to tell me that she was a ghost, are you?"

"Don't be an idiot, *comadre*, of course not. She was flesh and blood like both of us. Do you remember how she helped my Luisa bring the children up? As I sit here I can see her carrying in wood or doing the heavy work, so that Luisa would not have to do it. Right after her death, you remember no doubt, that Luisa moved to town that the children might go to school there. Manuel, Luisa's husband, stayed here to look after the farm. Luisa was not used to town people and in the evening after the children went to bed she often got lonesome. It was then that she started roasting cocoa beans and grinding the chocolate for which she later got so much money. One evening, it could not have been after eight o'clock, she started roasting two pounds, intending going to bed as soon as she finished. Much to her surprise, the beans were roasted in no time; and seeing how early it really was, Luisa decided to grind them. She got out the *metate*, the cinnamon and sugar and had everything in readiness. If you have ever done this work you know how hard it is to get the oil from the bean. But that night she had no trouble. It mixed beautifully with the sugar and cinnamon and it was ready for the molds in a short time. What usually took five hours to do was done in two. By ten she was putting up the chocolate squares. It was then she heard some one at the window.

'Luisa, Luisa.'

Thinking it was one of her neighbors she went to the door, but no one was in sight.

'Luisa, Luisa,' the voice continued, 'It is time for you to go to bed.'

'Who is that calling?' she asked not a bit afraid.

'My child, don't you know me?'

It was Tía Candelaria who had been with Luisa all the time and she did not know it. Luisa tells me it has always been that way since then. Whenever she is in trouble or in danger, she hears her voice consoling or warning her and whenever she is tired she feels Tía Candelaria's presence near. Luisa has never seen her, but she says that whenever she feels a breath of air caress her cheek, she knows the old woman is near."[7]

"Thanks be given to the blessed saints, that I have never been disturbed by spirits."

"You might just as well get used to them, María, you never know when you shall meet them. But bless my soul, who is this I see coming? If it is not Francisco and Rosita!"

"You were his nurse, were you not?"

"Yes, and I am the only one who is not afraid of him and treats him as though he were not a God."

Hardly had Nana Chita finished saying these words when Don Francisco and his daughter stopped their horses at the gate.

"The age of miracles has not ceased yet, I see," she called out.

"The saints alone perform them, Nana Chita," replied Don Francisco, "If you refer to my coming, Margarita is responsible for that."

"Sit down, sit down both of you. How is Margarita?"

"As usual, Nana. I don't have to ask you how you feel; your bright eyes and your sharp tongue tell me you are well."

"Yes, *gracias a Dios*, Francisco, I am always in good health. I was expecting you today."

"Expecting me? I did not know myself I was coming until this noon when Margarita asked me to bring Rosita to see you."

"Not you, particularly, but I knew someone was coming and I told Pedro so this morning."

"Did you have one of your symptoms?" laughed Don Francisco.

"Laugh if you must, but as sure as I get up with a jumpy feeling in my heart, I am sure to see someone I like."

"I bet it almost broke through your ribs this time."

"Don't flatter yourself, Francisco, a mere flutter it was and very indistinct besides," she said winking at Rosita.

"Do you really know when something is to happen?" asked the girl.

[7]Stith Thompson, Motif-Index number H 972—Tasks accomplished with help of grateful dead.

"Yes, indeed; if on getting up I have a headache and an upset stomach, some unfortunate thing will surely happen, a death, an illness, or some unpleasant thing."

"Everyone is as the Lord made him, blessed be His name," interrupted *comadre* María.

"True, true, María, but I did not come to discuss your symptoms, Nana Chita. Rosita came to ask you something or other about I don't-know-what."

"What a fine errand boy you are!"

"Why should I worry my head about women's trifles?"

"Oh, father, don't say such awful things. Don't pay any attention to him, Nana Chita."

"As though I would, Rosita!"

"Mother wants to know if you can come some day next week to help her make soap. She lost her recipe—"

"I think she did it on purpose," interrupted Don Francisco, "she likes yours better and knowing how selfish you are, she knows that's the only way she can learn the secret of yours."

"Father, please."

"I don't mind him at all, child! I never pay attention to simple-minded people."

"Your charming words gladden my heart, oh, seeress of the *chaparral*."

"Sure, I'll come, Rosita," answered Nana Chita ignoring Don Francisco's banter.

"Mother said she would send the buggy any day you could come."

"Let me see, tomorrow is Tuesday, no, I can't go then. 'On Tuesday never sail and never marry,' says the proverb, and I never start anything on that day. Wednesday—no—Thursday, yes, that'll be a good day."

"Be sure you have no 'symptoms' then, Nana, and if you do be sure they are pleasant ones."

"Go straight to the deuce, Francisco!" said Nana Chita getting up. "You keep them company, María, while I set the table. I had *merienda*

---

[8]Here approximately six pages are missing in the original manuscript. However, stored separately in the archive I found a self-contained version of a story here narrated by Don Francisco, which I believe takes up most of this narrative space. I know that this extracted narrative goes here because, later, after the missing pages, the manuscripts picks up and concludes the story with Ernesto as its central character (see footnote). The extracted story has the title "A Border Tragedy."

prepared for my expected guests; I really should not give him anything, the long-tongued fellow. Anyone who minded him would certainly be a bigger fool than he is."

Some minutes later the four were enjoying their *merienda* of orange blossom tea and flour *tortillas.*

"If you were half as good a prophetess as you are a brewer of tea—"

"Father, please," begged Rosita, "can't we talk of something else?"

"Let him be if it amuses him; he knows full well though that...[8]

On a bend of the Río Grande in the heart of the Texas brush land, nestles a sleepy little town. Its white stone and adobe houses enclosed by walls, its narrow, dusty, winding streets, the mosque-like tower give it the appearance of an oriental town. With its showers of sand that prick and burn like sharp needles of steel, and a tropical sun which hurls its angry rays at the unfortunate inhabitants, it could be an oasis town of the Sahara. But the nights! Glorious—silvery—a limpid sky shimmering with the glittering jewels of the gods.

Here lived, years ago, two families of old and aristocratic lineage. Their ancestors, impoverished grandees from Spain, had come many generations past to the new world hoping to fill their empty coffers with the gold and silver of the Indies. Time passed and the descendants, now Texans, had no love for the country across the sea. However, they kept the customs and traditions of the mother country and when the land passed from Mexico to the United States, both families clung more tenaciously than ever to what they called the "customs and the language of God."

They shut themselves in their big houses, seeing no one, remembering and living over the past glories of their ancestors. High walls hid the houses from the gaze of the common folk and all that could be seen from the street were the tops of palm trees and the pomegranates in bloom. The two houses gave access to each other through a small gate and the two families could visit each other without having to go out of their premises.

Each family had one child; the Mendozas, a son, the Olivares, a daughter.

Often on moonlight nights, the two young people were heard singing in the garden, now ballads from old Spain, which told the loves of Moorish princesses and Spanish knights, now "Cielito Lindo" or "Adelita." People hearing their blended voices remarked, "Their lives would be equally harmonious if they married." And this, which was public opinion, was the dearest wish of the two families. The marriage would unite two old names, two large fortunes, and two handsome young people.

Clementina, if not a beauty, had the wit and charm of her Spanish forbears. The oval of her expressive, olive-tinted face was startlingly set against a frame of auburn hair inherited, no doubt, from some distant Asturian ancestor. Ernesto, temperamental and romantic with the innate courtesy of the Latin, was the handsomest youth of the town. Everyone expected these two who had been reared together to marry when the time came.

In their childhood games Ernesto had always considered Clementina his sweetheart. The children grew; and what had been a childhood whim became real love for the boy. In his adolescent dreams he could see her, queenly in her bridal gown, meeting him at the altar. She, on the contrary, had never taken Ernesto seriously. She expected to marry some day, it is true, but someone else. Her dreams and illusions were more ambitious. She wanted to see the world, go to Mexico City, perhaps Spain. She longed for the salons she had never seen where men in uniform and braid kissed the hand of the woman they loved. Her father and mother had consented to make her dream come true and she lived in expectation of the day when she might leave the little town for better things and a gayer life.

Great was Ernesto's disappointment at the decisive "no" which ended his dreams and shattered his hopes. Sad and gloomy he wandered through the brush country. He could neither eat nor sleep and the fire that consumed him was fiercer than that of the tropical sun.

"Don't be a coward, men must be men," his friends counciled him. "Make love to other girls, show her that there are more flowers to pluck."

"No one would treat me that way," added the town bully, "she has deceived you like no man should ever be deceived. Had she not accepted your attentions? Had she not led you to believe that she would marry you some day? Do you know what I would do? I'd kill her."

"No, no," moaned the unhappy boy. "Not that! I love her more than my life."

Months passed and Ernesto could not forget Clementina. No longer was he the courteous, well-mannered youth. He became a cynical man who wandered aimlessly through the lowest dives of the town. Between drinks, he would tell the story over and over again to the crowd of ruffians and gamblers gathered there.

"Ah, my friend, who would have thought her capable of such an action," the bully ever at his side remarked. "As for me, I have always shunned those sweet innocent girls with ruby-like lips and lily-white hands in which they hide the claws of a tiger. If I were you, I'd kill her—I'd show her she could not laugh at me."

"She has deceived you the way no man deserves to be deceived," ran through Ernesto's crazed mind. "She has deceived you!" And the boy wept.

The night was calm and peaceful. The bell from the tower rang for the Rosary. It was the Eve of all Saints Day and the faithful gathered to pray for the living and the dead.

After the services, the girls scattered in the courtyard of the church. Suddenly a shot rang through the peaceful stillness of the evening.

A white-clad figure fell to the ground.

A man, pistol in hand, fled into the darkness crying out—

"I killed you because you deceived me the way no man should be deceived!"

Ernesto was convicted and sentenced to life imprisonment.

The day before he was to be taken away his father went to...⁹

... jail to bid his son goodbye. Before leaving, he handed Ernesto a package with these words:

Open this package and when you see its contents, you will do your duty as a man.

Next day when the guards came to take him away they found Ernesto dead.

"The slow-moving wagon that passed by the ranch bore his remains. The father had kept his promise to his wife; he was taking the boy back to her."

"How terrible that must have been!"

"It was, but for a man of his position it was the only honorable thing for him to do."

"And the families, father, what became of them?"¹⁰

"Remained in the town. The gate that connected their houses was forever sealed; and they never saw each other again."

⁹Here I break off from the extended version and the original text resumes. The extracted version has a slightly different ending.

¹⁰Clearly, in the missing narration by Don Francisco, the two families are *not* identified as Olivares and Mendoza, otherwise Rosita would not be asking this question. The Mendoza family appears prominently in González and Raleigh: *Caballero* (1996).

"Why can't you talk of more pleasant things," said *comadre* María. "What with ghosts and killings I am not going to be able to sleep to-night."

"Oh, yes, you will, María, drink more orange blossom tea and you'll sleep like an infant. We must be going, Nana Chita; it is getting late."

"Wait a minute, I want to send Margarita a sample of the soap I made this morning."

"Thanks, Nana, greet Pedro for me and tell him I was sorry not to have seen him."

"*Adiós*, Nana Chita. We'll be expecting you Thursday, bring Pedro along, *Adiós*, María."

"I must go too. It is time to go to the well for water," said *comadre* María putting up her sewing. "I am glad it is daylight yet; were it not, I would be afraid to go home alone."

"I'll walk with you as far as the gate. Come back soon, *comadre* María, an old woman gets very lonely when there is nobody around."

# CHAPTER VII
## The Good Eve[1]

It was evening in the pasture. The clear, cold air had the crispness and sharpness of a Texas norther on a December night. The stars, like diamonds against a tapestry of black velvet, shone more brilliantly than ever for they were awaiting the coming of *El Niño Dios,* the God-child so tender and sweet. Tío Patricio and Cristóbal kept watch with the stars and sheep. The beauty of the night and the thought of Day kept them quiet. All of a sudden from a distance by the *cañada* came a soft murmur, a mournful, melancholy sound almost like a sob. "Listen, little one, do you hear that?" "Yes, Tío, what is it? It seems to say, 'Coo-coo, shepherd.'" "Tomorrow is Noche Buena, the Good Eve, Little Mouse," the old shepherd continued, "and we shall not be here to watch and wait for the coming of the little Jesus."

"But we shall be at Don Francisco's, we shall see the Crib and hear the singers on the *nacimiento.*"

"But it is not like being under the stars, waiting for the angels to sing, Little Mouse. I like to watch here in the pasture until midnight on the Good Eve. The sky becomes silvery then and the stars shine as they have never shone before. Everything hushes and if you listen closely you may even hear faintly but distinctly the singing of the angels in Heaven."

"Do you think they will sing this Christmas?" Cristóbal asked in an awed whisper.

[1]This chapter of the manuscript was stored separately and was in very poor condition—pages missing, heavy hand-written editing by González and unnumbered pages. It has called for more editing on my part than the rest of the manuscript in order to connect disparate fragments, but I believe that this result is more than less true to González's intentions.

"I cannot tell. Only those who are pure in mind and heart or who grieve have that great joy."

"And did you ever hear them, Tío?"

"Only once, little one many years ago. Not because I was good but because I had a grief in my heart. I was a young shepherd then. The winter had been a trying one and very cold. The coyotes had carried away many of the master's sheep. To make matters worse, *El Inocente* had died in a most horrible manner. That was a long time ago, even before your mother was born."

"And who was *El Inocente*? Won't you tell me about him?"

"Yes, since it was his death that made me hear the angels sing. Juanito, as *El Inocente* was called, was born without a mind. It had remained in heaven waiting for him. Perhaps the same angel that brought him carried his mother back; it was she, no doubt, who had taken his mind back to her Creator, not wishing her son to realize the sufferings of this world. Because he was lacking all understanding, he came to be known as *El Inocente*, The Innocent. His father, a good soul, better than holy bread and as harmless as a new-born lamb, soon followed his wife to join Juanito's mind in heaven. And the unhappy creature was left to the mercy of the good people of the ranch.

No one seemed to assume the responsibility, but Juanito, himself, solved the situation to his liking. One morning, much to the surprise of the whole family, the Master's wife found him sitting on the steps as she opened the kitchen door.

"*Pobrecito angel de Dios*, poor Angel of God," she said to herself. "He has come himself to shame us for our neglect." From that time, *El Inocente* became her property. He grew. His thin arms and legs filled, but mentally he remained the same, just a big boy with the mind of a baby. At the age of thirteen he was a big boy. It was about this time that in the same manner he had chosen a home, he decided to become a shepherd. One day he followed a sheep dog to the pasture and there he remained all day, caring for the sheep only to come home at night. After this, every morning he called his dog and went to join the bleating herd and in the evening when the sun, pale like the smile of an old woman, went to rest, Juanito returned to the ranch.

But one day the flock returned without him. His companion, the faithful shepherd dog came alone, his back and face all torn and bleeding from the bites of some wild animal. He barked and yelped to attract the attention of those around him. However, so preoccupied were they with Juanito's absence that no one paid any attention to him. Finally in desperation he jumped upon the Master Don Ramón, pulled him by the trousers, looked at him, and started running in the direction of the pasture. We followed for a mile or so. Under a mesquite we found *El Inocente* bleeding and unconscious. By his side was a dead coyote. Juanito had strangled it, but in doing so had been horribly mangled. Two days later *El Inocente* and his mind were reunited in heaven from where he often helps me."

"But how can he help you if he is dead?"

"Not he, my child, but his spirit. Sometimes when I cannot gather the flock together, I think of him and say, 'Spirit of *El Inocente,* help me,' and I have never known it to fail, the flock comes together as if by enchantment."

"And when did you hear the angels sing?"

"Oh yes, my heart was sad and I thought of poor Juanito. He had been a better shepherd than I was; he had given his life for the sheep. And I also thought of the Good Shepherd as I have seen him in a picture at the Master's house, carrying a stray lamb on his shoulders. And here I was, poor miserable sinner that I am, failing in my duty. I wept for shame and despair. All of a sudden the sky was filled with a radiance never seen until then and I heard the most beautiful singing. I could not understand the words, but I did make out the words, 'Gloria, Gloria.' I realized then I was listening to God's holy angels and I fell on my knees in adoration. It was beautiful and I felt my soul become like the soul of an angel. Had I died then I would have gone straight to heaven, no doubt."

"Could we hear them if we stay here tonight?"

"Tonight I shall take the part of the holy Joseph and you will be home once more. Listen, do you hear the roosters crowing at the ranch?"

"Not at the ranch, Tío, isn't it too far?"

"Ordinarily yes, but during the Christmas season they crow louder and clearer. It is like a clarion call announcing the coming of a great event. Morning is not far off," continued the old shepherd. "The turtle-dove is singing. Do you hear it?"

'Coo, coo, Christ is born.'

"Why, Tío, you told me before that it mourned for her lover."

"So I did. But on Christmas Eve she weeps because she, of all the birds, did not see the Christ Child."

"And how did that happen, Tío?"

"She was so humble, so unassuming, no one thought of telling her the wonderful news. All nature, the stars of the heavens, the beasts of the forest, and the birds of the air had been told that the Messiah was to be born. And when the Angel announced the birth of the Savior, all the creatures came to worship Him, all but one—the dove. Yet the sign that brought the birds and the beasts to the Manger itself was the form of a fluttering dove—assumed by the Holy Spirit. But the dove herself never saw the Christ Child and that is why her song is a sob at Christmastime.

The morning star is descending and the sun will be coming up, but late as usual. That lazy vagabond is like city people; he likes to sleep late. Lobo, Lobo, time to get the flock together and go; we must be at the ranch by noon."

Christmas Eve, the Good Eve, was the time for the patriarchal feast at the Olivareño. It was the time when all the friends and relatives gathered there for the annual Posadas* and Tamalada.** Old feuds and enmities were forgotten and people who were irreconcilable enemies during the year met as friends, at least while they remained under that hospitable roof. Even Don Ramón, forgetting his grievance towards Don Francisco, because of his attitude towards Carlos, had come.

Christmas in the border ranches would not be Christmas without the traditional *tamales*** and baked turkey. A hog had been butchered and dressed turkeys, hanging from the beams of the *portal,* exposed their fat, naked bodies to the wind. The living room, which had been decorated by Rosita and Nana Chita with garlands of cedar and rosemary, was filled with fragrance and brought happy memories to the old nurse's heart.

"When your father was born," she reminisced, "the first garment he wore was warmed with rosemary fumes to keep him from all evil and bring him happiness. I never smell this good plant without thinking of him as a child. My mother's words, may she be in Heaven come to me, 'Chita,' she used to say, 'if you want children to follow in the footsteps of the good Jesus, you must always keep rosemary bush in your garden.' And I always have. It is said," Nana Chita continued, "that the Virgin had a big rosemary plant growing by the door of her humble home in Nazareth. In the spring the swallows made their nest on the side of the house where it grew, hiding it from the bad boys that might

---

*The Posadas is a ceremony described later in this chapter.
**Tamalada—A supper of tamales and coffee.
***A Mexican dish made of corn meal rolls seasoned with chile and stuffed with highly seasoned pork meat.

rob the birds of their eggs. In the summer the nightingales serenaded her and the good Saint Joseph with their sweet voices. The good priest says that when the little Jesus was born, the whole world was covered with snow and when the Blessed Family returned from Bethlehem, the little Babe, even though he was God, got the colic like all babies do when they get cold. The Blessed Mother was beside herself with anxiety and did not know what to do. All mothers are that way with their firstborn. That's the way I felt about my Pedro, bless him. She must have a fire, and right away too. I can imagine she was even a little cross with her patient husband, Joseph, for not having any wood in the house. The good Joseph, not daring to leave her and the baby alone while gathering the wood for the fire decided to cut some branches from the bush growing by the door. The room was soon filled with the sweet smell and warmth, and the little Jesus began to coo and gurgle with contentment. The bush became useful in many other ways too; when the Virgin washed the Baby's clothes, she hung them on the branches to dry; when the bad soldiers were killing all the 'Innocents,' the branches of the rosemary bush, of their own accord, covered the door. And when they passed by and saw the gray-looking bush covering the entrance to the house they did not enter there thinking the house deserted. And because the rosemary protected Him, Our Lord blessed the plant and made it holy."

Rosita had lost no time during the old woman's recital. While listening, she made *El Nacimiento* (the crib) with figures of clay. Mary and Joseph stood in the Manger before the Holy Child and shepherds were kneeling in adoration. Around them had been placed all the flora and fauna of the earth, growing and living together regardless of climactic differences and natural tendencies; pines beside palm trees; tropical fruits growing on ice-covered steppes macaws beside ptarmigans; flocks of sheep peacefully feeding by the side of ravenous wolves. The three Wise Men, one white, one yellow, and one black brought their gifts of gold, frankincense, and myrrh. And surmounting all, the Star of Bethlehem shone with brilliancy and paper angels on invisible wires fluttered around on paper wings.

The *piñata*, an earthen pot filled with candy and nuts, patted its enormous belly foolishly as it hung from one beam of the *sala*. From its dizzy elevation it swayed and bowed much to the delight of the children. In a corner of the room stood its executioner, a big, heavy stick with streamers of paper and tinsel which in the hands of blindfolded children would convert its glory into a mass of debris and waste.

After a collation* of *buñuelos*** and coffee, the guests gathered in the *sala* to sing *Las Posadas*. Christmas Eve being the day of fast, the Christmas supper would not be served until after Midnight Mass.

The custom of singing *Las Posadas*, introduced from Mexico by Don Francisco, had become very popular on the border. There was a feeling of joy and expectation as the master led Tío Patricio into the room. The brown-robed, turbaned old shepherd, a very realistic Joseph, walked to the center of the room leaning on his staff. Radiant of face, and voice which vibrated with emotion, the shepherd explained the meaning of *Las Posadas*. It is, he said, the most beautiful and the most solemn service of the Christmas season, a service which those who are still Christians and speak God's language hold every year in remembrance of the wanderings of the Holy Family in Bethlehem, that cold night so many years ago.

"Tonight," he said, "they are to be given lodging in this house and the Angels will no doubt sing in unison to announce the coming of *El Niño Dios*, the God-child."

The guests divided themselves in groups, each representing a house in Bethlehem. The group nearest the Crib was the Inn. The young people, carrying musical instruments, guitars and mandolins, followed Tío Patricio to the *patio* where Rosita, wearing the white robe and blue mantle of the Virgin, was waiting.

In spite of the merriment, there was a certain subdued solemnity as the Holy Pilgrims began their weary journey asking for lodging from door to door,

> "In the name of Heaven
> We ask for lodging
> My beloved wife
> Can no longer walk,"sang Joseph.

Weary and foot-sore the Pilgrims made the rounds only to be rebuffed brusquely, even with threats of a beating. Finally Joseph made his last appeal,

---

*Collation, in the original sense of the word, was a reading from some edifying book at a gathering of monks in a monastery at the close of the day. During fast days the monks were permitted, if tired, to drink just before the reading. In this way the collation came to be accompanied by light refreshments; hence any slight meal allowed during a fast day came to be known as *collation*. This expression is still used in the same sense in the Texas-Mexican frontier.

**Buñuelos*—Crisp, fried cakes sprinkled with sugar and cinnamon.

> "My wife Mary
> Is the Queen of Heaven
> For she is to be the Mother
> Of the Child Divine."

The group at the *Nacimiento,* rejoicing at the wonderful news, sang joyfully,

> "Is that you, Joseph?
> Is that you, Mary?
> Enter Holy pilgrims
> We knew not who you were."

The Pilgrims and the guests, kneeling in adoration before the Crib, continued singing while two children, taking the image of the Christ Child from the Manger, rocked it in swaddling clothes to the tune of a lullaby,

> "Good news to you, Oh shepherds!
> A virgin just gave birth
> To a Child so beautiful
> As the light of day."

The *Posada* ended, the children were given whistles and serpentines and amidst much noise and merriment, the *piñata* was broken. At the first strains of the orchestra, the *sala* was cleared for dancing.

No sooner were the first chords of *Sobre las Olas*\* preluded when Don Francisco offered his arm to his wife. "Let's show these slow-minded, slow-moving boys how a waltz is danced." They whirled and glided across the room amidst the cheering and clapping of their friends.

"Bravo, bravo, Francisco," cried Don Ramón who had been watching him "You shame the girls, Margarita. I often say that things are getting worse instead of better since our time. No offense to you, young Ladies," he continued turning to the group of giggling girls, "but your mothers were better-looking and better dancers than you are."

"Bless my soul, there is old Alejo with his fiddle," exclaimed Don Francisco seeing the old man peeping into the room. "Come in, my good Alejo." The old man entered holding the fiddle under his chin precluding a polka, and bowing to the company gathered there. When he finished, he bowed again in all directions not wishing to leave anyone out. Then clearing his throat and wiping his wrinkled forehead he repeated his customary Christmas greeting,

\**Sobre las Olas*—A favorite Mexican waltz composed by Juventino Rosas.

"Praised be the Lord, forever be He praised. Goodnight, I bid you all assembled here tonight. Perhaps someone will think I am a drunken Indian. But whoever thinks that of me may his spine be shriveled forever. I am that good Alejo of whom you have heard. I am not an Indian beggar, but have some Spanish blood. On my father's side I am humble; of him I dare not say much, for although a man of honor, I understand he was hanged. Of myself, I do not speak; you see me here before you, whether good or whether bad that's for you to judge. I am somewhat of a student; I can sing a requiem Mass and play a good quadrille. Praised be the Lord and may you have your wish!"

Not waiting for an answer, old Alejo began playing a quadrille and started tapping his foot on the floor.

"Ay, ah! Alejo, you want the old people to dance." But the descendant of Spaniards did not deign to answer. He merely nodded his head in assent and continued playing.

"*Bien*, Alejo, you call the dance and we will follow you." And as old Alejo played, fathers and mothers, portly grandfathers and...[2]

[2]Here, the concluding pages to "The Good Eve" are missing. Again, these pages may have continued the story of Carlos and Rosita.

# CHAPTER VIII

## Saint John's Day[1]

Rosita awoke with a start. For no reason she found herself sitting up in bed. What could it be? Then with the swiftness of thought, a stream of memories rushed upon one another. It was Saint John's Day, the day of all days when lovers openly tell their love for each other.

She jumped from bed and ran to the window that opened into the patio. The moon shone luminously and floated serenely across the sky in her crystal-like bark. But more luminously still shone the path through which Saint John traversed the heavens. How clearly it was defined, even to the fine stardust which he left as a trail behind him!

[It was good to have such a path, but suppose she died when it was not visible! Why should she worry about that? She thought the good Saint John would take care that she, Rosita de los Olivares who was so devoted to him, could find the way.][2] As she stood there weaving dreams as only maidens can, she felt the cool air like the soft songs of a nocturnal bird. It was on such a night, just last year, that Carlos had declared his love at this very window where she stood. The carnations had been in bloom then as they were now. She remembered giving him one and as she passed it through the iron grills, he had taken possession of her hand. She struggled laughingly to get free, but that had only made him retain it more firmly in his grasp. She still remembered the fervent kiss; she even remembered the very words he had said:

[1]Chapter VII also presented a special editorial problem. González left two versions. I have opted for the more extended one which gives us a richer sense of the female characters and the hair-cutting scene. However, the second version tells us more about Carlos and Rosita and thereby lends the overall narrative greater continuity. For this reason, I have integrated and noted these latter passages from the second version into the first.

[2]Bracketed passage is crossed-out in the manuscript.

"This little hand belongs to me and I shall never let it go."

"Turn loose, I hear footsteps," she had told him and in a panic he had released her hand. Now he was gone, but she was sure that the good Saint would bring him back to her by next Saint John's Day. [He had done an unpardonable thing. Joined a band of cattle thieves! A father's curse was upon him and she had been forbidden to even think of him. As though she could! Somehow she did not believe him guilty. He could not be! He was so gentle, so handsome! Tears welled in her eyes. "Dear Saint John," she prayed, "help us clear this mystery. Carlos is innocent, I know, and please bring him back to me."][3]

She remained at the window watching the night mists float across the *maguey* fence—now like silvery wings, now as the gauzy veils of an oriental dancing girl—they glided across—now it seemed as though they might be caught in the thorny leaves of the century plants—but no, they floated on unmolested like happy spirits in a heaven of their own.

Morning would be coming soon! She noticed the moon becoming spectral with the glimmer of the coming dawn. What was that legend Nana Chita used to tell her early on Saint John's Day when she was a child? She remembered it distinctly, she even knew it by heart. Just to try her memory she began to repeat it softly to herself,

"Early on Saint John's Day, three hours before the dawn, a young knight took his horse and rode through a flowery prairie. As he rode into the valley he saw a tall, slender cypress; its trunk was of solid gold and the leaves, they were of silver. Under the cypress so slender he saw a maiden fair, her luxuriant golden hair covered the whole countryside. With a comb of gold in hand, she brushed it soft like silk; braiding it into a coronet, the damsel fell asleep. A mockingbird flew by with a gay and happy song and seeing the girl so beautiful, it lit upon her breast. With its wings it fanned her face, caressed her lovingly, and it whispered in her ear, 'Your knight has come at last.'"

A shout awoke her from her reverie! The cowboys were up. Soon they would be taking Saint John's bath at the tank. She left the window, hurriedly dressed, and went down to the *patio*. Her father and mother were already waiting there.

"The morning air is cool," she heard Don Francisco say, "and makes the blood run faster."

"I hope the water isn't very cold," shivered the girl joining her parents.

"For shame, Rosita!" answered Doña Margarita, "who ever minded how cold the water is on this day."

---

[3]The bracketed passage is taken from the second version of this chapter.

"I told Martiniano to fill the tank with fresh water,"said Don Francisco, as his words were interrupted by distant shouts and laughter, "the *vaqueros* are taking their bath" he added, "more prompt are they than your girls!"

"What can be delaying them? Ah! here they come," Doña Margarita said, spying a laughing and singing group who were coming towards the house.

"*Buenos días*, Don Francisco, *buenos días*, Doña Margarita."

"Blessed be this day and its holy patron Saint."

"Blessed it be forever," answered the mistress of the house, embracing each in turn as was the custom to do on this day. "You vain little creatures," she added laughingly, "want to make yourselves pretty so you can get a sweetheart! Francisco, why don't you join the *vaqueros* and take your bath with them?"

"I was merely waiting for the girls to wish them a happy day and to tell them what I think of your face-washing. If God destined you to be ugly," he called out teasingly to the disappearing group, "no morning dew will ever make you pretty!"

"We can only try, master," responded the black-eyed Carmela with a coquettish toss of her dark head.

"The *albahaca*\* bed is unusually large this year," commented Rosita, "I was just noticing it yesterday."

"Doña Margarita," asked one of the group, "is it true that the Olivares brought this *albahaca* seed from Spain?"

"Yes, Lucía, it is said that when Don Juan José was leaving home for the Indies, he cut a branch of it for good luck. He put it in his breast pocket and it remained there forgotten for many years. Sometime later when he and his commander were exploring this land, he found the dried leaves of the plant and threw them away. A few days after that he happened to be passing by the same place and much to his surprise he found a few *albahaca* plants growing. This made him feel as though a little corner of his home had been transplanted to the New World. He put a pile of stones around the plants to protect them from the wild animals, and when he decided to stay, he built his house right where the seeds had sprung. And since then we have always had *albahaca* growing at the Olivareño."

"Do you always bathe your face in its dew on Saint John's Day?"

"Yes, my child."

"No wonder then the Olivares women are so pretty."

\**Albahaca*—An aromatic herb native of Spain.

"Thanks for what is due me," answered Doña Margarita, laughing at the girl's remark. "Here we are," she added, "who'll be the first to put her face in the dew? You, Lucía?"

"Carmela should be the first," someone said, pushing the giggling girl towards the *albahaca* bed.

"*Válgame Dios*, am I that ugly that you think I need it most?"

"No, but you are the only one who has a sweetheart and you should be the prettiest."

"*Niñas, niñas*," called out Doña Margarita, "remember you must do it before sunup and remember we have to bathe in the tank yet. Someone has to begin first; Rosita, you begin please."

Following her example, the girls buried their faces in the fragrant herb. Rosita's rosy face and the brown faces of the daughters of *peones* and *vaqueros* emerged fresh and dewy from the early morning bath.

"No, no, don't do that," warned Doña Margarita, seeing one of the girls wiping her face with her skirt, "the charm will be off if you do. Let the air dry it! That's right, pat it into your face. Just see how pretty you'll be the rest of the day."

"Just today, Doña Margarita?" asked the mischievous Carmela, "I thought it lasted all year!"

"Isn't one day of beauty sufficient to get a sweetheart?"

"Not these days, Doña Margarita."

Carmela's tart reply was answered by more giggles and Doña Margarita, ignoring both the answer and the giggles continued, "the men must be out by now. We really should hurry. If we want to profit by the waters on Saint John's Day, the bath must be taken before sunrise."

"Why, Doña Margarita?"

"I am surprised at you, Lucía! Hasn't Mariana ever explained to you the virtue water has on this day? Anyone who is submerged on Saint John's Day will be cleansed from mortal sin."

The men, already cleansed physically as well as spiritually, were leaving when Doña Margarita and her flock arrived. Respectfully they bade her good morning and wished her the happiness of the day.

The tank, as Don Francisco had said, was filled to the top; the rippling waves curling lazily along its placid surface.

"I get the goose flesh when I see the water, so cold it looks," one of the girls remarked.

"My teeth chatter before I get in," added another.

"Stop your talking," commanded the mistress of the *Olivareño,* "and do as I say. Stand on the edge of the tank and when I say, 'Saint John, we take this bath in memory of your baptism of Jesus in the river Jordan,' jump into the water, now ready! *Oye,* Carmela, stop your giggling and stop pulling Lucía's hair! Do you want to anger Saint John? Your sins will not be forgiven unless you do this with faith! Ready now!"*

Splash—splash—shouts broke out from fourteen young throats as the firm brown bodies struck the water.

"All out," commanded Doña Margarita swimming to the edge, "run home, everyone of you before you catch a cold. After breakfast we trim the hair on the block, don't forget!"

"*Sí, sí, señora,* we'll come—*adiós,* Doña Margarita—*adios,* Rosita."

The custom of trimming the hair on Saint John's Day which prevailed among the border people, and was practiced by all the women, particularly by the girls who were proud of their long hair, was as old as the country.

Whether transplanted from Spain or whether it originated in the new world, this custom was no doubt reminiscent of the decapitation of Saint John for the tresses were laid on a mesquite block and chopped off with a sharp ax or hatchet. It was believed that if the hair was trimmed on this day, it would grow four times as long by the next anniversary. If Doña Margarita wielded the ax, the effect was more efficacious; in fact this custom had become a ceremonial rite in which the mistress of the Olivareño acted as priestess.

As one girl after another laid her hair on the block, Doña Margarita cut it off repeating the words, "shorten our sinfulness, beloved Saint John, as we do our hair; let us grow in grace as our hair will in stature." And while the girls braided their hair, interweaving it with strips of buckskin leather to help in the growing process, the mistress told them the weird story of Salome's wicked dance and the beheading of the Saint.

That afternoon the quaintest custom connected with the day, known as *correr el gallo,* was to take place. Picturesque, but somewhat cruel, it savored much of the brutal sport of the Romans. Since it was a test of horsemanship, the men, except the *peones* who never rode, took part in it. The man owning the fleetest horse was selected to be the *corredor,* the runner. This year the honor fell to Martiniano. He it was who, riding ahead of the others, would hold the rooster to whose legs, wings, and neck had been tied the ribbon for which each *vaquero* was to ride.

---

*This multi-faceted celebration of St. John's Day following Christmas likely extends from December 27, feast day for St. John the Evangelist, to January 8, the Baptism of our Lord.

East of the house and shaded by mesquite and huisache trees was a square which boasted the name of *plaza*. It was from this place that the spectators would watch the riding and it was also from here that the racing would start down the *Camino Real* as far as the south gate.

All day Martiniano had pranced on his *moro** showing off before the gathered visitors at Don Francisco's house. The other *vaqueros*, equally excited, rode their horses getting them ready for the afternoon's ride.

The rooster selected as the victim for the afternoon's sport was one which Nana Chita had offered as a gift to the Saint. It was old, she had told Pedro her son, so old that it was not worth killing and its meat would be so tough and tasteless it would no doubt taste like chewed sugar cane.

"Why then, if it is so old and tough, are you giving it to Saint John?" Don Francisco asked her.

"Your years have not made you any wiser, I see," the old woman replied. "What is a Saint good for if not to perform miracles? If the meat is not to his liking, he can make it taste as though it were a young chicken's."

The rooster in question was now the center of attraction and animation. Little did the innocent victim know what was in store for him. At present his main problem was to eat all the corn placed before him. Never before, not even in the days when he was a young carefree sultan, had he gorged and feasted like this! Never selfish, much less in his old age, he called in vain for the harem that, too shy to approach, merely eyed him from a distance.

"He's eaten enough now," said Martiniano, entering with the attitude of bravado that characterized him whenever he felt important. "Don't get him too heavy. Why haven't you tied the ribbons on him? Do you think we have all afternoon to waste?"

"Mine is the blue," said Carmela, tying it to the rooster's neck and looking at him coquettishly.

"What is that to me?" Martiniano replied petulantly, "Capul is the one interested."

"Red for love," added Lucía, tying a red ribbon to the rooster's wings.

Each girl in turn tied her color where she thought it would be more conspicuous. Each *vaquero* knew which color belonged to the lady of his choice and each would race for possession of that color.

---

*\*Moro*—black-colored horse.

The beribboned rooster was brought in triumph by the girls. The *plaza* was crowded with people who came from the neighboring ranches either to see or participate in the race. Much rivalry and competition was exhibited among the contestants who, riding ostentatiously before the audience, displayed the color they were riding for. Doña Margarita and her guests sat on benches; the women of the *peones* crowded together in another section of the square, not daring to come near the *señora*. Apart from the women were the men who talked and gesticulated among themselves, taking an occasional drink from a too popular bottle that moved about the group with astonishing rapidity. The girls stood in a group of their own, admiring the riders who passed in review before them. Each pair of eager eyes followed the one who, wearing her colors, had singled her out from among the group. If he would only get the ribbon, was the prayer in each heart! Then she would not remain single another year.

The band started playing! Now the riders lined up! Now Martiniano, rooster in hand, ribbons trailing like a rainbow, galloped twenty paces ahead of them! All stood still! A minute of suspense! A shot rang out! As arrows expelled from the taut strings of a bow, the riders shot out!

"Hurry, Capul, Carmela is cheering for you! Juan, Luisa is waving her ribbon! Antonio, Pedro, Miguel, hurry, hurry, the others are gaining—Now Juan is ahead; he almost has the red ribbon within his grasp—Miguel, the green is almost within your reach—Ah! Capul is ahead! Carmela, say a prayer, he needs it! The others are gaining!"

"*Viva* Capul!" burst from the crowd, "*Viva* Capul and *viva* San Juan!" Capul waved the blue in the air—Victory and Carmela!

But where is the rooster, so proud and so gay a few minutes before? Nothing remained of him. A few feathers scattered to the wind told the pitiful tale.

Capul, triumphant and smiling, rode past the girls looking for Carmela. He spied the blue ribbon and the red carnations in her hair. Seeing no one and not caring where he was going, he went through the crowd. He came to where Carmela stood expectantly and without saying a word, picked her up, and placed her on the croup of his horse. The traditional ride of San Juan began. Each rider followed his example and the lovers rode around the square before the eyes of admiring friends and relatives. Saint John was a good matchmaker this year; not a single girl refused to take the ride.

But the climax to the day's festivities had not yet come! It would be that night when Don Francisco and Doña Margarita in person presided at the dance. There would be good music, good food, and drinks to make one forget the worries of life. It was the annual dance which Don Francisco gave to his people in honor of the Saint of the day.

The dance was held in the open. The dirt floor which had been packed, smoothed, and sprinkled for days before was now hard as brick. Rough lumber benches were arranged in a square around the dance floor. Kerosene lanterns, hung under the *portal,* gave the place an air of gala festivity.

Everyone came, young and old, from the toothless grandmother who smoked her shuck cigarette to the toddling baby. Early in the evening the guests began to arrive. The girls dressed in bright muslin dresses made brighter yet by corsages of red carnations and *albahaca* leaves. On this day they were allowed to show the state of their heart; if they had a sweetheart the spray graced the right side of the breast; if they were looking for one, it decorated the left.

The *vaqueros* wearing new shirts opened at the throat and shiny leather boots, looked boldly at the girls who were beginning to occupy the benches.

They took in at a glance the spray of flowers. The girls sat demurely with downcast eyes knowing full well their charms were displayed.

A group of mothers chattered and talked, their glib tongues moving incessantly about one thing and another.

It was not such an easy thing to have a daughter these days, sighed Mariana, the leader of any gossiping group. Not that her Lucía had ever given her a minute's trouble, but a girl's reputation was as fragile as the delicate petal of a flower and there were so many insects that wanted to taste its sweetness. She should be thankful though that Lucía was not like others she knew.

What did she mean by that, asked the other mothers in a chorus, she was not insinuating, was she? Oh, no, of course Mariana was not. She was merely saying what every mother knew; the responsibility she had with pretty unmarried daughters, especially these days when customs were so free; and besides, as they all knew, Satan never sleeps. No, that he does not do, assented all the others seriously, crossing themselves. So well was that known by everyone that there was even a verse about it, had they heard it yet?

That well drill Don Francisco had brought to the ranch was singing it the other day.

> If the pretty maidens do not beware
> the Green Devil will take them
> no one knows where.

What truer evidence was there than that? Oh, yes, they had to be careful, so very careful. At this they looked in the direction of their daughters who, arranging the ribbons in their hair and the flowers at their breast, were anxiously waiting for the dance to begin.

The musicians were coming and so were the *vaqueros*. Now was the time for the mothers to be more watchful. Each one had to see that her daughter did not catch the eye of any of the men. There was a general stir. Well did everyone know the meaning of the first dance—a declaration of love. Alejo, the fiddler, raised his bow, lifted his right foot at the same time, and on the downward stroke began to play.

A general flurry, a scurry of feet, the frightened palpitation of hearts. Each *vaquero*, hat in hand, rushed to the girl of his choice. A sigh of relief, a sigh of contentment as each mother saw her daughter asked for the first dance. Now followed the usual *"puema"** used for such occasions:

> He—In the east the sun doth rise,
> She—And sets in the west in splendor
> He—And the lovesick shepherd lad?
> She—He dies of a broken heart.

And with the last words the chosen damsel placed her hand on the arm of the gallant and the dance began. The mothers redoubled their vigilance now. Sitting rigid and straight, a white apron over their laps to receive the *regalo*, for custom decreed that the men should give their partners a present of candy after each set. They were the dragons that watched over their daughters' behavior. They had to see that the girls did not talk to their partners while dancing and above all, they must watch that no one danced two sets in succession with the same partner. No decent, well-bred girl would do that, and to do so might create scandal. The younger children crouched or sat on the floor watching the dance and munching the candy that the older sisters were providing for them.

No doubt Capul was the best dancer, his long, slender body swayed to the rhythm of the music as a reed does to the wind. No one could take such intricate steps. No one could hold his partner with the graceful abandon that he could. No doubt he was the best-dressed man too; his white bell-shaped trousers, the blue shirt, and the high pointed hat he wore tilted to one side marked him as the man of the hour. He and Carmela were the handsomest couple.

*Correct form is *poema*. (Here, apparently González is using "puema" as folk speech.)

"Look, look, *comadre*," Mariana nudged her neighbor, "just look at that shameless Carmela; the third time she dances with Capul and she talked to him too."

"Mark my words, he will not marry her; no man who treats a girl that way in public has good intentions."

"Her poor mother! Disgraced she must feel too, in having such a daughter!"

"*Mira, mira*, Don Francisco, is he going to dance? And with Carmela too."

"A polka, *muchachos*," shouted the master from the middle of the floor, "my bones need a little shaking and Carmela here has promised to do it."

"The ranch will not hold her now, the bold creature."

"Look, they stop," murmured Mariana. "What can be happening? I bet Don Francisco is disgusted with her."

"Come here, Capul," called Don Francisco, spying him among the group that had gathered to see them dance, "finish this dance with Carmela; I shall wait until your wedding next month to finish it with her."

"A wedding!" shouted Martiniano, "*Viva*, San Juan who arranged it. *Viva*, Don Francisco who announced it, and *viva*, Capul and Carmela who are the happy couple."

"*Viva, viva*," answered all.

"We go now," added the master, "continue the dance until day-break."

The dance continued. By midnight the dancers were enveloped in a cloud of dust. It might have been a whirlwind and the dancers, spirits of the desert. But what is dust when hearts are in the springtime of life and love is young.

Saint John had been good! There would be many weddings after the harvest and after the cattle were sold in the fall!

[Where was Rosita? Had Saint John brought her a message from Carlos? Sitting in the dreary solitude of her room, she sat on the window sill listening to the *vaqueros* and their sweethearts make merry. Let them be happy, she thought. "Beloved Saint John," was the prayer in her heart, "deny them not the happiness that has been denied to me."

The distant strains of *La Golondrina*, the farewell song, told her the dance was breaking. Her vigil was over. She looked up to the sky; the Milky Way, dim and pale, was disappearing! Saint John's path and his day were gone! Carlos had not come!][4]

[4]The bracketed passage is taken from the second version of this chapter as it provides continuity to the Carlos-Rosita story.

# CHAPTER IX

## The Cupid of the Brush Country[1]

No people of the north feel cold more than do the border people when a winter norther sweeps down upon them. In the teeth of one of their northers, Don Francisco and his *peon de estribo* (outrider) left the *Olivareño* just before dawn, bound for the nearest railroad station, Hebbronville.

The day proved to be as dreary as the dawn and Don Francisco amused himself counting the stiff jack rabbits that crossed his path. At a turn of the road their buggy almost collided with a forlorn-looking two-wheeled vehicle drawn by the sorriest nag imaginable. On the high seat, perched like a bright-colored tropical bird, sat a figure wrapped up in a crazy quilt. On seeing Don Francisco and his man he stopped, motioned them to do the same, and in mumbled tones bade them good morning, asked them where they were going, what might be the news at the ranches, and finally, were they all right. He seemed to ask these questions for the sake of asking, not waiting for a reply to any one of them. At last, having paused in his catechism for some kind of an answer, he put out one of his hands gingerly from under his brilliant cape to wave them good-bye.

"That's Tío Esteban, the new mail carrier," Don Francisco explained, and that is how this employee of Uncle Sam and the taciturn, square-jawed *peon de estribo* met. It was also the beginning of a lasting friendship.

Tío Esteban was the weather-beaten, brown-faced, black-eyed Cupid of the community. Often when some lovesick *vaquero* did not have a two-cent stamp to pay for the delivery of the love missive, he

---

[1]Manuscript contains two nearly identical versions of this chapter. I have opted for the more extended version.

personally delivered the letter. Not only did he carry the letters, but he served as secretary to those who could not write. He possessed a wonderful memory and could recite without any difficulty *The Secretary of Lovers,* from the first page which consisted of advise to lovers, to the last which explained in detail the language of flowers and the movements of the fan. He recited letter after letter, whether a declaration of love, an acceptance, a letter of condolence, or any other as found in *The Secretary.* Much to the amusement of Don Francisco and Doña Margarita, he organized an Academy wherein classes were given to the *vaqueros* and *peones* "in the delicate art of lovemaking," all for the sum of *cuatro reales,* four bits. On the nights when he was at the ranch he found himself surrounded by those who were seeking information in the *delicate art.* No girl or woman was allowed. "Females get their information from Satan himself," was his excuse, "they know enough without being told." And as the seekers of wisdom gathered about him, he recited verbatim what he knew by heart.

"Giving advice to those in love," he began, "in the ways of pleasing each other helps to contribute to the conservation or cultivation of that beautiful sentiment called love, which in all its manifestations is the expression of the beautiful and agreeable part of life. Remember this above all other things; when a man marries, his honor is in the hands of his wife. Never show too much love to a woman; like all daughters of Eve, she will not give her love to anyone who shows himself meek and humble. In other words, be like our first ancestors who wooed her less delicately than is our custom today. Exercise all ingenuity, sagacity, in your declarations of love. Learn of Solomon who in spite of his many wives could always make love to one more woman. In writing love letters the first thing to consider is the character of your ladylove.

If the lady to whom you wish to declare your love has had no experience in love affairs, make your letter simple and natural. If she is of a romantic nature, a dreamer, compare her to the great heroines of the past, Juliet, Eloise, Elaine, and express your sentiments in a flowery language and elegant figures of speech. If she should be inclined to religion, love must by expressed in a mystical and sentimental manner.

As to the paper that is to be used in declarations of this nature, change according to the character of the person or the intimacy of the relations. Many prefer a wreath of flowers in the right-hand corner, while others prefer a picture that will reveal the state of their impassioned heart. White paper is always in good form and unruled stationary is preferred. When the young lady corresponds to your declaration, wait at least three days before answering her, and when done it must be on flowered paper; a wreath of pansies to show her she is forever in your thoughts, red roses to reveal your passionate love, or a wreath of laurel symbolic of the glorious triumph of love to which both hearts aspire, although white paper is always best.

The first love letter must be sent with artifice, strategy, and delicacy. A novel or any other book might be borrowed from her and on returning it, the letter might be placed within its pages. The love missive can also be placed in a bouquet of flowers. If the beloved person is a neighbor, wait for the moment when she might be alone in her room and throw the missive through the window. This is not only considered good form but gives the appearance that it might have dropped from heaven.

Interchange of letters is very essential among lovers. Arrange with your beloved the means of communicating in safety and with secrecy. The letters might be left in the hollow of a tree, under a statue, in a piece of furniture, or any other safe place. It would prove inconvenient and most disagreeable if anyone found out the secret. Never trust the mail unless you can give the letter personally to the mail carrier."

No one was more attentive to these instructions then Marco, and it was because of this, no doubt, that he and Tío Esteban became fast friends. On the days when the mail carrier came to the ranch, the outrider went about his work with winged feet and a song in his heart.

"When Tío Esteban comes, the happiness is so great I feel as though the *Angelitos** were taking a walk through my body," Marcos had confided to his master.

"Perhaps he has some secret love that we know nothing about," suggested Martiniano, "and Tío Esteban brings him the love letters."

"A girl would be in great need for a sweetheart to love an Indian like him," answered another cowboy, who with Martiniano was smoking his after-supper cigarette in the bunkhouse.

"You'd be surprised how many tricks these Indians know about making themselves loved. They have all kinds of amulets, I am told. Some carry a piece of magnet tied around their necks; brings the good luck to them, they say, and draws love to the person who wears it."

"Is that so?"

"Yes, but that is like treating with things of the witches and I want none of that. Others have the powdered seed of the *tolohache* which weakens the mind but quickens the senses. It is an old Indian herb and its secret power is well-known among them. But the worst of all are the powders of *La Madre Celestina.*"

"What is that?"

*Angelitos*—Little angels.

"What is what?"

"The powders of *La Madre Celestina*?"

"*Madre de Dios!* where have you been all these years? They are a love charm which if used will make anyone fall in love. Suppose you have given your heart to someone who does not return your affection. All you have to do is sprinkle a little of it on a flower or a letter which you send her and as she inhales the powder she will fall in love with you."

"Does it ever fail?"

"Never. Sometimes though, it might make a person go crazy."

"*De veras,* is that so? I wouldn't use it then. I know of something better."

"What is it?" queried Martiniano, getting interested in the subject.

"An old *curandera* with the mustache of a witch, the kind that uses prayers to make conjure, told it to me in return for a favor I did her. Skinned a live horned toad for her, I believe. This charm works best in October towards the last of the month when the spirits get restless in their graves as the day of the Dead approaches. The sun begins to get sleepy then and goes to bed early. It is about this time too that all the creatures related to the world of the dead begin to fly about. The owls talk to each other in Spanish which they pronounce backwards so no one will understand them; they even take liberty with holy things and talk with impunity about Susej (Jesús) and Airam (María). The bats leave their roosts in colonies when their master, El Diablo, calls them. By the light of the moon have I seen them standing in a circle with out-stretched wings, playing a game in his honor. They sing in a mouse-like chirp which no Christian can understand unless you have been smeared with the blood of a witch. The *curandera* had and she told me the meaning of the game.

'Tan-tan,' sings one who outside of the circle must be Satan himself.

'Who is he, who is he, that is knocking at my door?' the lender asks.

'I am he, I am he, the Devil with his fiery horns.'

'What do you want?'

'A soul.'

'The soul of —,' and here he mentions a name, 'and may the bald Saint Peter take me this very moment if I do not say the truth. The person named dies before the Day of the Dead.'

"Jesús, María y José, the Sweet Names protect me!"

"But what was I talking about? My head goes from me when I think of such things."

"The love charm."

"Ah, *sí*. Before they fly away you get a bullbat and a female bat, and right then and there pierce their head through from temple to temple with a sharp steel needle. And here lies the charm; save all the blood in a small glass bottle without losing a single drop. You mix it very well, saying a Hail Mary backwards and before the blood has time to clot, go to church and when she comes out sprinkle the blood on her."

"On who?"

"The girl you are in love with, of course."

"But how do you know she is in church?"

"That's true, I had not thought of that."

"Well go on, we'll just imagine she is there."

"Then you look up to the sky and say these words, 'I see three stars in the heavens and the Star of Jesus is four, by this sign I swear that,' and here you mention the girl's name, 'will neither eat nor drink nor sleep until she marries me.'"

"Pretty hard on the girl, isn't it?"

"Not so much because she'll be in love and I am told that people in love do not eat at all. One thing worries me though, there is no church around here."

"The main trouble," answered Martiniano, "would be getting the bullbat and female bat, how are you going to know which is which?"

"That's true," answered the other scratching his head pensively. "The powders of *La Madre Celestina* might be better after all."

"They are dangerous; I'd be afraid to use them. Did you ever hear about Lucita? She was related to Don Francisco, the daughter of one of his cousins, I believe. She was as pretty a girl as could be found anywhere, full of the joy of living and of devilment. She was a little beauty, quick, vivacious, though somewhat proud. Her hands, as I remember, were the prettiest I'd ever seen, so white and so small. She had spent most of her life in the convent school in town and when she returned to her father's ranch she lacked no suitors. But she did not want to marry. She wanted to go away to school, college I think they call it, and learn all that is found in books. It would have pleased her mother had she married Fernando, the master's nephew. But she paid him no mind; not that she was a flirt and liked to play with man's affections; she just did not love anyone. Neither did she pay any attention to another suitor she had in town. He was a much older man, a widower I believe, who had lots of money. Some said he had made it smuggling, others said he was a gambler. Anyway he was a man that could not be trusted and Lucita hated him. Hearing that the girl was to go away he came to the ranch and asked for her hand, officially. He was not discouraged at their refusal. It is said though, that he swore he would have her some way or another. She laughed at this; but her mother was somewhat perturbed, fearing that he might use some dark means to win her. The next day she was driven thirty miles to the station. At the hotel where she and her father stayed, she was given a letter that had come for her. Her father noticed how pale she turned, but she offered no explanation as to the contents, neither did he inquire. A letter from some lovesick suitor, he thought, and let it go at that.

She was going to some school where teachers are made, but she was to live at the convent. The nuns who met her at the station told her mother later that she seemed very tired on her arrival and went to bed without any supper. Sometime after midnight the whole convent was awakened by the girl's screams. The nuns found her screaming and beating her head against the walls of her room. A doctor was called, but there was nothing that he could do. No doubt the powders sent in the letter had already entered her brain. The doctor had to place her in a straitjacket and in that condition she was brought home to her mother.

She became as a wild beast, could not walk like a human being, but crouched on the floor and lapped her food the same as an animal. She jumped on all fours about the padded room and dashed her body against the walls. Her mother realized that some evil spell had been cast upon her and to make sure, placed a Crucifix under her pillow and she who had been so religious screamed at the sight of it. The priest from town came to see her and when she saw him enter she flew at him scratching his face and spitting on him.

Don Francisco used to send some of us every evening to help watch. I'll never forget the change that had come upon her. The little hands that I so loved to see, the little fingers once so pink and nimble were out of joint and hung yellow and limp like a calf's tail. The sight made the marrow in my bones turn cold. The shaven head, the black curls had been cut off because she pulled her hair out by the handful, the look of madness in her eyes, the face distorted and bereft of all beauty. She would not lay down and even when death was upon her, she continued jumping and leaping like a frog. She died crouched on the floor like a sick lamb.

After the funeral her mother examined all the letters and she found the one she had received. It was from the rejected suitor and was covered with a yellowish powder."

"Was nothing done about it?"

"What can be done about such things? The scandal would have been too great. It was thought best to forget."

"If I knew Marcos had such powders, I would not rest until I found and destroyed them."

"Yes, and then you'd pay for it."

"Why should I?"

"Suppose the powders fell on you and you fell in love with Marcos. That's the queer thing about it, you fall in love with the person who owns them whether you want to or not. Wouldn't it be funny though if you went about making love to him," laughed Martiniano.

The other cowboy, somewhat piqued at the insinuation, said nothing but continued smoking in silence.

"Look, look," whispered Martiniano nudging his companion, "here he comes and Tío Esteban with him. Let's hide and see what they are talking about."

"Right here under the bed, suggested the other," and as both cowboys crawled under the cot, chaps, spurs and all, the mail carrier and the *peón* entered.

"It is early in the evening and no one is here yet," said Marcos. "We'll sit here and talk."

"Look around first," suggested Tío Esteban, "walls have ears you know."

"Not this time, Tío Esteban. Everyone is still at the master's house. You sit on the bench and I'll sit on this box."

"Very comfortable indeed," began the mail carrier. "I think I shall smoke a cigarette. No, thank you, I always use my own tobacco cured with the best *mescal* too," he said. "I see you can't wait to tell me all about it; who is she?"

"Lucía."

"Not Mariana's daughter!"

"Yes."

"My Lady Santa Lucía bless me! What an eye for beauty she has given you!"

"I can't see what Santa Lucía has to do with my falling in love."

"I see you are a bigger simpleton than if you had been made-to-order. Come here to the window. Do you see those two little stars so close together that they might appear *cuates*?* Those are her eyes which she gave up for the love of God. She wanted to remain a Virgin and serve the poor, but there was a persistent suitor who pursued her with his words of love.

*Cuates*—twins.

'What is it you love in me most?' she asked him one day.

'Your star-like eyes,' he replied.

The next day the suitor was horrified on receiving the eyes which the maiden had plucked out with her own hands. The good God put them up there in the sky as a reward for her sacrifice. She has become the guardian of the eyes of people, specially of those who are in love. That's why everything appears more beautiful then. When lovers are either separated from each other or are jealous, they often go to her with their troubles:

> 'Why did you give me sight
> my lady, Saint Lucy
> If I can not see my beloved
> During the day and the night?
>
> The eyes of that lovely maid
> Guard them, Saint Lucy, forever,
> And should she betray me ever
> Let them be devoured by worms.'

is what they say.

But what a mother-in-law you'll have. May the good saint blind you to all her faults. If you love the cabbage you'll like the leaves around it. As my mother, may she in glory be, used to say, 'If you love the girl, you'll like the mother too.' Let me hear all about it."

"I don't know how it started or how it came about."

"Nobody knows that, Marcos, not until you find yourself in love. And then it is too late. 'But if you like being an ox, you'll lick the straps that bind you.'"

"Do you remember when I first came to the ranch? It was a day in late fall. The geese were flying southward, perhaps to Mexico; and I thought of *El Nacimiento*, the little village at the foot of the Coahuila hills where I was raised, and my soul wept and I wished I might have wings to fly home with the geese. I wanted to be alone and I walked to the windmill where I knew no one would be at that hour.

But someone was there. And when I saw her for the first time my heart stopped at the wonder of such beauty. She was washing at the edge of the *laguna** and the rhythmic movement of her body made me think of the mountain palms as they are swayed by the wind."

"Did you say anything to her?"

---

*Laguna*—A small lake.

"I could not. My throat was tight as though there had been a rope around it. She smiled, and to me that smile was like seeing a rainbow after a storm or like finding rest after a hard day's work."

"But how then have you declared your love?"

"I haven't. I dare not, and yet I believe she knows about it."

"Why didn't you follow some of my advice? A letter in a book, a note in a bunch of flowers will do the trick."

"Oh, no, I couldn't do that. I want her to find out some other way. Whenever she goes to the well for water I follow her at a distance and once I was bold enough to sing to her. She must have known who it was meant for because she joined me in the last verse."

"If you repeat the words to me I might be able to tell better," advised the love physician.

"It is my favorite song, one which I learned in my village. It goes like this,

> 'Little Dove, come to my bower
> and the blessing of God will be ours;
> We shall go from the hills to the valley
> And happy we ever shall be.
>
> "I promise never to leave thee
> But will worship with love at thy feet.
> Little Dove, come to my bower
> And the blessing of God will be ours.'"

"She sang that with you?"

"Yes."

"Ah, Marquitos, assure yourself a married man. I shall yet dance at your wedding. No doubt she loves you. Singing a song...I must add that to my list of declarations," added the mail carrier to himself.

"*Muchas felicitaciones*, Marcos *amigo*," shouted Martiniano rolling from under the cot.

"*Ánimas benditas de Purgatorio,\* d*id I not say that walls have ears. But it was not the wall this time."

"You win *el premio gordo\*\** in the lottery of marriage," added Martiniano, ignoring Tío Esteban's remark, "were I not your friend I would make love to her myself."

"Not a word of this to anyone until Marcos speaks to Don Francisco," advised Tío Esteban, "promise?"

"*Sí, sí, seguro.* Of course we promise."

---

\**Ánimas Benditas de Purgatorio*—A small lake.

\*\*El primo gordo—fat prize.

"*Muy bien,* Marcos, you come with me. I cannot keep a secret long. My chest was not made to be a granary. You two keep your mouths shut; no flies will enter a closed mouth."

An hour later found Don Francisco and Tío Esteban at Mariana's. The old woman was in a rage, bemoaning the loss of her hens.

"Ah, Don Francisco of my soul, the most beautiful hen at the ranch! She was stolen from me I know, may the days of the thief be shortened. May the person who killed her get the evil eye, a pain in the side, sores on the hands. Ah, my beautiful hen; an egg as big as a turkey's did she give me every day. My curse, my curse be upon the evil doer."

"Too bad, too bad, Mariana," sympathized Tío Esteban.

"Your condolences will never console me for my loss. But if you'll pardon me, Don Francisco, I must see what has become of Lucía. An hour it is since I sent her on an errand and she has not returned."

"'A house of two doors is difficult to guard' is a good saying. While she mourns for a hen the daughter runs loose. The blood freezes in my veins though when I think of what she'll say when she knows what we came for. With your permission, Don Francisco, I think it is best for me to retire."

"Oh, no, Tío Esteban, you are in a way responsible for this and you have to remain."

"*Muy bien,* Don Francisco, as you say. I am merely thinking of the proverb, 'A woman's tongue and viper's bite are sent from Hell.'"

"My good Esteban, why did you not think of that before? Here she comes now.

"Tell her right away so we can terminate at once."

"And to what do I owe the honor of this visit?" asked Mariana standing with folded arms in front of Don Francisco.

"Sit down, Mariana, I cannot speak so well when I see you before me like a ghost."

"*Como usted mande.*\* I'll sit down, but I expect no good from your visit."

"Mariana, without any *rodeos,*\*\* I shall hit the nail on the head," said Don Francisco clearing his throat nervously. "I have come to see you about a family matter. You have a daughter, a pretty girl she is too and I have a very nice *peón.*"

"Don Francisco," interrupted the old woman with fiery eyes, "if you mean that Indian Marcos—well I did suspect something like this

---

\**Como usted mande*—as you command.

\*\**Rodeos*—In this case—beating around the bush.

\*\*\**Alcahuete*—A go-between.

when I saw that *alcahuete*** sitting there so smugly and looking so innocent as though he would not even break a plate."

"Mariana," replied Tío Esteban with all the dignity he could gather under the circumstances, "be careful of the way you speak to an employee of the American government."

"Don't be a *sinvergüenza** and above all don't come to me with talk about employments and governments. Very well do you know what I refer to."

"Calm yourself, my good Mariana," urged the master. "Whether Tío Esteban does what you accuse him of is no business of mine and I want to hear nothing about it. I am here merely to do my duty as Marcos' master and I expect you to do yours as a mother."

"Does Lucía love this Indian?"

"Who knows the secrets of a young girl's heart? That's for you to find out. You know the custom, Mariana. If we do not hear from you within a week, we'll know you have accepted Marcos as a son-in-law and we'll prepare for the wedding. But don't wait too long to give us your 'yes.' The blood of young people is not slow like ours."

But as Tío Esteban often said, 'the way of love is like roses, the more beautiful and desirable it is, the more thorny'... Old Mariana would not give her consent to the marriage. Weeks and months passed and still she would not give her answer to Don Francisco.

Marcos continued doing his work as diligently as ever, but he was losing heart. As to Lucía she was kept a prisoner by her mother who watched her as carefully as she would a barbecued steer head.

One afternoon, some six months later, Tío Esteban was met at the gate, not by Marcos as usual, but by Martiniano.

"Ay, Tío Estaban," he confided, "how true is your saying that the devil never sleeps, much less take a nap."

"What's happened now?"

"A well driller has come to the ranch, a foreigner too; some kind of tobacco-chewing American with strong arms and shoulders all painted with blue and red figures."

"Where does the devil come in? Not in the pictures he has on his arms?"

"Oh, no, Tío Esteban! He has the most beautiful picture of a flaming heart pierced with arrows! It's not that. He is making love to Lucía and old Mariana likes it."

"She would, the old hypocrite."

---

*Sinvergüenza*—A rascal; a shameless fellow.

For a while all the girls had been agog with excitement wondering which one the stranger would favor with his smiles, but it was soon noticed that he had no eyes for anyone except Lucía. One Monday, upon the stranger's return from town he had brought a present which he displayed one evening to the group of *vaqueros* around him.

"For the prettiest girl at the ranch" he had told them with a meaningful look.

Marcos thought nothing of it; his stolid mind worked only one way; he had implicit faith in Lucía. A girl who looked like our Mother of Guadalupe could be trusted anywhere, he thought.

However, much to everyone's surprise, Lucía was seen wearing the stranger's gift the next day. That could mean just one thing, Marcos and his suit were sent out 'for a walk.'

Again Don Francisco made his way to Mariana's house.

"*Mire, usted,*\* Don Francisco," she said to him, "I know why you are here, but what I am doing is my business. Lucía is my daughter and she will marry whoever I select for her. Even though I have no book learning like others I could mention, I know best what is good for her. What will she gain by marrying? And why should she work like a mule when she can marry an *Americano* who earns much money?"

"Does she want to marry him?"

"When did any girl want to do what is best for her? A good beating did I have to give her before she would wear those most beautiful earrings."

"Mariana, this is a fiendish thing to do. You are selling your daughter for a few baubles. How do you know who this is? He may be already married for all you know."

'The heart cannot suffer what the eyes cannot see,' says the Proverb. If he is married that's his wife's affair, not ours. Don Francisco, your coming has saved me making a trip to your house. I'll tell you now what I would have told you then. Lucía will marry Mister Luis within a week; you can tell your Indian *peón* so. *No faltaba más,* my daughter marry a common *peon* when she can marry a man like Don Luis?"

"All I can say to you is this, Mariana, may God forgive you the injustice you are doing Lucía. One more thing. I will not permit the wedding to take place at this ranch! I owe that much to Marcos. I have allowed you to live here since your husband's death because of the children, but from this moment you can start looking for another place to go."

---

\**Mire usted*—look you.

"Don Luis will provide for that. What care I now whether you drive us away from the ranch or not?"

The news of Lucía's approaching marriage spread through the ranch as only such news can. The ranch was kept in a state of excitement. Whispered conversations, discussions of how Mariana had talked disrespectfully to Don Francisco and how the old woman went about the ranch bragging of what she had told him. It had been noticed too that Tío Esteban had delivered several packages to Lucía. And like the inquisitive old soul that he was, he had torn off a corner to see the contents. "Silk," he told later, "all white and shiny, the wedding dress I suppose. Little does Mariana realize who is going to profit by it," he chuckled to himself. "But don't worry, Marcos, things will come out our way."

In fact the only two who were not excited were Lucía and Marcos. She went about the wedding preparations with a smile and a song and Marcos was indifferent to everything around him. Two days before the wedding Mariana was to move to a neighboring ranch. All the wedding clothes had been packed and Lucía had insisted that the mail carrier should take the box to its destination. And the mother, seeing how docile the girl had become, thought it well to humor her. She had also insisted on spending the night with Rosita who, she said, had a headache and as Lucía explained to her mother, she alone could rub it off.

No harm in that, thought the old woman, she'll be as safe there as she will be here.

But she was not.

A little past midnight, Tío Esteban drove his buggy cautiously to the master's house. "*Señorita* Rosita," he called out softly under her window, "all is ready."

A white figure jumped from the window. Like the dove of the song, Lucía had gone to join her mate, the Indian *peón*.[2]

---

[2]A brief rendition of Tío Esteban, the mail carrier, appears in González (1932).

# CHAPTER X

## The Barometer of the Ranch

After Christmas the winter became unusually cold and dry. But then since the fall, the coyotes had announced it would be so, for their fur had been heavy and thick and they had stayed close to the ranches, not daring to go to the hills. All vegetation had been killed by the *hielo prieto*\* and even the cactus, the always reliable food for the cattle, had wilted.

Spring came and with it, new hope. But whatever young green thing sprang up died for need of water. The mesquites were mere ghosts; the huisaches, shameful for not bearing their sweet-smelling blooms, hid their leaves. All the water holes dried up and death and starvation ruled the prairie. The buzzard was lord of the plains and as it flew over the trees, was a constant reminder of death. The cattle once so plentiful and fat had diminished to a few and those that remained looked at the world with sad, death-like eyes.[1]

"*¿Por qué no llueve, Dios Mío?* Why do you not make it rain, my Lord," Doña Margarita despaired one day, when she could no longer bear the prolonged, mournful bellowing of the suffering cattle. With a sign of resignation Don Francisco answered her,

"*Así es la suerte*, it's just luck."

"Francisco," said Doña Margarita with a sudden inspiration. "It will rain and soon too! Why hadn't we thought of it before? We'll have a procession, a procession of the Miraculous *Santo Niño de Atocha*. He has never refused me anything before and will not now."

"What the Lord has questioned, will be; saints cannot do what He does not wish."

---

\*Hielo prieto—the black forest.
[1]We are definitely into the spring of 1905 in this calendrical novel.

"Don't be stubborn, Francisco, go get Martiniano. Tell him to call the man from the pasture. You go get the children! Run, Francisco, run! And while you go I shall get the *Santo Niño* from His altar. I make a vow this very day that, if He sends us rain, I'll make the pilgrimage to Zacatecas and place a silver box and wax candlesticks at his shrine! Now go, Francisco, hurry! Hurry!"

"I'll go to please you, but I have little faith in your prayers and in your *Santo.*"

"*No le hace,* it doesn't matter. The rest of us have faith and that suffices."

Twilight found the courtyard filled with the *vaqueros* and their families who had come in answer to Doña Margarita's call. When she appeared at the door bearing the niche with the *Santo,* there was a hushed, reverent silence.

"Aquí, Martiniano, and you too Pedro, carry *El Santo Niño.* Francisco, distribute the candles, Rosita, you light them!"

The Saint in his niche of carved wood was raised to the shoulders of the carriers. Outbursts of veneration broke out from the lips of the faithful,

"Miraculous *Santo Niño,* help us,
Bring us rain, Blessed Child."

A young girl carried away by her enthusiasm cried out,
"What a beautiful saint he is and what lovely curls he has."

*El Santo Niño,* a popular version of the child Jesus, was represented as a traveler. The sixteenth century brown cape he wore reached to his sandaled feet. As a symbol of his spiritual and material protection, he held the shepherd's crook in his left hand and in the right, a basket filled with fruit and flowers. The plumed hat of a *conquistador* partly covered the ringlets that fell to his shoulders and hanging from the belt at his waist was a gourd where He no doubt carried water during his peregrinations through the earth. For *El Santo Niño* was a traveler and had appeared in this guise to the humble shepherds and *peones* of Mexico.

The procession started, the Saint leading the way, followed by Don Francisco, Doña Margarita, and Rosita. They wended their way through the uncultivated fields into the nearest pasture, the candles gleaming through the bare trees like so many fireflies.

The chanting of the prayer led by the mistress of the ranch was repeated fervently by all.

"Very pious Child, we beg of you that as you liberated the chaste Susanna from false witness, you may free us from the torments of Hell and of drought. Most Pure Child, we beg of you that as you liberated

Daniel from the lion's den you may free us from drought and other tremendous necessities; giving us now what we need most and at the end of our life a happy death."

*El Santo Niño* was taken to view the now empty, slime-covered tank, the now useless well at the bottom of which croaked the bull-frogs; the windmill, so quiet and still, the dying cattle. Surely He would take pity when He saw the calamity that would befall them if He did not intercede before the Divine Throne! A final prayer was said and the niche was placed between two branches of a mesquite overlooking a long stretch of bare *potrero*.

"Here you will remain, blessed *Santo Niño*, until it pleases you to send the rain we so much need," promised Doña Margarita.

The procession went back to the ranch, leaving the Saint in a punishment of solitude until He should do what was expected of Him.

A few days after the procession, there was much excitement in the quarters of the *peones* at the ranch. The women talked and gesticulated looking at the sky. One of them more excited than the rest was running hither and thither, calling someone in a shrill, nasal voice,

"Serafin-n-ne, Serafin-n-ne, where is that imp of Satan? Where are you, Serafin-n-ne. Just when I need him most he can not be found."

"Ah, Mariana!" called another woman from the door of her *jacal*, "not a bit of wood have I in the house. Hard enough it is to start a fire with green mesquite wood, but much harder will it be tomorrow when the wood is wet."[2]

"Have you seen the boy of mine? Serafín, Serafín," cried the woman again, not deigning to notice her friend's comment, "with all the washing to bring in and the chickens to coop up and the calf to turn into the pasture before the rain starts."

"Rain?" interrupted Don Francisco riding into the servant's quarters, "who said rain?"

"I did," hastened Mariana to reply, "we'll have rain before night."

"Were our mouth the mouth of a prophet! What are you so excited about? Here we're praying to Saint Isidore for rain, have even taken *El Santo Niño* in procession through the fields and now because you think it is going to rain you are more frightened than Old Noah was when he was expecting the flood."

"May Saint Isidore, blessed farmer that he is, send us his holy rain. May *El Santo Niño* intercede for us, but this will be a storm."

"How you talk, Mariana, not a cloud do I see in the sky!"

[2]The Mariana from the previous chapter? Probably not.

"Just you wait, Don Francisco, and that Indian cook of yours is to blame!" she said with vindictiveness. "A thousand devils take him where he belongs!"

"Ambrosio! What has he to do with the storm you are expecting?"

"He's been singing his songs, songs of Satan they must be too."

"And when he sings it rains," added the other woman, "a storm this time it is sure to be."

"Oh, just look at him," wailed Mariana covering her face with her hands, "he must be calling his heathen gods to help him."

"With hail and wind too. Oh! Saint Barbara, Virgin protect us from the hail and storm! Oh, master, whatever shall we do now?"

"Do about what?" thundered Don Francisco, beginning to lose his temper, "what's all this nonsense about?"

"When Ambrosio sings, it rains and storms, just look at him, Master; just look, Don Francisco. There he is."

Don Francisco looked and saw nothing uncommon in what the Indian cook was doing. He was chopping wood and singing. As he swung the ax in the air he sang a lilting melody which he punctuated in the downward stroke driving the ax into the wood.

"*Oye,*\* Ambrosio, stop your singing."

"Won't do no good now," moaned one of the women, "the harm is done already."

Ambrosio stopped, and beckoned by his master, came to where the women were.

"What was that you were singing?"

"Singing, me singing, master?"

"I should say you were, and you have frightened Juana and Mariana here. They say it is going to storm."

"Singing, master?" repeated Ambrosio again in surprise. "I no sing. Ambrosio think," he answered with the unclouded face of one who is satisfied with himself. "That no singing, master," he continued, "Ambrosio think aloud. He think he is Aztec warrior. Spring come soon, cactus bloom, flowers will smell and Ambrosio think of his home in far Xochimilco."

"What were you thinking about?"

"Of Aztecs coming, walking, walking many years. Looking for rich land, for lake, for eagle on cactus," and again he burst forth into song, this time skipping in a circle and throwing his hands up in the air at the end of each verse,

"Axtatzitzinti, ti, ti
tihúi, tihui, ti hui

"Campa tizaxqueh eh, eh?
campa tiyohueh eh, eh?

"Fine Words master!"

"Little Azteca come! come!
Where shall we go? eh? eh?"

"You see," said Don Francisco to the women, "Ambrosio means no harm. He is singing of his people. Do you think it will rain, Ambrosio?"

"Maybe so it rain, maybe so it no rain, maybe sun shine, maybe so it no shine. But Ambrosio is happy."

"See how you accuse him of something he does not know a thing about. He does not even know himself it's going to rain."

"You just wait and see," said Mariana with conviction. Hardly had she uttered the last word than a gust of wind blew away the towel, which in the manner of a turban she wore around her head.

"What did we tell you? It begins, it begins," wailed the women. "Excuse us, master, the clothes must be brought in and other things have to be done."

Credit was given to Ambrosio and not to the *Santo Niño* for the rain that came that night. The heaviest rain ever known to have fallen descended upon the Olivareño. The tank broke through, overflowing the *corrales;* a dry *arroyo* which had always been thought to be harmless became a seething current. No one slept that night. The men were up rescuing goats and sheep and the women and children huddled together at Don Francisco's house.

"Might be a good thing to have a procession of the Virgin to show Her the harm Her Son has done," suggested old Mariana, "though for the life of me, I believe the heathen Indian had more to do with what happened than the Holy Child Himself."

From that time, *"el año de la creciente,"* the year of the flood, Ambrosio became the barometer of the ranch. The next few days were days of magic at the ranch and in the pastures. The *huisaches*, now a mass of golden velvet, scattered showers of fragrant pollen, and the cactus converted the pastures into a chaotic symphony of yellow, bronze, and crimson. It was at times like this that Ambrosio became a poet and told myths of remote times when the Indians were lords of the land and the gods walked freely among them. Seeing the glory of the cactus in bloom, he told how the first cactus flower came to be and how the *pitahaya*\* had been sent by the gods.

"Like a *nopal*\*\* blossom you are, *señorita* Rosita, and sweet like the fruit of the *pitahaya*." And it was to the girl alone, that Ambrosio confided the legends of his race.

## The First Cactus Blossom

For some unknown crime that had been committed, a thing of evil had been sent to punish the Indians. It was a black shapeless beast that walked over the land, flew through the air, burning with his breath all vegetation and living things and blasting all hopes. Sometimes in the shape of an Indian warrior, gloomy and forbidding, he was the forerunner of wars, pestilence, and famine. He spoke to no one, and no one dared to address him as he passed through the villages, leaving panic behind him. Like all evil things, he was most unhappy and he longed for the companionship of man, the touch of a little child, the smile of a maiden.

Tired of his solitary life, he went to the medicine men. The solution to his problem was difficult indeed. He would cease to be evil and become a mortal being when a maiden with hair like the rays of the sun, eyes like the royal emerald, and face like a magnolia blossom would kiss him. And because of this dim hope he grew more restless, tramped over the earth, and brought more death and destruction upon the people.

Now on the hill beyond was the city of the chief who was mighty and brave like a mountain lion. But a strange thing happened in the household of the king. A child was born to him, not bronzed like all people, but fair, with hair like the sun god's and eyes like the emerald. All the soothsayers and witches were called to a council to interpret the meaning of it all.

"Oh, king," said the oldest of all, "a great joy and sorrow awaits thee. This child will bring happiness to your people but only through her death."

Then the king commanded the building of a big house in the heart of a desert island. A thick cactus wall was built all around it and a double one of *maguey*.\*\*\* In this island the child and the wisest witch that could be found were placed. In time the cactus grew so tall that the leaves touched the sky and the thorns were so sharp and pointed that not even a bird could fly through the fence.

---

\**Pitahaya*—Cactus pears, pinkish edible fruit known as Mexican strawberry. The blossom, cerise in color, is beautiful.

And the king, seeing that his child was free from harm, was happy.

In the meantime the baby had grown into a lovely maiden. She sang all day and no lover robbed her of her dreams of peace. One night the old witch was awakened by the princess's screams. In her dreams she had been pursued by a black something with huge bat-like wings that filled her with terror. The witch knew that the time appointed by the prophesy had come and she began to study the means of saving her charge. Every night the princess had the same dreams and each time the monster grew nearer and nearer and scorched her with his fiery breath.

One evening as the princess was walking by the wall, she was attracted by a waving plume, black as night. It reminded her of the dreams she had had, but the voice that called her was like the playing of a reed flute. She approached him and there heard the most wonderful things of the outside world and the people who lived beyond the cactus fence. That night she had the most dreadful dream of all, for the black monster took her in his arms and flew away to unknown regions. The old witch then knew that nothing could save the princess. She told her good-bye and gave her a cactus thorn with this admonition, "When in trouble, prick your hand with the thorn and you will be safe."

Next morning the princess heard the song of the unknown warrior and she came out to meet him. Forgetting himself, forgetting to be gentle, he pressed her to his heart. With a cry of fear, she broke loose for his touch burned like the touch of the black beast of her dreams. She, remembering the cactus thorn, pricked her hand with it as the witch had advised her. To the warrior's astonishment, the princess flew at once into space, getting smaller and smaller, and finally settled on a cactus leaf. But even then she was beautiful and pale. The cactus blossoms have been so ever since.

And then he wept, and kneeling, kissed the little flower that he had loved so well. As he did so something was born within him, a good heart.

## The Gift of the *Pitahaya*

Woman had brought unhappiness to all people, but to the Indians she proved a blessing for through her the *pitahaya*, a most refreshing fruit, was brought to them.

Many years ago there lived a maiden quick as a squirrel, quarrelsome as a magpie, and graceful as a gazelle. As may be imagined, she had more love affairs than a honeycomb has honey. She favored all with her smile, but accepted no one. But her father, disgusted with the state of affairs and the great number of warriors who wasted their time courting his daughter, wished to put an end to the shameful situation so little flattering to a chieftain. Calling the maiden to his presence, he commanded her to chose a husband from among the braves gathered there.

"I shall, only when I please," said the girl haughtily. "But from among them, I shall select the warrior who brings me the gift that resembles me the most."

The chief no doubt gave a sigh of relief as he saw the suitors leaving. But soon, to the consternation of the father and the merriment of the daughter, they returned. They brought the most unheard-of gifts. One who imagined her to be perfect brought a dove, another a milk-white fawn. Others brought wild flowers, gay colored feathers and butterflies. And one who imagined his fate as a husband, a wild cat.

Although the flowers and butterflies flattered her vanity, the willful princess who in reality did not want a husband, refused all gifts. She would have none of these meek braves who wooed her not like warriors should. The suitors did not despair, but the old chief who saw his tribe in turmoil, did. The corn fields were abandoned, the chase was neglected, and the braves, instead of looking for flints to make arrowheads scoured the country for presents.

One day heralds announced the coming of a prince from the far-away land of the Aztecs. He was tall and straight and walked the village streets in pride and disdain. His look was bold and defiant like the eagle's. The feather mantle he wore rivaled in beauty the flowers of the prairie. Heavy bracelets of gold and precious stones circled his arms.

He asked permission to present his gift to the princess. As the fearless eye of the maiden met the piercing, dominating look of the warrior, something like lightning flashed through the heavens.

With slow, determined steps he approached her, fixing on her the eyes of a charmer of snakes. He took something from under his mantle and presented it to the princess. It was a *pitahaya* in bloom.

"Princess," he said, "this is symbolic of you who are fair like its flowers, but sharp and forbidding like the thorns that cover it. Under its thorns, however, hides a most delightful fruit sweet as nectar and refreshing as dew. And you are like that. Under your rudeness and capriciousness hide sweetness and love. That I will discover as I discovered the fruit of the *pitahaya*. Come."

And with his mantle of feathers he covered the maiden who followed him far south where the cactus bloom and the mockingbird ever sings of love.[1]

---

[1]The stories of the cactus blossom and the *pitahaya* were published separately in González (1930a). These appear to be strictly local legends. I am unable to identify any versions in Aztec oral tradition.

# CHAPTER XII

## The Last of the Mendozas

It was Saint Isidore's feast day and the patron saint of the fields must have blessed his day.[1] The evening before, a shower had freshened up the *potreros*. Morning came and the remaining raindrops, imprisoned by the sun in the mesh of spider webs, added a diamond here and there to the already brilliantly arrayed *nopales*.

True to the saying that coyotes and *vaqueros* make merry after a rain, Martiniano, surrounded by a group of his companions, was singing in the ranch store. In keeping with the bright mellow morning they sang of what was nearest the *vaquero's* heart, the woman he loves and rain.

> What lovely little morning
> as though it may want to rain
> reminds me of that other morning
> when for you I began to yearn.

The catchy tune was hummed or whistled by everyone within hearing distance and soon the ranch was enveloped in music.

"Sounds like heaven," responded Martiniano. "I have never been there, not even in dreams, but I know everything looks as gay as a saloon on election day."

"*Mira! mira!*" interrupted one of the men, "who or what is that coming down the road? *Viva Dios*, if he does not look like the messenger of famine."

---

[1]According to the Catholic feast day calendar, this is May 15, Saint Isidore the Farmer.

The man approaching was indeed a sorrowful sight; a most dejected-looking man riding an old melancholy nag was seen dismounting.

He walked wearily into the store and between sighs, told the clerk what he wanted. With another sigh he paid, [and sighing again, left.][2]

The *vaqueros* crowded around him waiting for him to speak, but he said nothing, looked at them with the eyes of a slaughtered lamb, got on his mount, and rode away in the direction from which he had come.

"The *señor* of the sorrowful figure indeed," said Don Francisco who at that moment was entering the store.

"Who is he?"

"That's Don Luis."

"The one who used to write love letters?"

"*El mismísimo,* the very same. Caught at last!"

"You mean married?"

"Yes—*¡Pobre hombre!*—He is not much pleased about it, though. However he has no one to blame but himself; 'so many trips takes the water jug to the well that it ends by being broken,' is the saying. You can't tempt providence the way he did without being punished. He found his punishment in his reward."

"How can that be? I don't understand that, master."

"Easy enough. When I tell you about him, you'll understand."


"He lived in his plain, rambling adobe house alone, but surrounded by pets and accompanied by an old servant, the relic of a former splendor. His family, once one of the big landed proprietors of the border country, had come to less with the years. A series of consanguineous marriages, which had served to increase the family possessions, had at the same time sapped, little by little, the stamina of the descendants of the once powerful family of the Mendozas. As one generation succeeded another, the prolific fecundity that characterized them diminished until at the time of Don Luis' parents, there had been only two children, Don Luis and his older brother, Don Pablo. I knew Don Pablo well. A libertine by nature who had inherited, to a certain extent, the good looks of the Mendozas, he wasted his health and money in debauchery and dissipation.[3]

"The younger son, Don Luis, however, was a good-natured, simple-minded youth who at the time of my story, had reached the somewhat undefinable period at which people stand still for years, only to

---

[2]Bracketed passage crossed out in manuscript.
[3]Cf. the narrative of the Mendoza y Soria family in González (1996).

have old age rush in at a time when they have come to consider themselves eternally young.

"Possessing neither the energy nor the desire to work, he had come to the conclusion that since his family had always had plenty, he would never be in need. Little by little he mortgaged and lost what had taken the family so many years to accumulate. The banks of two counties had taken over the pastures and land which had once been the pride of his ancestors; where once roamed herds of long-horned steers and innumerable flocks of sheep and goats, was now uninhabited and bare. Don Luis retained what the law allowed him, the home and some two hundred acres of land. But he still imagined himself the sole possessor of the once big estate and every morning he rode out as usual, accompanied by his old faithful servant.

"Different in temperament from his brother Don Pablo, he was meek, gentle, and chaste. He had never been known to have had an escapade and he had never married. However he had one great weakness, if it could be called that. He was always falling in love, but in a passive way, with some girl of the neighboring ranches. Like the ingenious Manchegan Knight, he alone was aware of his love which he kept hidden in the innermost recesses of his heart until the springtime of the year when he blossomed out in amatory outbursts. He had made love to two generations of girls. As one crop grew up to maidenhood, Don Luis declared his sentiments to each in turn. One by one they outgrew him, married, and had daughters of their own. As the second generation came on, he remained ever ready to offer his heart and hand to anyone that would listen to him.

"He had not been favored by looks, as you very well see for yourselves. His tall lanky figure, his coconut-head pivoting on some eight inches of neck, his triangular ears, big hands, and splay feet prevented him from being a handsome man. His mustache, as I remember, was the barometer for his emotions. When he was not in love it hung limp and unkempt; but in the spring when the world was aglow with prairie flowers and all nature invited him to love, it was waxed and triumphant.

"No sooner had the first birds mated when Don Luis, his dyed hair shining a reddish-purple against the sun, his mustache curled aggressively, went out on his amorous quests. Mounted on his once powerful horse, he rode leisurely along, a forlorn, solitary rider on lonely ranch roads. As soon as he was seen approaching, the girls scampered away from the house to some safe retreat until the love-bent gallant left with many a sigh and backward glance.

"He often came to buy the most necessary things for his maintenance from the ranch store. In the spring he was a daily visitor, either to mail a love missive or in expectation of one which never came.

"'Look here,' he once approached me mysteriously, displaying a package of ruled paper with a wreath of red carnations at one corner, 'beautiful, isn't it? This time the carnations are bound to work. Last year the paper I used had violets and I did not get a single answer. But that was because violets do not inspire love. Just wait until they see these flowers that can almost speak with their beauty and fragrance,' he said caressing the paper with his long, bony fingers.

"'But now,' he added confidentially speaking, '*entre nos,* between ourselves, I will get so many answers that it will be most difficult for me to decide which girl I want. And listen, Francisco,' he continued frisking about like a young colt, 'this is what I am going to say.' Then he showed me the letter which he sent every year; his one declaration of love, for he always used the same whether sent by mail or uttered one hand over his heart and eyes looking up to heaven for inspiration:

"'Most esteemable young lady:

"'I can no longer bear the pain which devours this your captive heart and I would like to know whether my love is returned or not. Should I be so unfortunate as to be rejected, then I will put between us the immensity of the sea.'

"But in spite of his many rejections and more ignorings he never left on his threatened voyages. He might for a few days go about in a mood suitable to a rejected lover, but the coming of the terrific summer heat evaporated his love-sick spell and melted away the wax of his temperamental mustache.

"'What I cannot understand,' I overheard one of the *vaqueros* say to him one day, 'is why, when having broken so many hearts and when so many girls pine for you, you have not married yet.'

"'I am well aware of that, my friend,' Don Luis replied, not realizing that the cowboy was merely making fun of him. 'I'll tell you my secret. I'll tell you the reason why I have preferred to remain in this holy state of singleness. I prefer not to make any girl unhappy.'

"'Nonsense, any girl would be happy with you.'

"'Ah no, my friend. You do not know the evil impulses that are buried here,' he said, pounding his heart. 'I have the most diabolical desires that would keep me from being faithful to one woman. I love one today, another tomorrow, in fact I love them all.'

"'Who would have thought that of you, Don Luis?'

"'That's the kind of man I am,' he continued, beating his chest, 'I am a wicked man, a most wicked creature.'

"'You know who you remind me of? The locust that we hear on summer days.'

"'Compare me not with such a common insect,' he replied with indignant haughtiness.

"'But it really is a compliment, wait until I tell you about him. The locust, like you, was a gay person, in fact too gay to suit his wife.'

"'Ah, married.'

"Yes, but in spring when the huisache was in bloom, he became intoxicated with the balmy perfumed air and joy of living. It was then that, forgetting the duties of a faithful husband, he made love to the butterflies which, like flying flowers, tempted him with their beauty.'

"'Like the girls tempt me with theirs.'

"Exactly. His wife became jealous and when her erring husband returned home in the evening, satisfied with himself and life, you should have heard her garrulous voice rise above the stillness of night. But he said nothing and merely sat heavy-eyed with love and too happy to hear. As summer came on and the July heat made his life unbearable, his romantic adventurous habits were transformed into a languorous lassitude. Perched on the bark of a mesquite, he complained in his shrill voice of the cruelty of the sun. It was then that his wife, forgetting his past offenses, bathed his feverish forehead with the cool morning dew. The butterflies, seeing him so domesticated, flew to more venturesome lovers and the hummingbird forgot him in disgust.

All was peaceful again until spring...

"'Ah, spring, she comes scattering flowers, scattering flowers,' sang Don Luis.

"Yes, until spring, when passions were stirred in his heart and his roving disposition returned. At last his wife became disgusted with the state of affairs and she went to the Eagle, the monarch of all flying beings, and presented her plea. After due deliberation the king replied, 'Only one thing can check his roaming ways and that is to make him ugly in the sight of the ladies. From now on he will be a changed creature; his eyes will be popped and round, and his colored wings will become an ashy gray. If this does not stop him nothing else will.'

"And it did, for the butterflies laughed at his owl-like eyes and colorless wings. Chagrined and morose, he came home and for months refused to speak. His wife's wishes had gone beyond her expectations; she wanted him at home, it is true, but expected him to keep her company as in the days of their courtship. Realizing that she could never be happy with this ugly creature who did nothing but complain, she went to the king again, this time asking him to make her like her husband. And with her change she became fretful like him. So to this day the shrill voices of the cicadas are heard in the heat of summer, the male complaining and shrill, the female shrill but contented."

"That's it, that's it," exclaimed the descendant of the Mendozas, "I am like the locust, but unlike him I will not have my wings trimmed and no one will ever tell me what to do."

After that he was always very careful to explain to everyone the reason why he had never married. "Unlike the locust, I want to remain free as the air, free as the birds that fly across the sky."


"He who boasts is due for a fall" is an old saying, and it was no doubt because of his boastfulness that he met his nemesis.

On a neighboring ranch not far from his diminished, ancestral domain lived Tío Felipe, a well-to-do farmer whose possessions were a well-cultivated farm, a few fat cows, enough horses and oxen to run the farm with, and a daughter.

Lola, as the daughter was named, was what we call an overripe young woman who was getting along in years as well as in flesh. As a young girl she had been a slender, black-eyed coquette, but she had gone the way of all flirts. Plainer and more demure girls found a husband and a home while she had remained "to dress saints,"* as the saying goes. It was said that Saint Elias, as he went about in his yearly peregrinations through the world looking for virgins to adorn his altar, had already doomed her as an old maid. But she had not yet reconciled herself to her fate. "Marriage and death are sent from heaven," she would console herself. She was already approaching that age dreaded by all women and was beginning to show all the symptoms of a crabbed spinsterhood.

"So people say Saint Elias has already claimed me as one of his virgins," she said. "Just to get the best of him I'll marry this year, even though it be to that simple-minded idiot Don Luis."

Spring came and the unsuspecting love-sick gallant sent his accustomed circulars. As was his habit during the spring months, he came regularly to the post office. One day he received a letter and everyone crowded around him to see him open it. He tore the seal with a flourish and as he glanced at the contents, turned as pale as a ghost and would have fallen had there not been someone to hold him up. After he had somewhat recovered, he said to me in a choking voice,

"Look, look."

*To dress saints—to be an old maid.

I looked and read

"'I am greatly honored by your offer which I accept with the consent of my father.'

"'You must be congratulated upon your good fortune. Lola is as fine a girl as you could find anywhere. She will make you an excellent wife.'

"'But you do not understand,' wailed the 'fortunate' man between sobs, 'I never meant to marry at all. I merely sent those letters because I enjoyed thinking myself a great lover. Whatever shall I do in the spring now?'

"The wedding took place some time that summer and no one saw Don Luis again for many months.

"I shall never forget the first time I saw him after his 'marriage and death were sent from heaven.' He was the most disheartened figure imaginable. His once beautiful mustache was the most forlorn part about him.

"It was in the spring, and the first of his married life. Everytime I see him he looks worse and worse. Married life in spring does not seem to agree with him."

"Does he have a family?"

"Not unless you call his wife that. He is the last of his name. As I told you before, they were as well-known here as they were in town."

"Could he be Doña Juanita's brother-in-law?"

"He is Don Pablo's younger brother."

"Why doesn't she help him then? Wealthy as she is, the crumbs from her table would make him feel rich."

"She has tried it several times I am told, but he will accept no help from one whom, he says, was so greatly offended by one of his own blood."[4]

"I never did know just what happened," said one of the *vaqueros*, "do you, Don Francisco?"

"Very well. I was not there when the incident occurred, but Capul was. Why don't you ask him to tell you?"

"He is not here," answered Martiniano who as always was the spokesman for the group. "Besides you can tell it better. But start from the beginning, master, *por favor.*"

"I knew Juanita's family very well; in fact we used to visit them in town long before she was born. Her father was my cousin, a stern, severe man. As to Juanita, she was in the opinion of all a saint, a dove, a

---

[4]The story of the forlorn lover is reported separately in González (1932a). The imbedded story of the locust is reported separately in González (1930a).

virtuous girl who on her death would immediately go to heaven, shoes and all. She had been educated in the manner of her class and time, with much austerity and nothing of pretension. Her parents had sent her to the convent where she had been instructed in the Christian Doctrine, etiquette, a little arithmetic, grammar, and enough writing to sign her name; for in those days women were not taught to write, that they might not correspond with their sweetheart, if the time ever came when they had one.

This rudimentary education completed, her mother had applied her to domestic duties. Though rich, there were certain household duties that she must learn; to cook, that she might know how to have it done, and to direct all the household expenses. In her idle moments she embroidered shirt fronts for her father and altar cloths for the village church. Every morning at the crack of dawn, her head covered with the traditional black shawl, she and her mother attended Mass, returned an hour later, and went to the vast and austere dining room where foamy cups of spiced chocolate and glasses of newly-milked milk awaited them. She occupied the rest of her time in pious reading, the cultivation of flowers, and the care of her many caged birds.

In the afternoon when the ringing of the Angelus broke the clear stillness of the sky, she, her mother, and the servants repeated the Angelus, and the Rosary, and the Litany of the Saints. At eight, with the arrival of the master of the house, supper was served; meat broiled over the coals on a spit, rice, beans, and corn *tortillas,* hot and fluffy just out of the *comal.** The older people discussed the gossip of the day; after the meal, Juanita would approach her father and say with the timidity that characterized her, 'your hand, my father.' And after she impressed her filial kiss, the old town *ranchero* would say, 'May God bless you, my daughter.' The girl then went to her bedroom and, after saying the evening prayers, slept peacefully in the canopied bed with white drapes. An hour later nothing was heard but the snoring of the master and the occasional barking of the dogs.

On very special days, the girl, accompanied by an older woman, visited the Sisters in the convent, either to take a gift or to ask the nuns to say a prayer for some special intention.

The closed and cloistered life she led had made Juanita somewhat reserved and melancholy, but it was a serene and smiling sadness which made one feel that perhaps she enjoyed being sad. She knew very little of the world and certainly nothing of human passions and emotions. She ignored the existence of novels. Her only readings had been limited to

*Comal*—flat iron where tortillas are baked.

the lives of the saints and their struggles to attain spiritual perfection. When she reached her eighteenth birthday, her father thought it time for her to marry. Not even then was she a beauty. She was too cold and her features too severe for that, but her alabaster skin, chestnut hair, and pale blue eyes set her apart from the rest of the girls of her age. She was slender, perhaps too much so, with no feminine curves to grace her carriage. She lacked the coquetry so innate in the girls of our race, nevertheless such was the tranquillity of her face, her candor and innocence, that she won the respect, I cannot say the love, of Don Pablo Mendoza. Past thirty now, he had been a gay blade in his younger days; he had loved and had lived and now, needing the peace and rest of home, had decided to marry. His features were to be noticed among the offspring of some of the servant women, but that did not interfere with his marrying the pure, chaste girl that was to be like a balm in his turbulent life. In fact, her ignorance of life had led her to consider his escapades a necessary evil. She did not love him, neither was he repulsive to her; since her parents wished the marriage, she raised no objections. Juanita's father had seen in this dissipated landowner the husband for his daughter. Both were rich and their marriage would unite two old families and two big fortunes. Juanita also suited Don Pablo who saw in her a submissive wife that would never complain.

I have been told that since early childhood Don Pablo showed the evil inclinations which were to characterize him through life. He had been cruel to the smaller children, incited them to quarrel, and what was worse, when he reached puberty had shown disgusting signs of licentiousness. His tutor told me that once, not knowing what to do with the boy, he had taken him to his parents, telling them that he could teach the boy nothing and that his tricks and pranks were too much beyond his poor understanding. The boy's mother, ignoring the hypocritical whimpering of the boy, had replied, 'Punish him! I have already told you that I gave him to you, skin and all.' As to his father, taking the boy by the arm he had led him to the *corral*. The boy cried, begged him not to whip him, but to no avail. The whipping was a masterpiece of its kind after which he had been locked up for the rest of the week. But this punishment and others did not correct the boy's evil tendencies. Another time the tutor found him by the well in conversation with the servant girl, saying things that burned the teacher's ear with mortification.

'You imp of Satan,' the tutor had exclaimed, 'who has taught you those things? Pedro de Urdemañas himself must have instructed you. You'll see for yourself, my fine young man, how the green devil himself will carry you in a cloud of sulphur one of these days.'

As Pablo grew he began to show a certain liking for ranch life and often after a stormy scene with his father, had gone to the ranch. There he had given bent to his desires, working with the cowboys in the pasture by day and making love to the girls by night. Many times returning from the *potrero* at twilight, not even waiting for the *peon* to take off his spurs, he had escaped unseen to some *jacal* where lived some girl whom he liked. *El Güero*, as he was called because of his reddish hair and gray eyes, was, if not liked, tolerated by the candid ranch girls who saw in him not only a town boy but the master's son. He gained their good will by presents of bright-colored calico dresses and an occasional silver coin. When Pablo reached the age of twenty his father died, leaving the boy to care for his mother, a younger brother, and the vast estate which they had inherited. And with no one to fear now, Pablo continued his life of pleasure and excesses, until weary of so much sordidness, he had decided to marry.

After the wedding which took place with a ceremony due his rank, Don Pablo decided to make his home in the old family ranch. The ranch house was remodeled and Juanita's mother gave them the furniture which she, as a bride, had inherited from her mother. But marriage did not change him and Juanita, not versed in the wiles of the world, could not hold him. Don Pablo continued living the life he liked, looking after the estate and making love to the ranch girls.

One day he happened to see Dolores, the niece of the overseer. And that was his undoing. Her oval and expressive face, the color of a piñon nut, her black curly hair, and smiling, brown eyes made him forget everything else. She was an orphan and now, at the age of eighteen, had changed from a thin, lanky girl to a luscious beauty. To see her dressed in her Sunday best was a sight to remember with pleasure. Her stiffly starched percale dress, the *rebozo** gracefully draped around her slender waist and crossed over her firm bust, the black hair braided down her back helped to enhance the beauty with which the saints had blessed her. Unfortunately for Don Pablo but fortunately for her, she had a sweetheart, the handsomest *vaquero* on the ranch. Bernardo, such was his name, was the best at throwing a lasso, taming a bronco, or riding a steer. He always had a ready word and knew how to spend his money on the best *mescal* and *tequila* that money could buy. He had two loves, his widowed mother whom he called his 'Madrecita,' and Dolores whom he loved with the passionate abandon of youth. Don Pablo had come too late; but the fact that the girl had a sweetheart made him more determined than ever to make her his. But in spite of her innocence,

*Rebozo*—Silk shawl.

Dolores was a woman and she soon learned to avoid him without once hurting his position as master.

On the other hand, Bernardo hated him with the concentrated hate of one who sees the honor of his woman in danger. And had it not been for the traditional and almost feudal respect which he felt for the master, he would have dealt with Don Pablo differently.

Spring came and with it the wedding day of Bernardo and Dolores. Early in the morning on the appointed day, the bridal couple and their friends went to the master's house where the wedding, arranged by Dôna Juanita, was to take place in the chapel. The ceremony finished, the bridal party went back to the *caporal's* house where the wedding feast was to take place. Everything was ready there. Under the spacious *portal* and along the wall, rows of chairs had been placed. At one end sat the musicians, two guitar players, a fiddler, and an accordion player. Doña Juanita, the priest, and Don Pablo presided over the *fiesta*. Everyone was happy. Everyone laughed, except Don Pablo who, from the place where he sat, eyed Dolores and Bernardo with anger and envy. What right had they to be so happy while he, the master, suffered the tortures of the damned? Until now no girl had ever escaped him. Why had Dolores, the only girl he had ever loved, preferred a common *vaquero* to the love and the wealth that he could have given her? Never for one moment had the idea come to his libertine and vicious mind that the girl might have preferred to be the wife of an honest man to being the plaything and the passing fancy of the master. He would make them pay for the offense, he thought as he sat there in the seat of honor, his face convulsed with anger and hatred. He would see that Bernardo and Dolores would never belong to each other.

While some of the *peones* were amusing themselves, others with the master's permission were preparing for a *rodeo* in honor of the bride and groom. At noon, dinner was served on tables which had been placed under the *portal*. The priest, Doña Juanita, and her husband sat at the head of the table; Bernardo and Dolores at the foot; the guests placed themselves wherever they could find a place. In the center of the table were placed large platters filled with barbecued meat, stuffed turkeys, and bowls of rice and beans. At intervals, piles of *tortillas* and pyramids of bread were placed within reach of all the guests.

With dinner finished, Doña Juanita retired to take her nap. The priest went back to town and Don Pablo remained to participate in the afternoon festivities. The musicians were about to begin playing when El Capul arrived. I am told he looked striking that day. His face, like a carved statue of ebony, was the exact color of the black horse he was riding. He was greeted with shouts of joy because he was then, as he is now, the best singer and could improvise songs for every occasion. He took in the situation at a glance. Don Pablo's sullen and vindictive face, the lascivious look he cast upon Dolores; the bride's timid and downcast expression; Bernardo's disdainful and almost arrogant attitude towards Don Pablo, as though he meant to imply, 'I am the master here.' Bernardo asked El Capul to sing and without further insistence, he borrowed the guitar from one of the players and began to improvise, looking at Don Pablo with a malicious smile:

> 'Speak to me, little guitar,
> speak with your strings of gold,
> tell in words so brave and bold
> the story you would relate.
>
> There was once a gay hawk,
> who lost his way in the valley,
> looking around for a dove
> to steal away from its love.
>
> But listen to the moral
> young hawk, lost in the valley,
> doves that have a mate don't sally
> in search of another love.
>
> The man who goes a-courting
> the affection of a pure girl,
> resembles a toothless man
> who is given jerky to chew.
>
> The man who goes a-wooing
> the wife of another man
> will be like the bad thief
> crucified, but not rewarded.'

I am told that Don Pablo paled at the second stanza, but as the song advanced and the insinuations became stronger, his face turned purple and the veins on his forehead seemed to burst.

'Enough,' he shouted with bloodshot eyes and foaming mouth, 'were I but living in my grandfather's time I would have your living tongue perforated with a red-hot iron. This insolence will be reported to Don Francisco.'

'A good thing God does not grant everyone's whim,' muttered El Capul to himself as he mounted his horse and rode away from the *corral* very well pleased with himself at having touched Don Pablo's vulnerable spot.

The pause in the festivities caused by the master's outburst was broken by one of the *peones* who came in to announce that everything was in readiness for the *rodeo*. The cowboys hurried away, both to escape Don Pablo's wrath and to put on their chaps and to get their rawhide *riatas*. One by one they returned, some whirling the lassoes in the air, others tightening the horse's girth. The *peones*, impassive to everything, sat bareheaded on the *corral's* fence, while the women, somewhat frightened yet, sat under the canvas-covered swats that had been arranged for the occasion. Bernardo and Dolores occupied a central position near the musicians and the overseer who was to supervise the *rodeo*. Don Pablo pranced like a wild Centaur near the *corral* gate, *riata* in hand.

In spite of Dolores' protests Bernardo was persuaded to ride a steer. As expected of him, he selected the fiercest, the one all were afraid to ride. The beast was roped and Bernardo mounted it. Once he had a good hold with the stirrups he cried to the other *vaqueros*, 'Turn him loose. I am the fiercest bull in this *rodeo*.' The steer rose formidably, snorted, pawed the earth with its front feet, and began to jump. Bernardo, spurs nailed to the side of the steer, smiled and waved to Dolores. Then something like a black snake was seen hurling through the air. A cry was heard. With an oath, Don Pablo galloped away dragging Bernardo's body out of the *corral* into the pasture beyond. Blinded by fury and hate, the rider saw nothing ahead and both he and the horse hurled themselves into the trunk of a tree by the road.

Don Pablo's body, a deformed bleeding mass, was carried into the house.

A month after the funeral Doña Juanita called Bernardo and Dolores to her house. She ignored completely the incidents leading to her husband's death; only once did she mention anything that might lead her guests to suspect she was thinking about it, and that was when she asked Bernardo if he had completely recovered.

'Now that my husband is gone,' she said, 'I need someone to look after the affairs at the ranch and after much thought I have selected you to be the administrator.'

Without waiting for a reply she left the room. The next day she moved back to town. In her father's house she took up the thread of her former existence. The years have passed and Doña Juanita, in the opinion of all, is a saint, a dove, a virtuous woman who on her death will immediately go to Heaven, shoes and all."

"You talk like a book, Don Francisco. That story is as fine as one you read to us once, from the thousand and I don't know how many other nights."

"The Thousand and One, Martiniano," laughed Don Francisco. "Here comes Capul with his guitar. He will entertain you now. Amuse

yourselves today, *muchachos*; tomorrow we go to the *potreros* at day-
break."

El Capul entered and began to sing:

> "No learned singer am I
> but when I begin to sing,
> I never know when to stop
> but can sing to my dying day.
> The songs burst from my heart
> like water from mountain stream."

# CHAPTER XIII

## Distant Rumbling[1]

*Mexicans at the cry of war,*
*Prepare your war steed and sword.*
*The earth from its center will tumble*
*At the sonorous cannon roar.*

The school for boys was beginning the fourteenth year of its existence and the third at the Olivareño ranch. Following a system of rota-
tion encouraged by the patrons, the school was moved from ranch to
ranch and for the third time since its foundation, Don Francisco, as head
of the directors, was bringing it back to his ranch.

Seated on crude, backless benches, some fifty boys ranging from
seven to twenty years faced the teacher who stood before the class open
book in hand. A man in his early fifties, he was slight in structure but
gave the appearance of being taller because of the lion-like, well-shaped
head and fine brow. The bronzed features, made more strikingly so by
steel blue eyes, might have been carved out of metal, so definite were
they in their symmetry and proportion. He was a man born to command;
but it was only when he smiled that those around him lost the combined
fear and awe which he inspired in them.

---

[1]González left two versions of this chapter which at one point was numbered XI, leading me momentarily to believe that this was the missing chapter.
However, the second more extended version is re-numbered as XIV and later
XIII. XIII seems to make the most narrative sense here. This and the final chapters clearly provide a sense of an ending for the preceding representation of a
rich Mexican folkloric culture that is now facing the changes brought on by
Anglo-America.

As usual, school began with the singing of Mexico's national anthem. What if the school was in Texas? He was paid by the parents to make good Mexicans out of these boys and he was doing it. In fact he had surpassed his own expectations. As the boys reached the age of twenty-one, of their own accord they crossed the Río Grande into Mexico; those born in Texas to naturalize themselves as Mexican citizens; the others to pay allegiance to the land of their birth and reinforce their citizenship.

Educated in Mexico during a period when the French trend of thought predominated, Don Alberto had become saturated with the teachings of Rousseau, Diderot, Montesquieu and the other encyclopedists. The philosophy of Voltaire and Victor Hugo was his religion; the reading of the classics his diversion; the outstanding passion of his life was instructing the border boys in the culture and traditions of their race. He tolerated the United States as a nation of blue-eyed barbarians who were the born enemies of anything Mexican or Spanish. Married to the daughter of a Texas landowner, he had been persuaded by the *rancheros* to stay in Texas and conduct a school for boys. No one was more fitted than he to instruct the Texas-Mexican youth in the spirit of their race. He remained; he had introduced books that opened new horizons before the eyes of the border youth.

The texts, with the exception of Mexican history and grammar, were Spanish translations of the French books he had used as a boy. The mornings he usually devoted to reading from books of travel, writing, arithmetic, and grammar. The last subject was especially stressed. "A gentleman is recognized by the language he uses, and you as such, must use only the best of Spanish," he insisted. The afternoons he dedicated to what he liked to call general culture. It was then that he made use of the most astounding and outstanding instrument of his career, his voice.

Classical in its sonority when describing the past glories of Greece and Rome, it became caressingly soft as he discussed the *Moonlight Sonata*, Schubert's masterpieces, Chateaubriand's *Atala* or the painters of the Renaissance; eloquent in his denunciation of ignorance and illiteracy; thundering as he told of the "robbery of Texas by the insidious cupidity and avarice of the Colossus of the North."

He might have been a pedagogue of ancient Greece as he wandered through the fields followed by his boys, teaching natural sciences from nature itself, the elements of botany in the woods, elements of physiology from animal life, and in clear evenings he gathered his group around him and taught them the most rudimentary things about the stars and planets. No natural phenomenon escaped his teaching; a hailstorm, a rainbow, a sandstorm presented occasions of which he took advantage. He was an inspired teacher who transmitted the thirst for knowledge to his pupils.

His most noteworthy achievement had been the introduction of vegetables. In a land devoted entirely to ranching, no thought had ever been given to farming. Corn, beans, and pumpkins were planted occasionally, but that was as far as any agricultural endeavor went. In a few acres of land which he used for experimental purposes, he raised all kinds of vegetables which were distributed among the *rancheros* and their families.

After fourteen years of hard work, he was beginning to see his efforts repaid. His pupils were beginning to be the recognized leaders of the border; others following his advice had gone away to American institutions; those who had married, inspired by his teaching, wished for a broader education for their children.

In accordance with the common belief "that learning spoils them for work," the children of the *peones* did not attend school. Yet during his free time and in his own home, Don Alberto instructed those who wished to learn. Whereas Father José María was the "father" of the ranches, Don Alberto was the teacher. And these two men, who disagreed about every religious principle, were of the same opinion about one thing, education for all.[2]

The *rancheros*, believing themselves masters of everything, looked down from their self-appointed eminence upon the *peones* as mere instruments to work for them. It had never occurred to these *hidalgos**  that the *peones* were human beings with a mental capacity to learn and spiritual possibilities to appreciate the beautiful things.

"Their fanciful imagination needs an outlet which only instruction can give them," Don Alberto told the priest.

"Their spiritual hunger and lack of proper religious environment makes them have a pagan soul," was the *Padre's* always ready reply.

That conversation had taken place some years before, and now for the first time, through the teacher's persistent efforts and Don Francisco's liberal concession, the children of the *peones* joined the children of their masters in the singing of the national hymn.

For their benefit Don Alberto had prepared a special talk that morning. He related to his boys the past greatness of the indigenous races; he told them of the city of the Aztecs, the great Tenochtitlán, that had surprised the Spanish conquerors with its splendor and its wealth. He told

---

[2]See González (1930:69-75) for an historical account of such schools.
*Lords.

them of the valiant prince Cuauhtemoc who, when tortured by the Spaniards because he would not reveal the hiding place of Moctezumas' treasure, had merely smiled and said, when his anointed feet were placed over the burning coals "Verily this is no bed of roses." He unfolded before their avid minds the miracle of the dark Virgin of Tepeyac, the Blessed Mother, who as an Indian maid appeared to the Indian, Juan Diego as proof of God's love for his Indian children. "It was an Indian boy, Pipila," he said, "who set fire to the strong Spanish fortress of Granaditas when the patriot Father Hidalgo was fighting for our independence; it was Morelos, a man with Indian blood who carried on when all hopes for freedom were lost. It was a pure-blooded Indian, Benito Juárez, who struggled for our sovereignty when French aggression threatened Mexico, and today," he ended, "it is a *mestizo,** Don Porfirio Díaz, who directs our destinies. So you see my boys, the heritage of this race of bronze, the race of strong heroic men. *Viva la raza de bronce! ¡Viva México! ¡Viva Don Porfirio Díaz!"*

"*Viva, viva,*" answered the boys with enthusiasm.

"This day should be the proudest of your life," the *Padre*, who was making a visit to the ranch, told Don Francisco and Don Alberto that afternoon when informed of the innovation at the school. "How many times have I not prayed that I might see this day before I die. The first task before me is to eradicate their belief in witchcraft and evil spirits that is so deeply rooted in their souls. But that cannot be done until something else is offered in its place. And that, Father, is what I propose to do. They need something to believe in and finding nothing better, they revert to the primitive beliefs of their race."

"What you have just said," offered Don Francisco, "brings to my mind something very strange that happened just last week. You know Paula, don't you, *Padre*? I believe you do, Alberto. Well, one night last week I heard her scream, the most terrific screams I'd ever heard. It sounded like the howling of wildcats and coyotes combined. I wanted to go and see what the matter might be. 'Don't meddle in other people's affairs,' Margarita said, 'most probably she's been having a love affair with another man and she is getting what she so well deserves.'

I said no more and went back to bed, but not to sleep for her screams kept me awake all night. I never knew a woman could scream that long and that loud. The next morning she came for water to the well and when she saw me there, she covered her face with a towel she was wearing around her shoulders.

'*Buenos días*, Paula,' I said to her, but she did not answer my salutation. How strange I thought! Whatever her faults might be Paula is never discourteous.

'I heard you scream last night,' I continued, 'was anything the matter?' She shook her head and started lifting the water bucket to her head. It came as a surprise to everyone, so much so that I could not believe it at first. He is very tenderhearted, as you know, in fact he has never been known to have done a mean act. His neighbors often borrowed his yoke of oxen, his team of mules, his plow. It was quite usual for them to keep his things as long as they wished, and as he never complained they continued doing so. One of his friends, who was a-courting and who wanted to make a good impression on the lady of his choice, asked for the use of his new five-gallon hat and Bacho, characteristically willing, was glad to lend it. He is a soul without malice and he allowed himself to be imposed on. One of his *compadres** came to see him one day and after much hesitation said,

'*Compadre,* I have a small favor to ask of you; it is not much and I am sure you will accommodate me.'

'Speak, *compadre,*' responded Bacho, 'consider yourself served.'

'It happens that my wife wants a new dress and I would like to take her to town, but sad to say, my team is resting now and I thought you might...'

'Why, certainly,' Bacho replied, 'I can lend you my team and the wagon besides.'

'I knew you would, may the Saints repay you for I never will; but there is something else which my tongue dares not utter... you see my land needs plowing and I thought you might...'

'Why, yes, you can borrow my yoke of oxen too; but if you are going to town, who is going to plow the land?'

'That's it, *compadre,* I am just coming to the point; since I am using your mules and I have just borrowed your oxen and you have no way of plowing your own land, I thought you might complete me the favor by plowing it for me.'

'Sure, a friend is a friend, and what is a little plowing among people who like each other?'

Well, dawn found Bacho, yoke of oxen, and plow, bound for the field while his friend went to the city. Pole in hand, Bacho led the oxen over the field once and then again. It was a warm spring morning and the birds fussed and scolded as they flew about. He watched them for a while; particularly did his eyes follow two blackbirds. One sat on a limb of a tree and directed the work of the other, while he quite cool, rocked lazily in the breeze. The bird looked at Bacho mischievously with round yellow eyes and then gave a cry that might very well have been one of

*Compadres*—Close friends.

derision. 'Laughing at me, eh?' thought Bacho. That was more than he could endure. Of late he had come to suspect that his friends considered him a *guaje*,* but to have even the birds know that too, was too much. He was through—no more would he be the laughingstock of his friends. He stopped his work, unyoked the oxen, and sat determinedly on the plow. The oxen switched their tails philosophically and the young moon, like a golden crescent, rose in the sky. But like all newborn things the moon went to sleep early. Bacho alone remained at his post. Soon smoke from the ranch houses perfumed the damp morning air and the roosters proclaimed another day. Bacho's friend came to see what had been accomplished while he was in the city and he found two furrows neatly plowed and Bacho sitting on the plow, staring, far, far ahead.

'Are you ill, has anything hurt you?' his friend queried. Bacho got to his feet and started away with no explanation. To all but himself and the taunting blackbird, the incident remained a mystery. Since then he stays to himself and we never see him.[3]

I've often heard it said, 'Like Bacho he became mulish at his task', and have wondered what it meant. But going back to this belief in witchcraft that can easily be explained," continued Don Francisco, "but I certainly cannot see Ramón's attitude towards Cristóbal."

"That's the point I want to stress," contested Don Alberto emphatically, "the need for education. If Ramón had been properly educated he would not believe such foolish things; to this very day he believes the child is possessed of an evil spirit—what a foolish thing! And as a result Cristóbal has really become possessed, not of the evil spirit they tell you about, but of a hopeless feeling of despair."[3]

"That's where your work comes in, Alberto, free their minds from such beliefs, dispel all superstitions. Get your people ready, train them for what lies ahead of them. I have been here longer than either of you," continued the priest. "It is fifty years since I left France and I have seen this country grow. I blessed your house when you returned from Mexico. I married you, Alberto, and I have christened all your children. I still hope to marry them."

"With the favor of God, *Padre*."

"That's right, my son, without His will we can do nothing. But great changes are coming still. I shall not live to see them, but you will, Francisco, and you too, Alberto. I have been happy here. There's much

---

*Guaje*—literal translation, gourd, empty headed, simpleton.

[3]Here González picks up Cristóbal's story last seen in chapter VII.

about your simple life that has often reminded me of my youth in the simple French village where I was born. But things will change. I hear the rumble of progress at my heels. I see these peaceful ranches passing away to other hands, and my eyes weep for you and yours."

# CHAPTER XIV

## The New Leader

Unlike Don Francisco, his younger brother Fernando had always lived in town. Soon after his return from Mexico, much against Doña Ramona's wishes, he had married the little playmate of his boyhood, Isabel, the youngest daughter of the American Juan Preston.[1]

"It is not that I do not like the little Isabel," she had explained to Fernando when he asked for her permission, "but in her veins flows the blood of the people who are not the friends of our race, and that, my son, should be sufficient reason to oppose the marriage." But in spite of her many protests they were married. The following year on the first of May, 1871, the second Fernando, like all the Olivares children, was born in Mexico. His mother, always frail and delicate, died two years later.

"Bring the child to me," Doña Ramona had written her son. "I shall raise him like an Olivares should be raised." And thus it happened that a grandson of Juan Preston was brought up in the traditions of a Mexican *caballero*.

Fernando grew up, and realizing when very young that he had American blood, felt different from the rest of the boys. He had a feeling of resentment against his heritage that made him feel he was an outcast among his friends. Doña Ramona's teachings, the stories that she had him read about these people, made him feel that he could never have anything in common with his American grandfather. The death of Doña Ramona brought him to Texas, a youth of nineteen, handsome, proud, and somewhat reserved.

[1]Here González picks up the story of Don Juan Preston last seen in Chapter I.

He met Don Juan Preston shortly after his arrival, and reticent as he was in his feelings towards him, the boy could not help but admire the fine old gentleman who was his American grandfather. Much to his surprise he realized he loved him with the same love that he would a father. They became fast friends; the boy and the old man spent many hours together talking about the things they liked to do or discussing the books that both had read. During their long walks together Fernando often boasted of the greatness of the Olivares, of the proud name he bore, and always with an air of condescension towards the old man who rarely spoke about his family.

One day much to Don Juan's surprise, the boy, somewhat hesitatingly asked, "Grandfather, are there more nice *Americanos* like you?"

"My boy," the old man had replied, "there are good people everywhere, regardless of nationalities and racial differences."

That had been the beginning of an enlightening education for Fernando. Don Juan told the boy the history of his family in Virginia and much more about the country of his birth. To his great surprise and astonishment Fernando found himself interested in learning English and in knowing the Americans better. Unlike the men of his class he wanted to work, and much to his father's surprise and Don Francisco's mortification, he had himself hired without their knowledge as a clerk in a general store in Corpus Christi.

"I want to know my grandfather's people better, learn their ways, see how they live," he told Don Francisco when the Patriarch of the *Olivareño* remonstrated about what he called a disgraceful arrangement.

Thus it was that he acquired in a practical way much more than the English language.

Great was his surprise at the treatment he received in the American town. Had he received a slap on the face he would not have felt worse. The fact that his family had been in the country for five generations meant nothing to these Americans whom he had come so prepared to like. The fact that his grandfather was Mr. John Preston from Virginia made no difference to them. In their eyes he was just a Mexican, and a Mexican was something to be treated as an inferior being. Had he been hated he would not have considered the insult so great, but to be merely tolerated was more than his proud spirit could bear. But he would not go home, he would stay! He had come to learn English and that he would!

In the loneliness of his room he often went to sleep shedding tears of hate and mortification. And these were the people his grandfather had told him were kind and good. These were the people who had declared all men were equal!

The words which as a child he had heard from Doña Ramona's lips came back to him in a rush, "Never trust them, we were born enemies, and enemies we shall remain." He had wanted to be their friend and they had rejected him, had treated him as he would not have treated one of the *peones* at home.

He withdrew to himself and would not come near any American except when his work at the store demanded that he do so. The owner of the store, recognizing the boy's superiority over the rest of his employees, had more than once tried to befriend him. However Fernando's courteous but aloof attitude had let him clearly see that he wanted to be left alone. One day he was called into the office after working hours.

"We would be very happy," his employer had told him, "to have you come for supper Saturday night."

"I thank you, *señor*," Fernando answered rising from his seat, "I work for you, and you can command me, but an Olivares never accepts charity."

"You misunderstand me, my boy, it is because we like you that we are inviting you."

"I have suffered the insults of your race once,... I shall not expose myself to more."

"Your attitude will not help matters any. Didn't you tell me once that you came here because you wanted to know Americans better? How can you expect to do so when you never mingle with them? You keep too much to yourself."

"I came prepared to like them, I came prepared to learn your ways and be like one of you, but how can I do that when not for one moment am I allowed to forget that I am a Mexican? That being the case I am not going to thrust my society where I am not wanted. I came willing to become an American, but instead of that I am now more determined to remain what I have always been, a Mexican and a gentleman."

Fernando did not accept.

The news of his father's death brought him home. Don Juan was also gone, and there was no one in whom the boy could confide the things that had hurt him so much. He remained at home; it was then that he began his threefold career as businessman, a ranchman, and a politician.

The experiences that he had met and the history of his people made him see that the border needed a leader, and what better leader could they find then he who understood and knew the *Americanos*? It was fifty-five years since the land of his ancestors had become part of the United States, and all this time the *rancheros* had lived happily ignorant that they were foreigners in a foreign land. He could see that they were unprepared politically and educationally to cope with the situation that would soon be theirs to solve. He saw what his work was to be: to awaken his people to the fact that they were part of the country in which they lived, and to urge them to exercise their rights as American citizens.

"It is our duty to learn English," he told them, "to send our children to American schools. Not that we are ashamed of our Mexican traditions, but because this will make us know how to protect ourselves against them."

And so it was that he became the leader of his people. His keen alert mind saw what the *rancheros*, impregnable in their racial pride and blinded by their belief in their rural greatness, could not see; the inevitable invasion of the Americans to the border country. Seeing that it would not be long before that happened, he wanted to prepare them to meet the new arrivals on equal grounds.

His financial success, his magnetic personality, and handsome appearance made Don Fernando become the recognized leader of the community. He became the political boss because the people were willing to follow him and wanted him to be one. And since all the landowners of the border country were either a branch of his family or were related through marriage, he had no trouble in getting the *rancheros* to do his will.

He often made trips through the ranches urging the landowners to get their poll tax and be ready to vote at the next election. It was very important that they do it he told them, because an American living in the northern part of the county was running for office and the only way to keep him out was for them to vote against him. Little by little Fernando convinced all; little by little the *rancheros* made special trips to the county seat to get their poll tax.

Only one remained deaf to all his pleas, his Uncle Don Francisco. Six months before election day, Don Fernando made one more trip to the Olivareño ranch. Once more he pleaded with his uncle. "It is time for us to band together," he had told him. "We are threatened by the encroachment of the *Americanos*. They want to divide our county, take the richest part for themselves and leave us the sand dunes of the desert plains and the sandbars of the Río Grande."

"They do!" Don Francisco had replied deeply aroused, shaking his fists at his unseen enemy. "They shall not! I'll become an American citizen if necessary and so will my *peones* and *vaqueros*; we'll show them we are still rulers of the land."

"Which suit shall I get ready for tomorrow, Francisco?"

"My American suit, I suppose, Margarita; if I am going to vote, I want to do it right and dress as the Americans do. Who would have thought the day would come when Don Francisco de los Olivares would vote in an American election?"

"Do you have to do it, Francisco?"

"You heard what Fernando said when he was here last week. Unless we border *rancheros* vote, the *Americanos* will rule the land. And he is right too! It seems strange though that we should have to become Americans in order to remain Mexicans."

"You know best what to do," sighed his wife, "but I do not like it. Are the *vaqueros* and the *peones* voting too?"

"Everyone will. They leave for town tomorrow; the *caporal* alone remains. Even Tío Patricio has asked Ramón to let him go. 'Don Fernando needs me,' he told Ramón, 'and I must go to him.' He is a strange old man. Proud of his beard as he is, he volunteered to shave it off if necessary."

"But why? Can he not vote unless he is shaven?"

"Sure he can, but he told Ramón, 'If Don Fernando needs votes, I give him two. First I vote as I am, and then without a beard.'"

"*Válgame Dios*, Francisco. I like this voting less and less; it turns men's heads and makes them do such foolish things. How glad I am we women do not have to do it too."

"Who knows, Margarita, what this will bring to us! I feel a traitor to all that I have treasured in my heart. But Fernando is one of us and we must fight for him."

"You are right, Francisco! He is your nephew and we must help him now. Your saddlebag is all packed. I will see about my suitcase now. What time do we leave?"

"I told Marcos to have my horse saddled and the coach ready before daylight. We'll leave at the crowing of the first rooster."

"*Muy bien*, my love."

Early in the afternoon of the day previous to the election the *rancheros* began to arrive with their voters. Both political parties were ready and both were ready to vote, not only with the ballot but with the gun, if necessary.

The town caroused all night, and to prevent the stealing of votes from each other, the antagonistic parties locked their voters in a safe place. Don Fernando enclosed his men within the walls of the Court

House, his opponent did the same in a *corral* on the opposite side of town.

But in spite of all these precautions, Don Fernando's candidate was not in bed that night.

The next day found the leader and his party despairing at what the result of the election would be. With no candidate to oppose his opponent, it was evident that the election would be lost.

While the party mourned for and buried its dead two things happened; the opposition took control of the polls and a new candidate was found by Don Fernando. Himself.

The opposition, undaunted by the news, continued at their post at the polls and refused to allow Don Fernando and his men to vote. Riot ran high. There was much drinking and shooting and the town people did not dare leave their houses. Fearing for the safety of the inhabitants, Don Fernando, contrary to all his principles, called on the Rangers for help and under their surveillance, the election, which turned out to be a victory for him, took place.

"A man of brains and of courageous heart is Fernando." Don Francisco told his wife the following day when relating the incidents of the election. "You should have seen him as I saw him, eyes flashing, wine glass in hand, toasting to all the *rancheros*. That blue-eyed, long-legged *Americano*, the one who wants to create a county for himself came in with three of Fernando's enemies. He asked for a drink and Fernando told the barkeeper to serve them. Don Bill, I think that's the *gringo's* name, refused to drink with him. Fernando was very angry. His face turned the color of wax and his hand went to his hip.

'An offense like this must be washed with blood,' he shouted. 'I could kill you like a dog, but I prefer to fight you man to man. Choose!' he told Don Bill, presenting two pistols the bartender had brought.

'I use my own and you use yours,' Don Bill responded.

The news of the duel spread and soon the place was filled with people. Friends of both men tried to stop it, but neither one nor the other wanted to give in. I was Fernando's second and there was nothing for me to do except to see the thing through.

'Take six steps, turn around, and fire,' I advised them. Not a sound was heard as these two men, both so handsome and in the prime of life, played with fire.

'One—two—three—four—five—six,' I counted.

Two shots rang out simultaneously. Don Bill and Fernando stood unhurt. Both had fired into the air. They looked at each other for a few seconds. Fernando walked towards Don Bill. The American met him halfway, and they shook hands and embraced.

'*Muy hombre amigo*,'* said the American.

'A brave man you are, my friend,' answered Fernando.

You should have heard the *vivas* that rang out.

'*Viva* Don Fernando, *Viva* Don Bill,' shouted the men gathered there.

They parted personal friends but political enemies still."

"*Válgame Dios*," exclaimed Doña Margarita, "what things do happen at these so-called elections. Do people have to fight when they vote?"

"Oh no, my Love, Fernando says this happens because we are not used to voting and are like children with a new toy. But once we become accustomed to it, I imagine it will be as easy as branding a calf or roping a steer."

"God grant it, Francisco! When do we leave for home? I do not like it here at all."

"Not until tomorrow. I must see Father José María this afternoon. While I am gone you and Rosita can visit friends or perhaps you'd like to buy a dress or a hat. Is this enough?" he asked, giving her twenty new silver dollars.

"*¡Madre de Dios!* American money," gasped Doña Margarita, "where did you get it?"

"From the bank. I went there this morning and changed a few hundred *pesos* to American money."

"American money! But Francisco, I know not the value of it!"

"That's another thing we must learn, my Dove. Fernando says we can never hope to be good businessmen as long as we persist in using Mexican money."

"You and Fernando with your new American ways. I hope you will not try to change the black eyes of Our Lady of Guadalupe to blue!"

---

*Muy hombre amigo—A brave man.

# CHAPTER XV

## The Woman Who Lost Her Soul[1]

Late in the afternoon Don Francisco was sitting in the town Rectory waiting for his old friend Father José María. A polite copper-hued maid had told him that the priest would see him in an hour and having nothing with which to occupy his mind, he stood at the window to view the town and watch the passersby. From the courtyard opposite the parish school came the sound of children's voices, now urging someone to make a home run, now cheering the victor, now showering strong Spanish interjections with Latin vehemence on the defeated. Outside the glorious sunshine of a Texas afternoon, the last rays of the sun tinted the blue sky with brilliant hues, garnet, purple, and gold; a gray-colored sky, a gray-colored neighborhood. Here, an adobe house painted a brilliant blue, there a tin-roofed shack shamelessly flaunted its title to the world, *El Viento Libre*, Free Air. In the house beyond, sitting on a vine-clad porch, a girl lazily strummed the guitar. Across the street two youths plucked feathers from their game cocks to arouse their fighting spirit for the next day's fight. The languorous indolence pervading the atmosphere was that easygoing way peculiar to the Mexican temperament. This quietude and stillness was broken by a childish cry,

"*Le Desalmada, La Desalmada.*"

The girl on the porch, presumably frightened, dropped her guitar and hastily crossed herself. The children in the school yard ceased their play; even the youths ran into the yard, roosters under arm. As the cry of alarm floated down the narrow street, the same demonstrations of fear

[1]Again, González left several copies, versions and fragments of this chapter including one paper which she read at the 1928 meeting of the Texas Folklore Society in which she substitutes herself for Don Francisco and presents the paper as a personal field experience. By carefully integrating these various versions I have produced this account.

were shown. With a natural curiosity Don Francisco looked out the window to find out the reason for such demonstrations of fear and consternation.

He peered down the street and saw nothing alarming. He noticed, however, two women braver than the rest standing on their doorsteps, gesticulating and uttering curses on another woman coming down the street.

"*Maldita, maldita,\**" he heard them yell, shaking their fists at a woman in black. The woman stopped as though in fear. She drew a black shawl over her face and in a moment disappeared into a dark alley. Forgetting his mission, forgetting that night was swiftly descending, he ran after the woman determined to find out more about the strange incident he had just seen.

Stumbling over the rocks and rugged cracks, he followed the fleeting black figure now almost hidden by the darkness. She turned from one crooked alley into another. He followed fascinated by a morbid curiosity. At the end of a blind alley Francisco saw her enter a hut, hurriedly closing the door behind her. He pushed. The door was locked. He knocked; no answer. Francisco knocked again and again. A trembling voice, like that of a frightened child, asked,

"What do you want?"

"I want to see you; let me in."

"But you cannot come near me, *Señor*. I am accursed. I am *La Desalmada*."

"*La Desalmada*?"

"Yes, the woman without a soul."

"That's why I must see you," Francisco replied, humoring her, not having the least idea what she meant.

"Just a moment; let me unlock the door."

He entered. The room, if it could be called that, was dark and damp. A sputtering, tallow candle furnished the only light. By it Francisco could see that the woman before him was beautiful, but beautiful in an unearthly way. Her face, pale as wax, reminded him of the face of an ivory medieval statue. Her eyes were black, fathomless pools, shimmering like black diamonds in the night.

"You…" he stammered, not knowing how to begin—

"Yes, *Señor*, I have no soul," she said with the simplicity and conviction of a child.

---

*\*Maldia*—accursed.

"You are the only one that has come near me in such a long time—and for that I am very grateful. Because you have been kind to me, and that others may profit by my sinful actions, I will tell you my story. But you must promise to tell it again and again. Do you swear it by the ashes of your ancestors? Do you swear by the salvation of your soul?"

He nodded his head in silent assent.

"May your children and your children's children be stung by scorpions and devoured by worms, if you fail to keep your promise. But please sit down. I am sorry I have no better seat to offer you," she said, pointing to an empty apple box.

Like one in a trance Francisco sat opposite her, his eyes fixed on hers.

"I have not always been as you see me now," she began. "Once I had a home and was happy, and because my parents had no other children, I was spoiled and selfish. Our friends considered me beautiful and were proud of me. No one could play the guitar and sing as I could; the castanets fluttered like black butterflies in my hands. The praises of those who knew me turned my head and I became arrogant and haughty. My admirers were many. In the mellow evenings of summer, when the perfume of the night blossoms and the singing of the birds intoxicated the senses of youth with the gladness of living, I was serenaded by someone who courted my love. It was not uncommon to hear a serenader in the early morning hours when all was covered with dew, singing a love song at my window.

Like all the girls of my class I lived a life of seclusion, was not permitted the company of young men. But what does that matter when flashing dark eyes speak? I encouraged all, but I accepted no one. Why did I not marry? Because my perverse nature wanted the only thing that I could not have. I loved the only man whose love was prohibited by all that was true. I loved Julio, the promised husband of Rosario, my best friend. My eyes told him what my lips would not utter. Every evening when all was quiet, he came to the *reja* of the window to talk to me. At this time something happened that made me more determined than ever to keep Julio for myself. The month of May came around and with it the coronation of Our Blessed Mother; when Rosario was chosen to crown the Virgin, my heart was filled with anger and envy. Why should she have everything while I had nothing?

As the day of the ceremony drew near, Julio's love-making became more ardent and persistent. I promised to give him my answer after the Virgin's coronation. That evening always will live in my mind. The Virgin herself must have blessed it. Balmy, yet cool, sweet-scented with many flowers. The white-clad, white-veiled girls, the singing of the Ave

Maria, and the flickering of the candles in the dusk as we wended our way into the church, made me forget that I was a child of Mary. As I knelt at the Virgin's feet to offer my flowers, I also left another offering—my love for Julio—I gave it up that Rosario might be happy.

When he came to see me I told him of my resolution. I let him see the enormity of our sin and our wickedness and I urged him not to see me again. How bitter our parting was! But in spite of the heartache, I felt free and lighthearted because of my sacrifice. As Julio kissed my hand in a last farewell, Rosario came in. She did not say anything, and since I was sick with remorse I did not offer an explanation. 'She will know all from him when he sees her later in the evening,' I thought, for he had promised me to call on her that night.

Early the next morning as I was watering the flowers in the *patio,* Rosario came in, pale as death. She gasped a few words and fell at my feet. She was dead. She held something white in her hand. It was a note addressed to me. 'You have tortured me on earth,' it said, 'my spirit will torture yours from Hell!'

No sooner was Rosario dead than my soul began to be tormented... Call it remorse, call it Hell or what you may, my soul was in agony. My parents, disgraced because of the shame that had befallen them through my bad behavior, disowned me and I was shunned by our former friends as one unclean. My mother took to her bed and when she was buried a few days later, my father and I were the only ones who accompanied her to her resting place. My father left town but I could not. Something, some unknown force kept me close to the grave of my victim.

Now I am as one unclean, a living corpse, for my soul is with my victim in Hell. I cannot eat, I cannot sleep. I tramp the streets in hopes that the weariness of my body will make me forget. Sometimes at night, when tired of the day's wanderings, I close my eyes in sleep. Rosario comes to haunt me, an indistinct shadow that gradually takes shape. Then I see her as I saw her last. Her eyes pierce mine like a dagger and with a cry of anguish her voice rings out, 'My spirit suffers in Hell because of you.' I wake up in despair—Oh! the agony, the suffering and remorse of a lost soul!

Once I went to see the priest that christened me and prepared me for my first Communion. I opened my heart to him. There were tears in his eyes as he listened to my story.

'My child, my child,' he said, 'You have no doubt sinned, but your soul is where it should be, in God's keeping. Pray much, eat well, work, and end your life of wandering.'

I followed his advice and for a time felt better and had hopes of being happy again. But one night I saw Rosario again, surrounded by flames and writhing in agony. The torments she suffered drove me insane.

In desperation I went to see a gypsy witch, a fortuneteller, and what she told me filled me with terror. My soul, she said, was in the liver of a toad, and only through many incantations would it be restored to its proper place."

As she said the last words her eyes became distorted with fear. Like one in pain she shrieked, her trembling hand pointing to a dark corner of the room.

"It comes—it comes—for my soul!"

A toad hopped into the middle of the room blinking its eyes solemnly. The woman lay on the floor, moaning.

"My soul is gone—my soul is lost."[2]

Francisco looked around for a bed where she might be carried to, but the only thing resembling one was a pallet on the floor. He did all that he could for her, laying her on the bed and wiping the perspiration off her face with a wet cloth.

It was night when he left the hut, but before going back to his wife and daughter he decided to see the priest and explain his sudden departure. He directed his footsteps to the Rectory where Father José María was wondering what had become of him.

"What could have happened?" the priest was muttering to himself as he took his after-supper walk in the garden. "It is not like Francisco to run off without seeing me first. I must call on Margarita tomorrow. I wonder if the rumors I have heard about Carlos have reached him? What a terrible situation this is; Ramón's stubbornness, Francisco's squeamishness about what he calls family honor, Carlos' compromising silence, and Rosita's broken heart. She is the one who suffers most, but like the angel of God that she is, she smiles and is patient though it is breaking her heart." Don Francisco's footsteps interrupted the priest's thoughts.[3]

"You must pardon my abrupt departure, *Padre*," explained the ranchman after the usual salutation, "but when I tell you my strange adventure and the strange story I have just heard, you will surely forgive me."

[2]Stith Thompson Motif-Index number E 721.3—Wandering soul cause of sickness and E 721.5—Wandering soul assumes various shapes.

[3]González is picking up the story of the thwarted lovers.

"That was poor Carmen you saw," said the priest when Don Francisco had finished the story. "She was and still is a good girl. The trouble is that she took the affair too much to heart. She was somewhat to blame, it is true, but not altogether. I have often talked to her, but my words mean nothing. What happened was a terrible thing of course, that cannot be denied. But I blame her parents more than I do her. They spoiled the girl, encouraged her vain ways, were proud of her conquests, thought her coquettish ways charming, and then when she needed their help most, they disowned her and left her to bear the scandal and gossip alone. I cannot understand a parent's love that cannot forgive the misfortune that comes to a son or a daughter. They call it disgrace, shame, dishonor, and instead of kissing the sorrow away, instead of clasping the wayward child to their breasts they cast him away, perhaps to lose his life and what is more precious, his soul. Take Carlos for example…"

"Father, as much as I respect you, I must beg you not to speak of him."

"How do you know he is guilty?" the priest interrupted. "His father did a monstrous thing."

"'A man is known by the company he keeps,' Father, says the proverb. What was he doing in such company?"

"Was he ever given a chance to explain himself? Did Ramón for one moment give him the benefit of the doubt? He took it for granted that the boy was guilty; and then, in the presence of all, whipped him as though he had been a hardened criminal; shaming him before everyone, breaking his pride and his spirit. No, no, Francisco, you may think the same as Ramón, but let me tell you this, his father and all who countenanced the affair did him a terrible injustice."

"You are a priest, Father, and cannot see the ways of the world."

"The ways of the world, humph!" responded the priest scornfully. "I suppose you think they are superior to the laws of God?"

"But honor…"

"Honor is all you can think about. You'd sacrifice your flesh and blood for that. But let me tell you this, and you tell that stone-head friend of yours the same thing, I am for the boy. And until convinced of his guilt, I shall stand for him. And what's more I am going to investigate the matter, not for his father's sake, not for Rita's, poor unbalanced creature that she is, but for Rosita's."

"As a father I must ask you not to interfere with parental discipline."

"And I, as her spiritual father, will do everything to bring about her happiness. Don't misunderstand me, Francisco, never will I counsel her to disobey you, never will I advise her to go contrary to your wishes; but as one interested in her happiness, I will fight for her. Have you heard what people are saying about Carlos?"

"I have not and I do not care to hear it."

"Francisco," said the priest, placing a hand on his friend's shoulder, "I have always considered you a man of sense, a lover of justice, and I do not want to have to change my opinion of you."

"Well, speak then, I shall hear."

"He has left Camargo for Durango to work in the silver mines. Before leaving he told friends he was going away to get rich, but that he would return to clear his name and marry your daughter."

"How dare he!" sputtered the ranchman, losing his composure again.

"A man in love dares all. 'I shall return to proclaim my innocence,' he said, and I believe him. But going back to poor Carmen..."

"I came here with the best intentions in the world—I wanted to do something for her but your words have completely upset me and I do not know, Father—I cannot think right now."

"Come, come, if your intentions were of that kind, you certainly cannot change them."

"I had thought that perhaps taking her to the Olivareño might help her—but now I do not know that I want to do it."

"Now you shall, my son," said the priest embracing him. "You would be the best of men were it not for your stubbornness. That will be heaven for the poor girl; not to be here where everyone knows her, not to have to face the scorn of those whom she once loved."

"Don't count on it too much, Margarita might not consent. I have not talked to her yet."

"Of course she will not object, just wait and see."

"We shall talk about this tomorrow. I really must go now. Margarita will be wondering what has become of me. Until tomorrow, Father, come to see us, we are at Don Adán's as usual."

The following morning Don Francisco accompanied by his wife and Father José María went to see Carmen. They found her oblivious to everything, sprinkling the damp, dirt floor of the *jacal*.

"That's all she does," whispered the priest to his companions, "believing that her soul is in a toad, she keeps the place damp and cool that it may not go away."

"*Pobrecita*, how terrible that must be," exclaimed Doña Margarita, wiping the tears from her eyes.

"*Buenos días*, Carmen," cried Father José María, hoping to bring her out from her trance-like condition with a loud threatening voice.

She dropped the bucket, stared at her visitors and then with the steps of a somnambulist, walked towards the priest. With trembling fingers she touched his cassock, ran her hands down his sleeve, and at the touch of the Crucifix at his belt, withdrew her hand quickly. She looked at his face again, then at the Crucifix, and finally a smile of recognition shone on her face.

"Father—Father José María," she stammered.

"Yes, Carmen, we have come to take you away."

"Take—me—away?"

"Yes, my child, to a beautiful place away in the country where there are many trees and flowers and where there will be someone to love and care for you."

"Love—me—Care for me—Oh, Father," she sobbed, "that cannot be. I have not heard those words since Rosario died."

"Go to her, Margarita," said both Don Francisco and the priest.

"We love you, Carmen, and we want you to come with us, won't you come, dear?" said Doña Margarita, holding the girl close to her heart.

"But my soul—it is here—I cannot go."

"Of course you can, Carmen, we shall make you well again."

"My soul, Father," she said, turning to the priest, "can I go and leave it here?"

"Your soul, dear child, is within you and God will look after it."

"It is in the toad, the gypsy woman told me so," she added with the conviction of a child.

"Carmen," said the priest sternly looking her in the eye. "Listen to me, listen closely. You believe me, don't you?" The girl nodded. "Fine. Now listen closely, very closely, to what I am going to tell you. I, Father José María, say this to you; your soul is safe. It is in God's keeping. You understand?"

"You mean I am free?"

"Yes, free to go with us who are your friends."

"And can I go now?"

"Yes, dear Carmen, come with us now," and saying this Doña Margarita led the girl by the arm out of the miserable hovel.

"Perhaps with love and care she can become her old self again. Who knows what this will do for her. You are a good man, Francisco. Write me soon and tell me how she gets along."

"Father, there is something I must tell you; it has been in my mind since I talked to you last night. Ramón might have been wrong."

"God bless you, Francisco," and the good priest wrung his hands. He said no more, knowing how much that confession had cost his friend.

The family coach, driven by four white mules, drove into the ranch late in the evening. With a leap Don Francisco descended from the driver's seat, helped the three women down, led them to the door of the *sala,* and excused himself. He went into the kitchen where the coach-man had preceded him.

"She looks like a ghost and is crazy," he heard the servant say. Those were the last words the *peón* uttered. The lash of a whip cut him across the face. Don Francisco, eyebrows contracted in a frown, one higher than the other, stood whip in hand facing the men gathered there.

"Let that be a lesson to your lying tongues," he said. "She is not crazy. And whoever repeats that will live to rue the day."

"What could have happened?" the priest was muttering to himself.

# CHAPTER XVI

## Blessed Be the Moon and the Unfortunate Lover

It was two years now since Cristóbal had left home and life in the pasture with Tío Patricio to come to live with Don Alberto. The once-pale thin boy with the haunting eyes was now a strapping boy of seventeen who looked upon the world with the adventurous spirit of youth. Far different was he from the child that had at one time cowed in the presence of people and feared the darkness of night.

Rich in lore of the creatures of the woods, the boy's virgin and dormant mind had awakened at the magic touch of learning. He had been an inspiration to Don Alberto, and the school master had given himself body and soul to his development. The first task, more arduous than Don Alberto had imagined, had been to dispel the boy's fear of the supernatural, to free his spirit from the evil influences which Cristóbal believed held him in their clutches.

That accomplished, the rest had been easy, for Cristóbal's mind, replete with the knowledge of the creatures of the woods, was ready to plunge itself into learning as found in books. Avid for knowledge, his thirst for learning found satisfaction in the books which the teacher provided for him. Don Alberto saw in him the embryo of what, if properly directed, might be a genius.

"He must be encouraged," advised the priest late one afternoon when he and Don Alberto were having *merienda* with Don Francisco.

"If Ramón will let me, I'd like to take him home with me, teach him the classics, and send him to the American school to learn English."

"Who is the teacher now? Do you know him?" asked Don Alberto.

"He is a *señor* Davis, just returned from Kentucky," answered the priest. "His father, as I remember, came with General Taylor when the Americans took the country. I am told he was a very handsome, ambitious young man who hoped to make his fortune out of the war. He had an eye for beauty and a desire for riches and in Hilaria Garza he found what he was looking for, a pretty girl and wealth. She was a descendant of the founders of Camargo and her family possessions had at one time extended clear to the Nueces. To keep this young American home, Hilaria's father gave him a big tract of land. He founded the town of Davis, and anxious for more of his countrymen to come to this newly acquired territory, he gave the United States government the land on which the fort is now located.[1]

"Don Enrique was his name," added Don Francisco. "We were good friends, he was *un hombre muy simpático*, a very attractive man. And we liked him very much. He became as one of us; the same as did most of the Americans and other foreigners who came at the time. They were all bachelors, but they did not remain so for long. The dark flashing eyes of our *señoritas* conquered them the same as the sword had vanquished us a few years before. Those who were married and brought their families soon accepted our customs, our language, and even our religion."

"How different from them are those who are coming now!" exclaimed the priest. "Just last week I went to Brownsville to see Father Parisot and I could see the change. Instead of the friendly faces of people we've always known, the streets were filled with grim-looking men, their faces hardened by avarice and determination to get rich. I called on Judge Williams, Fernando's friend. What he told me about these newcomers made me feel a little better. It seems that after all, we are not the only ones who resent their attitude. He said that he and the old time families, whether American or Mexican, disliked their coming as much as you *rancheros* do. He told me of an incident that happened no less than two weeks ago. One of these new American families moved into his neighborhood. The family, it seemed, had two children of school age. The father, wishing to enroll them, took them to the convent one morning, but he brought them back home saying that he would not send his children to a school where Mexicans attended. Judge Williams was very angry. His own daughter, as you know, is married to a Mexican banker, and naturally he took it as a personal insult."

"Why do they come to our land if they don't like us? Why do they come to live here if they consider themselves so good?"

"They come for money, Francisco. This land is undeveloped, and there is much wealth to be gotten from it yet."

---

[1]Here González is referring directly to Henry Clay Davis who, after marrying Hilaria Garza, founded Rancho Davis, which later became present-day Rio Grande City in Starr County. The Fort is Fort McIntosh.

"It is because of this economic and social evolution that I want Cristóbal to go to town. I want him to learn to mix with people and above all I want him to see how other people live. In him I see Fernando's aide, perhaps his successor."

"You have done wonderful things for him, Alberto, the same as you and Margarita did for Carmen, Francisco, and speaking of her, how is she? I have not seen her yet."

"Do you hear that singing?"

"I have marveled at the beauty of the voices and I have wondered who the singers might be."

"Carmen and Rosita; like mockingbirds they sing all day. They have been good medicine for each other. Sometimes I even think Carmen might be in love."

"*¡La Virgen del Carmen*! How happy that would make me! Who with, Francisco?"

"With my cousin, Manuel de los Olivares. He often comes here for the mail and I have seen him cast loving eyes on her. I saw their glances meet and the look that came upon her face was one of fear and one of joy combined. Only lovers act and look like that."

"What are you going to do about it?"

"As one responsible for her, I shall speak to Manuel and if they love each other—"

"My blessing they shall have," added the priest.

"Several times we have persuaded her to dance," continued Don Francisco. "It is beginning to be like it was before my child had her sorrow."

"Does Rosita grieve yet?" asked the priest with interest.

"Yes, many times in the evening when the dove calls in the *cañada*, Margarita and I have seen her wipe a tear that she would hide from us. She can't forget."

"Women like her never do, Francisco..."

"Father," interrupted Don Alberto, "will you excuse me? I'll leave you now; I have to do something I left undone. I have a little business to settle with Ramón. Francisco, with your permission, most probably I shall see you later in the evening."

"May you go with God, and may you fare well, Alberto."

"It is in evenings like this, Father," said Don Francisco after their friend left, "when I feel the cool breeze on my face and all becomes still, so still that I can hear the silence of night, that my mother comes to me in thought."

"She must have been a great woman."

"Ay! that she was. She was like night, so quiet and so wise – have I ever repeated to you what she liked to call the beatitudes of the ranches?"

"No."

"I remember quite distinctly the first time I heard them; Fernando, my sister Rosa, and I were very young children. Rosa could hardly talk, Fernando was four and I must have been six. We were sitting in the *patio* of this very house, just about where we are now. That was before the family left for Mexico. My father had very sad news; his brother Juan had been killed by the Americans somewhere while on his way to San Antonio. He was sitting by my mother; his bowed head resting on her knee and great sobs shook his big body. I remember how I sat there fascinated, watching the rise and fall of his wide shoulders and I thought how much like a panting horse he was. My mother caressed his hair with the soft, comforting movement I knew so well. Rosa sat on her lap, Fernando and I were at her feet. The first star appeared just as it has now—

I remember very little of what happened while we sat there, but one expression of my father remains in my heart as though it had been burnt there with letters of fire:

'If everything is taken from me, if my dearest ones are killed one by one, why should we remain here?'

My mother's words, soft but firm, I can still hear.

'Cesáreo, my beloved, we shall return to the land of our ancestors and we shall begin anew building for our children, as your grandfather did for you and yours.'

She kissed my bowed head—'The world is so beautiful, Cesáreo,' she encouraged him, 'and we shall find there the same things to love as we have found here. Listen, my beloved,' she continued, 'listen to the things we can be thankful for, the things of which no one can rob us, because they belong to the soul. They are the blessings which we shall have there, the same as we have had in this land.'

And then she repeated in a voice so much like music:

'Blessed be the butterfly, the sweetheart of the rose.
Blessed be the star and those who sigh for her.
Blessed be the jasmine, perfumer of the garden,
Blessed be the mockingbird, sweet singer of the woods.
Blessed be the swallow who withdrew from Christ the thorn.
Blessed be the Moon and the unfortunate lover.'

"Blessed be the moon and the unfortunate lover," mused the good *Padre,* "exactly what I came to talk to you about."

"The moon?" asked Don Francisco somewhat surprised.

"No, the unfortunate lover. I want to talk to you about Carlos. 'Ramón might have done wrong' were your words when I spoke to you about this some time ago. Do you remember my words then? I have kept that promise to myself and have found out the truth."

"The truth, Father!"

"Yes, about Carlos; what I am going to tell you will no doubt surprise you as it did me. Listen.

One very stormy night last month, I was in my study reading and smoking. The wind was playing havoc with the trees, and the rain came down in torrents. I was thinking how fortunate I was to be sitting in my room and I shivered at the very thought of having to go out on a call. Just then I heard the distant galloping of a horseman. It kept getting nearer and nearer and as I sat there listening, I could not help but think what dire need the rider must have to be out in such a storm. Closer and closer the galloping came. I heard it stop at my door. There was a knock. Perhaps it is the wind, I thought! But no! The knocking became more insistent. I went to the door and saw a man stand there. I let him in.

There was something about him that made me think that I had seen him before, but where or when I could not remember at the moment. He might have been forty or he might have been seventy, I could not tell. His sunken cheeks, parched lips, and burning eyes showed me the man was not well.

'I am a sick man, *Padre*,' he told me, 'and I want to confess my sins.'

I could see that he was in as much need of physical help as spiritual. I made him take off the dripping coat and covered him, wrapping him in a blanket, and made him sit by the fire. I then went to the kitchen and made some peppermint tea with cinnamon.

He had a high fever and he was trembling so, he could not even hold the cup in his hand and I had to take it to his lips. I could see, though, that he was in no immediate danger of death and I proposed to him that he let me put him to bed in my spare room and the confession could wait until the next day.

'No—no—*Padre*,' he stammered, 'tonight—right now.'

So I took the key, put on my cape, covered him the best I could, and together we went to church. The confession was long and painful; painful to him because he was very weak and fainted twice, and to me, because what I was hearing would vindicate and clear Carlos of all guilt, and yet I could not use the information confided to me in the confessional.

Do you remember Traga-Balas? It was he who knelt before me. Once he had helped a penitent die like a Christian; he had brought me to the dying man on another stormy night, and now he himself had come to me, just like a truant boy returning home after a day of forbidden pleasures.

I took him home with me, put him to bed, and watched all night by his side. The next morning he was worse and I called the doctor. He verified my fears. The man had caught pneumonia and at his age, his weakened condition could not combat the disease. He had but few days to live, the doctor told me. My one thought now was to find the means by which he would confide in someone else what he had confessed to me. He was delirious most of the time, but during his lucid moments I talked to him about what was foremost in my mind. Seeing the precious moments slip by, I made up my mind to be cruel if necessary to save Carlos from shame and disgrace.

What were a few moments of distress to a dying man, one who had lived his life; I excused myself, comparing the life-long misery of two young people who were just beginning to live. I took the bull by the horns, as you *rancheros* say, and I said to him:

'Antonio, you will soon face your Creator and there is something you must do before you go,'

'"Am I really going to die?' wailed the unhappy wretch. 'Don't let me die, *Padre*. I am not ready to go yet.'

'Your actions have caused the unhappiness of many,' I said, ignoring his plea, 'you have confessed to me but now you must confess before men.'

'And if I do, will I be saved?'

'God will forgive you, and many people will bless you.'

'Alright, *Padre*, I am ready.'

Like one insane I ran to Fernando's house. He was at dinner and had company, but I did not care. I could not even speak. I dragged him by the arm and he followed me thinking me crazy, no doubt. And to him did Antonio tell what he had already confessed to me about Carlos' affair.

He had escaped from the penitentiary, he told us, when the incident occurred and had just returned home where he kept in hiding. No one knew where he was except some of his friends, escaped convicts like himself, who were to join him later. Together they carried on a very profitable business stealing cattle from the *rancheros* and selling them across the river. He knew all the pastures; he knew where the best cattle were kept and everything had come to his heart's content.

One day when his band was hiding in a motte discussing the next move, Carlos had come upon them. He recognized in the leader the man who at one time had disgraced the Olivares name. Realizing what a blow it would be to you if it was ever found out who the leader of the cattle thieves was, Carlos had pleaded with him to desist from his shameful way of living, had begged him to go away to Mexico, anywhere where he was not known. But Traga-Balas refused to leave. He could not abandon the friends that had been so loyal to him. They continued their depredations and when Ramón was elected head of the expedition sent to pursue them, Carlos, knowing that they would soon be caught, went to warn him. He had also taken another horse and a change of clothing so Traga-Balas could escape unrecognized.

You know the rest, Francisco, there is no need for further explanation."

"And he did it to save my name from further shame!"

"Yes, he suffered dishonor and disgrace to save the father of the girl he loved."

"Why didn't he speak?"

"Had he done so he would have exposed Antonio and that was what he would not do, not because of him but because of you. Antonio escaped, went to Mexico, stayed there three years, but feeling sick and seeing he was soon to die, came back to me to confess his sins as he always said he would. He died that same day and I gave him the Christian burial he so much wanted.

The next thing I did was to send a special messenger to Durango. I would not even trust the mail, urging Carlos to return.

He is back, Francisco. These years of suffering have helped to make a serious man out of the once care-free spoiled boy. He has become rich and is much respected where he lives. Do I have to tell you what has brought me here today?"

"No, *Padre*. There is no need. Has he seen Ramón yet?"

"Ay, Francisco! That is the hardest part of all. The boy cannot forget and he cannot forgive. That's why I came to see you first. He has respect for you and whatever you tell him, that he will do. Would you not want to see him now?"

"Now? You surprise me, *Padre*, where is he?"

"At Alberto's. I left him there this afternoon to see Cristóbal."

"Yes, *Padre*, what else is there for me to say? You have arranged everything."

"God bless you, Francisco. How proud Doña Ramona will be of you tonight! How true her maxim was, 'Blessed be the moon and the unfortunate lover.' I go now, Francisco, but I shall come back soon with Carlos, too."

Two hours later, on his return, Father José María was surprised to see the house all lighted.

"Courage, my boy," he said to the young man who walked by his side. "They are expecting us, I see."

They stood at the door. The good priest could not believe his eyes.

Don Francisco and Don Ramón, in holiday attire, waited at the threshold. Rosita and Doña Margarita stood in the center of the *sala*.

"Here I bring him to you; prepare the feast for his return," said the priest.

With an exclamation of joy and surprise Carlos flew to his father's arms.

"*Padre, mi padre.*"

"My son, *mi* Carlos," sobbed the *ranchero*.

"May I embrace you too, Don Francisco?" asked the boy, freeing himself from his father's arms.

"That you may, my son. Proud am I this day to call you son and to hold you in my arms."

Then taking Carlos by the arm Don Francisco led him to Rosita. He took the girl's hand and placing it in Carlos' eager hand said to her in a voice that trembled with emotion. "My child, it is for you to cage him; it is up to you to see that he does not leave his nest again."

# CHAPTER XVII

## We Stay!

One month later, the evening of a bright clear day found Father José María again at the *Olivareño*. He sat in the patio waiting for Don Francisco and his wife who were bidding their last guests farewell.

What a blessing it had been for Carmen to come to the Olivareño, he thought. She had become her former self; she was almost the same spirited girl that he had known years before in town. But he knew that she was not altogether happy yet. Doña Margarita, who had watched with maternal affection the changes that had come upon the girl, told him that occasionally she had seen something like a shadow of pain cross her face. He himself had often seen her move her lips as though in prayer. Was she saying a prayer for the friend of her girlhood days? Was she perhaps praying for Julio?

Inscrutable indeed were the acts of providence; without even trying to, he had found out what he had always wanted to know: Julio's fate. Carlos had known him in Durango. The sorrows through which both had gone had brought them together and they had become fast friends. Both young men felt the weight of misfortune and disillusioned and weary of life, both were reckless and both had gained the reputation of being oblivious and immune to danger. And because both did not care for riches, wealth had come their way.

Feeling that he had been responsible for Rosario's death and Carmen's unhappiness, Julio could not be happy. The riches which he had acquired meant nothing to him. Had he only known that Carmen was taken care of he would have been happier, perhaps!

One day a sudden explosion in the mines caused some of the men to be entombed. Julio offered his services in the rescue work. His fearlessness had saved the men, but he himself was killed. Carlos, being the closest friend he had, looked after his personal belongings. Much to everyone's surprise, it was found that he had over a quarter million *pesos*. This amount he had left to a hospital for unprotected women.

When Carmen was told of his death, she took the news serenely. Nothing was ever said again about the subject, but her eyes were often filled with tears.

Don Manuel, though, would make her forget all the unpleasant recollections of her earlier years. His love would surely make her lead another life. He was taking her to a world unknown to her, to a different land where no one knew what she had gone through. In Mexico she would, no doubt, forget.

He was proud of Don Francisco too. For the first time he had been at the wedding of one of his daughters. He had knelt by Rosita's side when the Church gave the blessing to the newly married couples.

After the wedding Don Francisco had teased him, telling him that he looked happier than either of the grooms.

Perhaps Don Francisco was right. But why shouldn't he be when through his efforts he had made four people happy! Ay, more than that, if he counted Francisco, Ramón, and Margarita. Poor Rita did not count. She knew nothing of what went about her. If only Cristóbal would not inherit her illness, he mused; some people had thought he would. How the boy had developed in the short time he had had him in town! He was such a bright promising boy, one after his own heart. He was learning English rapidly; as to Latin, he took to it as though he had been born in Rome.

He was happy! If only these *Americanos* had not come to upset the life of the *rancheros*. Just when everything was going so well, just when it seemed as though all the problems had been solved, another had presented itself. If only the *rancheros* would forget the injuries they had once received. If only the old wounds would heal completely!

But it was too soon for that. And these people, who were coming in crowds, were not helping the situation with their attitude towards the Mexican population. Perhaps they resented the air of reserve and arrogance with which the Texas-Mexicans received them. It was hard to say! But trouble there was to be, he could see that. And it was coming soon. It would be not only an economic and social strife, but a racial struggle as well. It would be a contest between an aggressive, conquering, material people, and a passive, proud, volatile race. It would be a struggle between the new world and the old, for the Texas-Mexican had retained more than any other people, old world traditions, customs, and ideals.[1]

His reverie was broken by the presence of Don Francisco and his wife.

"Dreaming again, *Padre*?" asked Don Francisco, putting his hand gently on the old priest's shoulder.

"Not at all, my son. I was seeing the future."

"And what does it say to you, *Padre*?"

"I see hundreds of strangers at your doors. I see them struggling for possession of this country."

"You almost make me laugh, *Padre*. If what they'll get is the worthless desert-land, what will they do with it?"

"They plan to chain the river with machinery, irrigate the land, make it work for them."

"Impossible."

"Not at all, my son," answered the priest. "They merely do what we should have accomplished long ago. They'll buy the land for a few cents, improve it, and later make a fortune. I tell the people not to sell," continued the priest. "I tell them to hold on to what they have. But they will not listen. They are dispossessing themselves of their land, selling their homes for a few dollars which they will spend on foolish things. It breaks my heart to see them do it for I can see what the result will be. They will become like *peones*, working for the owners of the land that once was theirs."

"Like *peones* to these people who dislike us and distrust us? What an outrage! Can we not stop this before it is too late?"

"Stop it?" asked the priest. "Try to stop a mountain torrent; try to stop a hurricane!"

"Must we submit like sheep led to the slaughter?"

"No, but the remedy lies within our hands. Heretofore we have lived following the customs and ideals of another nation; the time for that has passed. We must accept the changes that come without losing our integrity, and above all we must hold on to the land; fight for it if necessary; suffer hunger, privations, rather than let it go."

"Change! Change! That's all I hear now! I have sold my birthright. I've been almost forced to abandon the citizenship of my ancestors, and still am I expected to change more? What more can a man do? Must I also sell my soul for money?"

"God forbid your doing that. You get easily excited, Francisco."

"And you easily alarmed, *Padre*! Let's forget all concerning the land and the foreigners, and talk about something more cheerful—about the wedding, about our children so happy now. I've never seen Rosita

---

[1]The crisis is building toward the uprising of 1915-16 against Anglo-American authority. See Montejano (1986: 110-128). Recall also the incident of Gregorio Cortez in 1901.

look so radiant. I had never seen Carmen so beautiful!" beamed Don Francisco.

"Rosita reminded me much of you, my daughter, when you came here as a bride."

"I remember that occasion," Don Francisco added, "you came to see us when we had just arrived. No older than Rosita were you, Margarita. How many things have happened since then! Eight children did the Lord send us! And now they are all gone, married. Just my Pearl and I remain, but we are happy."

"Yes, we are happy, Francisco."

"It is time for the evening prayer," said the priest looking at his watch. "Margarita, will you play the Ave María?"

"Certainly, *mi padre*."

She went into the house. The strains of the evening prayer were heard. "*Ave María plenae de gratia*," played the harp and "Ave María the Lord is with thee," repeated the men with bowed head.

The peacefulness of the evening, the beauty of the music was too much for the good priest. Silent tears rolled down his wrinkled face. "The calm before the storm," he thought to himself.

Just that morning he had heard the *vaqueros* plotting to leave the Olivareño; the *Americanos* were offering big pay in the new towns they were building; they needed men and the *vaqueros* needed more money. What would Francisco say when he realized the situation? Would the *peones* be faithful to their master or would they follow the example of their more adventurous friends?

This would be the beginning of the downfall of the Olivareño. Without the ranch hands, what would Francisco do? He knew the tempest would break loose this very evening. It was for this he had remained. Both Francisco and Margarita would need him.

The music ended. There was a pause. The priest was the first to speak.

"I wonder what the *caporal* wants. He's been standing at the door for some time, not daring to come in."

"What is it, José," asked Don Francisco.

"Can I see you alone, master?"

"Alone, why should you see me alone? Speak! What have you to say that Father José María cannot hear?"

"I know not how to say it, master," hesitated the faithful José—"the *vaqueros*, not all of course—but some..."

"The *vaqueros*! Proceed," interrupted Don Francisco—"what about them? Are they not pleased with what was given to them at the wedding feast? Didn't I tell you to give them what my guests were to be served?"

"It is not that, master."

"A fight perhaps? Has anyone been hurt?"

"Would that were the case, master, the telling would be less hard."

"Speak, my son, speak," encouraged the priest, "what is it?"

"Father—Don Francisco—I cannot," stammered the corporal, "would that I had no tongue to break the bad news."

"José, your master commands you to speak; the *vaqueros*, what has happened to them?"

"Gone, Don Francisco."

"Gone, I do not understand you."

"They have just left—Martiniano—El Capul…"

"José, will you explain or will I have to get the words out of you?"

"Be patient, Francisco, will you ever learn to control yourself?"

"It's this way, master," began José, wiping the perspiration from his brown suntanned face. "A short time ago, just as the guests were leaving, Capul Martiniano and five other *vaqueros* asked me for their pay. I told them the money was not due until the first, but I suggested that if they needed something they should charge it at the store.

'We are free men and as such have no master to obey,' he continued, 'Tell Don Francisco that! We are going now whether you pay us or not; the *Americanos* pay us more in one day than what we get here in a week,' and with that they galloped away."

"And you allowed them to go," thundered Don Francisco.

"What could I do, master?…"

"Away with you," he said in a terrible voice, "away with you before I tear you to pieces with my own hands."

"Francisco."

"I am sorry, Father, but when a thing like this happens…"

"It has always been the same, my son, the new against the old. You and I are the relics of an epoch that is rapidly disappearing. The *Americanos* bring a new age. Men like Fernando and Alberto are the links that will join this incoming era with what is doomed to perish."

"With what is doomed to perish?…"

"Yes, my son, it will not be long now before this land will be invaded by the newcomers; it will not be long before you will become an alien in what you once considered the heritage of your ancestors."

Twilight descended. The long shadows of evening enveloped the *patio* in a purple haze. Don Francisco, bowed head in his hands, said nothing.

When hearts weep there is no need for words.

The priest, his white hair shining like a halo in the semidarkness, stood quiescent by his side looking out at the vague disappearing landscape.

The leaves of the mesquite and cottonwood trees whispered like toothless old women telling their beads.

Silence mingled with the shadows and with the depressed spirits of the men. The soul of evening sighed to the wind and the singing of the mockingbird made the spirit weep with the sorrow of living.

"Margarita, my Pearl," sobbed Don Francisco.

"I am here, Francisco, I heard all."

"The same story again, are we to be driven from our homes? Are we to abandon all that is ours?"

"No, Francisco, we shall stay," answered Doña Margarita with the pride of her race. "This land is ours. It was blessed by the blood of the fathers who made it a Christian land. It was blessed by the blood of our ancestors who fought and suffered for it and conquered it, that we, their children, might have a home. The *Americanos* may come. They may take the land, but our spirit, the spirit of the conquerors, will live forever. Texas is ours. We stay!"

# JOVITA GONZÁLEZ
# A BIBLIOGRAPHY OF HER WRITINGS

## Books

1996    (With Eve Raleigh) *Caballero: An Historical Novel.* Eds. José E. Limón and María Cotera. College Station: Texas A&M University Press.

1997    *Dew on the Thorn.* Ed. José E. Limón. Houston: Arte Público Press.

## Articles

1927    "Folklore of the Texas-Mexican Vaquero." In *Texas and Southwestern Folklore.* Ed. J. Frank Dobie. Austin: Texas Folklore Society. Pp. 7-22.

1930    "Social Life in Cameron, Starr, and Zapata, Counties." M.A. thesis. University of Texas at Austin.

1930a    "Tales and Songs of the Texas-Mexicans." In *Man, Bird and Beast.* Ed. J. Frank Dobie. Austin: Texas Folklore Society. Pp. 86-116.

1930b    "America Invades the Border Towns." *Southwest Review* 15: 468-477.

1932    "Among my People." *Southwest Review* 17: 179-187.

1932a    "Among my People." In *Tone the Bell Easy.* Ed. J. Frank Dobie. Austin: Texas Folklore Society. Pp. 99-108. (A longer version of González, 1932).

1933    *League of United Latin American Citizens: Regulations and By-Laws.* Brownsville: Recio Brothers.

1935    "The Bullet-Swallower" In *Puro Mexicano.* Ed. J. Frank Dobie. Austin: Texas Folklore Society. Pp. 107-114.

1937    "Latin Americans." In *Our Racial and National Minorities: Their History, Contributions and Present Problems.* Eds. Francis J. Brown and Joseph Slabez Roucek. New York: Prentice-Hall. Pp. 497-509.

1940    "The Mescal-Drinking Horse." In *Mustangs and Cow Horses.* Eds. J. Frank Dobie, Modie C. Boatright and Harry H. Ransom. Austin: Texas Folklore Society. Pp. 107-112.

1941    (With E. E. Mireles and R. B. Fisher) *Mi libro español.* (three volumes) Austin: W. S. Benson and Co.

1949    (With E. E. Mireles) *El español elemental.* (six volumes). Austin: W. S. Benson and Co.

The Texas Folklore Society publication series has been recently re-issued by the University of North Texas Press.

# Reprints

1951    "The Devil in Texas." In *A Treasury of Western Folklore.* Ed. B.A. Botkin. New York: Crown Publishers. Pp. 699-702. (Reprint of 1930a)

1954    "Stories of My People." In *Texas Folk and Folklore.* Eds. Mody C. Boatright, William H. Hudson and Allen Maxwell. Dallas: Southern Methodist University Press. Pp. 19-24. (Reprints from 1927 and 1930a).

1955    "The Ghost of Las Chimineas." In *Texas Tales.* ed. David K. Sellars. Dallas: Noble and Noble. Pp. 97-106.

1972    "With the Coming of the Barbwire Came Hunger: Folklore of the Texas-Mexican Vaguero." In *Aztlán: An Anthology of Mexican-American Literature.* Eds. Luis Valdez and Stan Steiner. New York: Alfred A. Knopf. Pp. 81-83. (Reprint from 1927).

1972a   "Among My People." In *Mexican American Authors.* Eds. Américo Paredes and Raymund Paredes. Boston: Houghton-Mifflin. Pp. 8-15. (Reprint from 1932a)

# Papers Presented at the Texas Folklore Society Annual Meetings

1927    "Lore of the Texas Vaquero."

1928    "The Woman Who Lost Her Soul."

1929    "Legends and Songs of the Texas-Mexican Folk."

1930    "Social and Economic Conditions of the Texas Mexicans before the Industrial Development of the Rio Grande Valley."

1931    "Some Border Characters, Traditional and Legendary."

1932    "Among My People."

1933    "Among My People."

1934    "Traditional Proverbs and Ejaculations of the Rio Grande Border."

1935    "Collecting Folklore on the Rio Grande."

1936    "The Cristo of the Cactus."

1938    "Poetry and Pots."

1947    "Nana Chita's Symptoms."

1948    "The Marquis de Aguayo's Ghost."